Shadows
of the
Midnight Sun

Graham Brown and Spencer J. Andrews

Cover design by Jack Hendrick

ISBN: 1482799448
ISBN-13: 9781482799446

Other novels by Graham Brown

Black Rain

Black Sun

The Eden Prophecy

Co-authored with Clive Cussler

Devil's Gate

The Storm

Zero Hour

Coming soon: from Graham Brown and Spencer J. Andrews

Shadows of the Dark Star
(Book 2 of the Shadows Trilogy)

Shadows in the Blinding Light
(Book 3 of the Shadows Trilogy)

The Gods of War (Volumes 1 and 2)

Table of Contents

Prologue:
The Dying of the Light

The Germanic Front, 396 AD

A COLD wind blew across the Germanic plain. It rustled the dead leaves and swept past a set of ancient stone walls. High atop the ruins, a set of ragged standards fluttered in the wind as the approaching darkness consumed the final rays of heaven's light.

A battlefield stretched out before the silent walls. Here and there, fires burned, illuminating a field strewn with the dead. Thousands lay where they'd fallen, their bodies gashed open, their blood soaking the chalky soil in an odd communion between earth and man.

A Roman captain looked out on the carnage from beneath a ruined archway. He was the only living soul for miles around. Clothed heavily, as winter was setting in, his face was youthful but weathered by war. His hair was blond and cropped short, in the style of the legions. Hints of pain and determination filled his blue eyes, and blood dripped from the sword he carried.

He slid it into the sheath at his side and took his horse by the reins. With a tired gait, he led the animal across the field, picking his way between the mangled shells of the dead. Traces of mist grew up between them, hugging the ground like spirits too broken to fly.

Perhaps the souls of the dead were not ready for the journey to Elysium, he thought, or maybe there were just too many for the Boatman to take all at once. Four days of pointless war had seen to that.

Struggling forward on weary legs, the captain kept his eyes focused on the brow of a low ridge a mile or so in the distance. It was the only thing that mattered now.

That ridge was the boundary of civilization. On this side lay the power of Rome. Beyond it was the wilderness, anarchy, and the Goths. That would be his home now. Until the end of his days, however few remained.

They will never forgive you for what you've done.

These words formed in the captain's mind. The thoughts were his own. But for reasons he could not explain, they rang with the timbre of another voice.

They will never take you back.

The sound of a horse neighing in the distance startled him.

In the dark, under a strand of dying trees, he spied a black horse standing beside a small fire. The animal was huge and sturdy—a warhorse, a soldier's horse.

It stood calmly, and then reared up and neighed again, vapors streaming from its nostrils like dragon's breath. The sound carried across the open field, sending a chill through the captain's veins, as if this horse belonged to death itself.

His own steed bucked at the sound, trying to break and run. He tried to steady it, pulling hard on the reins, but the animal snapped its head around and ripped free of the leash. The captain lunged after it, but stumbled and fell as the animal galloped into the distance.

Exhausted from the fighting and killing he'd done, the Roman captain remained on his knees for a moment, trying to catch his breath. With his own steed gone, his thoughts turned to the black horse on the hill. Perhaps he could take it for himself.

He looked back up the slope, but the stallion was no longer alone. A figure now stood beside it, cloaked and unmoving. It seemed the animal's master had returned.

Try as he might, the captain couldn't identify the man by his clothing. His face was shrouded, his cloak billowed in the wind, but it was not the coat of a Roman soldier or the rough garments worn by the Goths. Whoever the man was, he stood calmly, with a large sword drawn and ready at his side.

As he looked upon this figure, the punishing thoughts returned to the captain's head like a nightmare.

They will never take you back… They will never forgive you for what you've done… So where have you left to go but to death itself?

He fought to block the words but they only seemed to grow stronger. Somehow, he knew they were coming from the man on the hill.

They will never forgive you. So where have you left to go but to death itself?

With great weariness, the captain stood awkwardly, gripped by a kind of fear he'd never known. He reached for his sword, pulling the crimson-stained weapon from its sheath and holding it toward the dark rider in the distance.

"I have no quarrel with you!" he shouted.

The figure did not move or even react. He just stood like a statue.

The Roman captain took a step back, holding the sword out before him. He turned, looking for his horse. He scanned the open field, but the animal was long gone, vanished into the night.

He glanced back toward the hill.

To his astonishment, the cloaked figure stood directly in front of him, swinging his blade. With the reactions of a hardened soldier, the Roman parried the blow, but it rang his arm as if he'd struck a great stone.

He stepped to the side and swung for the stranger's head, but the attacker was too fast. The swords collided between them. The impact knocked the captain off-balance and sent him stumbling backward. He regained his balance just as the attacker swung again. This time the blow was far greater. The Roman's blade shattered, and the hilt was torn from his hand.

Before the captain could retreat, a gauntlet-covered fist cracked him across the side of the head, sending him flying to the ground. He landed hard, rolled, and grabbed for a dagger in his boot. Before he could reach it, the weight of the attacker crashed onto his back, knocking him face-first into the dirt.

Pressed down by the heavy foe, the Roman felt his head being pulled backward until his neck was stretched and exposed. A razor-sharp blade sliced across it, cutting his throat wide open. He dropped forward, choking on the warmth of his own blood.

As quickly as it came, the weight of his opponent vanished. But even freed from this oppression, the captain could do nothing but grasp at his neck.

A booted foot rolled him over and onto his back. Clutching his bleeding throat, he looked up.

The dark rider loomed over him now, sitting on his haunches like a vulture. He pulled back his hood, revealing angular features and short dark hair. He glared down at his victim with lifeless black eyes.

And then it came—a message, a whisper.

Do you want to live?

Memories flashed through the captain's mind. Thoughts of his mother, father, and sisters. The beauty of Rome. The taste of cool water and good wine.

The words rang out in his mind once again, louder this time.

Do you want to live?

Guilt, pain, and fear crashed over him, all at once. He wanted to say no, to die like a soldier should, but he reached out for the dark rider. He tried to speak, tried to say yes, but all that came out was bloody froth.

He felt his life slipping away. He could feel demons of Hades reaching for him from beyond the great void.

Yes, he thought, hoping the rider could hear him somehow. *Yes! Anything to live. Anything!*

As he pleaded with the stranger in his mind, the stranger smiled. It seemed he'd gotten the answer he had been waiting for.

Chapter 1

New York City, Present Day

A LATE-MODEL Audi sat parked in the cold rain on a darkened street in Morningside Heights. Run-down apartment blocks loomed around it like monoliths, lit only by the dim light of a few battered street lamps and glare from a neon sign at the corner bar.

Inside the Audi, a man with cropped blond hair, broad shoulders, and black eyes sat in the driver's seat. He waited patiently as the clock ticked past midnight and rain drummed steadily on the roof.

The weather was miserable. The windows were lined with drops on the outside and slightly fogged on the inside. The bitter cold had seeped into the car long ago.

Christian Hannover didn't notice. It'd been a long time since he felt it. In fact, it'd been a long time since he felt much of anything.

His gaze fell to the passenger seat and the twelve-inch hunting knife that lay there. He stretched his hand out to touch it, running his finger across the razor's edge of the blade. The slightest pressure would split the skin, the slightest thrust would punch the tip through flesh and muscle and bone. It was a weapon to kill with, and tonight someone would die.

Maybe it would be him? Would he care if it were?

His life was hollow, empty. His existence had been meaningless for longer than he could remember. What was the point of it anymore?

It was a riddle he'd considered often. At least once during each day, he thought of destroying himself, but so far, every day, he'd chosen to live.

He looked down at the blade. *No*, he thought, *this weapon was meant for someone else.*

He looked back out into the rain as a cab pulled up to the brownstone across the way and a crack of light appeared around the doorframe. A tall, well-built man who might have been in his thirties stepped out dressed in sharp clothes.

"Hecht," Christian whispered to himself. "So it is you, after all."

As Christian watched, James Hecht ignored the rain, walked quickly down the stairs, and ducked into the waiting taxi. The door shut, the brake lights went dark, and the cab began to move.

Christian turned the key, starting the Audi. Once Hecht's cab had moved off, Christian pulled onto the street, turning on his headlights. He didn't need to stay too close. He had a pretty good idea of where Hecht was going.

The two vehicles traveled north amid the steady rain, heading uptown along Broadway and moving past 155th Street and into Washington Heights. At this point, they weren't too far south of the George Washington Bridge. The traffic thinned as they entered an industrial area, and Christian pulled back farther.

In the distance, he saw the cab stop in front of a large factory with rusted steel walls and frosted glass windows, half of which were broken out. Weeds grew waist-high around the perimeter, while a hurricane fence carried signs that read KEEP OUT and NO TRESPASSING somewhere beneath the graffiti that covered them.

Christian parked the Audi down a side street and grabbed the knife. He climbed out of the car and threw the keys on the seat, fully expecting he'd never see it again. He pulled a black trench coat over his shoulders, stepped into the shadows, and all but disappeared.

Up ahead, Hecht was out of the cab. He didn't pay, just waved off the cabbie, and the driver sped away. Now on foot, Hecht glanced Christian's way.

Christian waited, wondering if Hecht had sensed him following. But Hecht had other things on his mind and turned quickly, heading onto the factory grounds.

Christian held his position for a moment, watching the rain fall in its endless, repeating pattern and listening to the repetitive thumping sound coming from inside the old factory.

When Hecht finally vanished around the corner of the building, Christian began to move. He hiked quickly down the street, crossed over it, and pushed through an iron gate. He crossed the vacant parking lot and made his way around to the far side.

Sheltered from the wind and protected by a six-foot overhang, the factory's warehouse-style doors were open a few feet. Three men stood in front of them as the heavy beat of club music pumped out into the night. Flashes of red and green danced through the crack in the door.

An illegal rave—rife with drugs, prostitution, and any other type of criminality one could think of—was raging inside.

Christian approached the bouncers—two black men and one white. The first black guy had dreadlocks, the second a shiny bald head. The white guy beside them had a full sleeve of ink on each arm and half his neck. All three of them looked like prison was a second home. Prison and the gym.

The black guy with the shaved dome stepped in Christian's path, holding up a hand. He tilted a pair of sunglasses down just enough to see over them.

"You got a reason for being here, my man?" His accent was Jamaican.

"I'm here for the rave," Christian said.

"You better have more than that," the dreadlocked man said from his spot against the building.

Christian looked his way.

Dreadlocks held out a hand and rubbed his thumb and fingers together. "This gig ain't free."

The inked-up white guy pressed close, a Glock pistol of some kind stuck into his belt.

Christian pulled out a small wad of cash, three C-notes folded up tight.

The white guy leaned even closer, his eyes darting back and forth. From the twitchy way he moved and the skull-like appearance of his face, Christian guessed he was a meth junkie and probably high right then and there.

"Smells like a cop to me," he said.

Christian turned toward him. "Surprised you can smell anything over the stench coming from your mouth."

The junkie put a hand on Christian's shoulder and went for his gun, but Christian's right hand snapped forward like it had been fired from a catapult. He snatched the gun from the man's belt before the guy could touch it.

At the same time, his left hand clamped onto the man's throat, half crushing the junkie's windpipe. He shoved the guy backward and slammed him into the metal door of the factory, which reverberated with a resounding *boom*.

Christian's fingers curled tighter and tighter around the tattooed guy's throat. He stared into the man's eyes, which twitched and jumped from the drugs and the adrenaline.

"If I kill you," Christian said, "will that prove I'm not a cop?"

The sound of guns cocking told Christian the others were ready to shoot, but he didn't let go. He continued to stare, willing the junkie to look at him, bending his thoughts.

The tension left the guy's body, and then the twitching in his eyes slowed and eventually stopped. Only then did the man really look at Christian, falling deep into a type of pain he could not escape nor understand.

A deep voice called out from behind Christian. "Best let my man go, if you want to live."

Christian ignored the threat. He stared into the meth addict's eyes. "You don't want to go where I can send you," he whispered. "Understand?"

Staring back at him, trembling now, the guy nodded slowly.

Christian let him go, and he fell to ground, clutching his throat.

Christian dropped the Glock, calmly put up his hands, and turned back to the bouncers. The bald guy held a Tech 9 machine pistol with a high-capacity magazine sticking out the bottom. Dreadlocks aimed a long-barreled, nickel-plated .357 revolver.

For a second, Christian thought they might fire. Then Dreadlocks laughed and de-cocked the pistol.

"You one crazy son of a bitch," he said, lowering the weapon. "Whatever you're on man, I wanna get me some."

Christian handed two bills to Dreadlocks and then crumpled up a third and dropped it onto the ground by the fallen bouncer.

Dreadlocks waived him inside, and Christian stepped through the gap in the warehouse doors, his right hand clutching the knife inside the sleeve of his coat. The bouncers he'd left behind would never know how close they'd come to dying.

Inside the factory, a few hundred people danced and mingled on three different levels. Green and red lasers bounced around as the music pounded the steel walls with so much force it seemed it might shake the place apart.

Christian moved through the room like a shark in calm waters, slow and menacing, looking for his prey. He knew Hecht wouldn't stay long in the populated areas. He'd be off in some dark corner feeding a different addiction.

A woman working the crowd in a fishnet outfit caught Christian's eye. She went from one man to the next, leaning on them, touching them provocatively.

No takers, Christian thought. But the night was young. She was just advertising at this point, figuring out who had money and who was just pretending. She'd planted the seed, and now every single one of them was thinking about her, thinking about later.

She noticed Christian watching, and a sultry smile appeared on her lips. As she slinked toward him, the lasers crisscrossed over her body, lighting up her surgically enhanced curves.

"You look like a man who gets what he wants," she said.

He looked her over. Tattoos made of invisible ink covered parts of her body. Under normal lighting, you'd never see them, but they appeared instantly under the black lights of the club.

He marveled at her ingenuity. Not a drop of dark ink marred her skin. She could mix with this crowd or take a call at a five-star hotel, and no one would bat an eye as she strutted across the lobby in a business suit.

"You're a professional," he said. "If you're any good at your job, you've put your hands on every guy who's walked into this place. I need to find someone who came in five minutes ago."

He slipped his hand into a pocket and produced some more cash. She put her hand on the bill, but Christian held it tight.

"Six feet tall. Close-cut dark hair, silver shirt."

"Half the guys in here," she said.

"No jewelry," he added. "Pale. No tracks on his arms, no drugs."

She exhaled loudly as if she was thinking. "I don't know."

"Forget it," Christian said, pulling the money back and pushing past.

"Wait," she said. "Gimme something else?"

Christian glared at her coldly. "You look your clients in the face?"

"Sure."

"If you saw his eyes, you'd remember."

"His eyes?"

"Hollow," Christian said. "Lifeless…Like mine."

She looked into Christian's eyes, and her face lost all expression, as if a cold wind had just blown across it. The eager smile, the fake gloss—all of it vanished. She stepped backward, flustered and unnerved.

Christian grabbed her wrist to keep her from leaving. "You've seen him."

"He went up top," she said, "with a new girl."

Christian extended his hand with the money. She didn't take it. Christian stuffed it into her palm and closed her fingers over it. "If you ever see eyes like these again, I suggest you run."

She nodded, blinked a few times, and then stepped backward into the crowd, moving quickly away from him.

10

Christian looked up. The place was cavernous, with three levels and a hundred hidden recesses. No doubt Hecht had lured the girl into one of them. Christian headed for the upper levels, hoping he wasn't too late.

Chapter 2

JAMES HECHT stood at the bar on the third floor of the abandoned factory. Red velvet drapes hung on each side. The girl next to him was less provocative than most of the others, in a black cocktail dress with an open back and a little chain in front to keep the low-cut sections together. She looked clean—clean enough for him.

Hecht pushed a double shot of Red Bull and vodka toward her and picked up his own. She downed it without hesitation and moved in closer to him. He sensed the warmth of her hand on his thigh, but it meant nothing to him.

She licked her lips. "I want you."

He pulled her in and kissed her, the taste of her mouth and scent of her skin arousing him, igniting his purpose for being there. He would take her in the back. No one would even notice. He wouldn't even leave the party after it was done. He might even stick around long enough to make it a double feature.

He grabbed the back of her arm, put his own glass down without finishing, and led her away from the bar. It had been so long. Too long. He pushed through the crowd, eager to reach the darkness. Too eager, perhaps, as he knocked into a group by the bar.

Someone stumbled, spilling his drink.

"Watch it, jackass!" the guy shouted.

Hecht's body tensed. He snapped his head around. His free hand went for the blade in his pocket, but he held back.

The guy looked at him, raising his hands and backing off quickly. Hecht turned, leading the girl away.

"Freak," someone mumbled.

They had no idea.

Escaping the crowd, Hecht took her into a hallway that once held the factory's offices.

"Where are we going?" the girl asked in a groggy voice.

"Someplace quiet," Hecht said.

He led her to the end of the hall. He still hadn't seen a place that would do, until he spotted a metal stairway that led up to the roof.

He scaled the stairway, pulling her along. She followed as if in a trance. A padlocked door blocked their path. He kicked it once, breaking the chain with ease. The door flew open. The loud bang startled the girl, even in her drugged state.

It was cold and the rain was still falling.

"I don't want to go outside—"

Hecht threw her out onto the roof. She hit hard and slid on the wet surface.

He pulled out a butterfly knife and whipped it open. Licking his lips, he stepped forward and let the metal door slam shut behind him.

—☓—

By now, Christian had reached the highest point in the factory, the third floor. He didn't know how close he was, but in the low light and the sea of people, he could have walked right by Hecht and never seen him.

He ignored the dance floor. There were too many faces to scan, and it wouldn't happen there, anyway. Hecht needed privacy to enjoy himself.

He spotted an open section filled with old, rusted equipment.

Darting into the room, he checked behind the huge machines. Nothing. He busted through the office doors, one after another. They were empty.

Time was running out.

Beyond the last office, he found another hallway. He started down it and then stopped. He'd heard a dull bang, like the sound of a shutter broken loose in a storm. It rang out again and then twice more in quick succession.

Christian turned around. At the end of the hall, a stairway beckoned. He raced toward it. A metal door at the top of the stairs was being pulled open by the wind and then released to slam shut again. *Bang…bang, bang.*

Christian climbed the stairs, slipping the carbon-steel knife from his sleeve. A hint of light reflected off its polished surface. He stopped near the unlatched door, seeing that it had been forced open. He knew what lay beyond it.

He eased it open. Hecht was across the roof, under the eaves of the old elevator housing. The girl was there, backed against the wall. Hecht was playing with the butterfly knife in front of her, opening it and closing it, waving it across her face.

"Scream all you want," Hecht said. "No one can hear you."

Without hesitating, Christian pushed through the door and charged at Hecht.

Hecht sensed him at the last second, turned, and swung the butterfly knife. It slashed through Christian's coat as Christian stabbed downward with his own knife.

Hecht blocked Christian's strike with his arm, and the two men tumbled onto the roof's surface and separated.

Christian sprang to his feet. As Hecht came up, Christian slashed his blade through the air, cutting across Hecht's face, slicing his cheek, and taking off half of his nose.

Hecht stumbled back, landing beside the girl, strangely colored blood oozing from the wounds to his face. Even in the dim light, the blood was dark, a deep-orange color, closer to rust than the bright red it should have been.

The girl pushed backward, trying to move away, trying to get as far under the eaves of the elevator housing as possible.

Hecht snatched at her, grabbing her ankle and pulling her out. Crouching behind her, he wrapped an arm around her neck and pressed the butterfly knife against her throat.

"I'll kill her," he snarled.

"You'll kill her anyway," Christian said.

Truth was, killing wasn't Hecht's goal. It was only a means to an end. He was after something else.

"This is none of your business," Hecht shouted. "What right do you have to interfere?"

The rain began to pick up. The wind seemed to blow a little stronger.

"You don't have to do this," Christian said. "You don't have to live like this. There's another way."

Hecht began to laugh. A laugh of disgust. "And what way would that be? Your way? Drake's way? Dead and barren as a stone?"

"You ran from the brotherhood," Christian shouted. "But your life doesn't have to end in misery."

"What do you know about my life?" Hecht grunted, backing up and dragging the girl.

"I know you're in pain," Christian said, stepping forward. "And I know you were once a decent man. And we *both* know where this road ends."

"Fire," Hecht whispered.

"Fire," Christian said.

Hecht seemed to waver, and Christian stepped forward, closing the gap.

Hecht recovered quickly. He snipped at the girl's skin with the knife, pricking her throat just outside her jugular vein. Christian stopped in his tracks as a trickle of blood began to flow.

"Please," she begged, squirming to get free.

Hecht kept her up, crushing her to him with his forearm.

Any hesitation was gone from him now, replaced with rage and anger. "Maybe I'll force you to watch," he shouted. "Maybe I'll bleed her right here in front of you. Think you can handle that?"

Her blood continued to flow. Hecht looked down as it trickled over his arm.

In that moment of distraction, Christian charged, grabbing for Hecht's arm with his left hand and swinging his knife around the side of the girl with his right.

Christian plunged the blade into Hecht's ribs, and Hecht arched his back, releasing a scream that sounded something other than human. It echoed across the rooftop.

Hecht flung the girl to one side and stumbled backward with Christian's knife stuck in his ribs.

The girl hit the roof hard and grabbed at the wound on her neck. Hecht fell, clutching at the knife. He slammed onto the roof, made a weak attempt to get up, and then fell again. He crawled a few feet, trying to grab at the knife and pull it out, but finally, he slumped to the ground. He lay there and began to shake, his hands twitching before finally going still.

Christian dropped down beside the girl. Blood was streaming over her fingers, down past her collarbone and onto her chest.

Christian reached for her. She pulled back.

"Let me see," he demanded.

He pulled one of her hands away and looked at the wound. An inch wide and straight across her neck, the gash had blood flowing from it, but not squirting. Neither artery had been cut. He placed her hand back on the sliced skin.

"You'll live."

He grabbed for her purse, riffled through it, and pulled out her cell phone. He dialed 911 and threw the phone down next to her. The operator would trace the call, and help would arrive soon enough.

Next, he looked at his own hand. The girl's blood covered his fingers and palm, spreading and thinning with the rain. He could feel it like nothing else in memory.

He stared at it for a second and then let the rain wash it away, slowly diluting the red color until no traces of it could be seen.

Finally, he turned to where Hecht lay. A sign he'd been waiting for had not come. It meant Hecht was still alive.

As if to prove it, Hecht began to move.

"Damn," Christian said.

Hecht got to his feet and wobbled on his legs, clutching once again at Christian's knife. He pulled at it, but the barbed edge held it in place.

The girl saw him and began to shake.

Christian readied himself for another battle. "There's nowhere left to go, James. This is how it ends. This is how it always ends for us."

Hecht glared at Christian with unyielding malevolence. "For you!" he shouted.

He charged, but instead of attacking Christian, he went for one of the factory's huge skylights—a giant ten-by-ten grid of dirty glass. He launched himself without pause, flying and dropping and crashing through the aging skylight.

He fell three stories, shards of glass trailing down behind him like glitter. He landed in the crowd, sending a shock wave of screams and stumbling people scattering toward the edge of the dance floor. Some were injured, others in shock. Curses flew everywhere. People covered their heads from the falling slivers.

The lights and lasers continued to pulse, the music pounded without slowing, but all movement stopped.

The crowd stared at Hecht, inching toward him.

They stopped in their tracks when he started to move, even after a thirty-foot drop, even with the twelve-inch knife sticking out of his ribs.

They gasped as he stood and put his hands on the blade and ripped it from his side, releasing a shriek of agony that swept through the factory and drowned out the music for an instant or two.

By now, the crowd was backing up, giving him all the space they could. And when he began to lumber toward them—stumbling and carrying the knife in his hands—they got the hell out of the way, tripping and pushing and all but climbing over one another to give the madman and his twelve-inch knife some room.

Watching from above, Christian shook his head. He grabbed the girl, brushed the slick, wet hair from her face, and gazed into her eyes.

"Let it fade," he said. "All of this. Let it fade."

She blinked once, and then her eyes glazed over. Christian left her in the rain and tore off down the stairs. Halfway to the ground floor, the sound of gunshots rang out.

The bouncers.

More shots followed, including the sound of the Tech 9 spraying bullets in all directions. The crowd scattered, stampeding for the side and rear exits.

Christian pushed and shoved his way through them toward the front entrance. Finally reaching it, he stepped through the gap.

He was too late. The two Jamaicans lay dead on the concrete, pools of blood spreading around them. The white guy was gone, dragged off to a fate only an unfortunate few would ever know.

People were streaming out every exit, running in a panic for cars and subway lines. Over the noise of the stampede, police sirens could be heard approaching through the rain.

Christian looked in all directions. Hecht was long gone, and despite a desire to chase him, Christian knew he had little choice but to run himself.

Chapter 3

Potomac, Maryland

A COOL mist hung amid the trees of St. Gabriel's Parish Cemetery as dawn graced the Maryland sky. It left the grass wet and the stone paths dark, shrouding the grounds respectfully and dampening out the noise of the world beyond.

In the middle of the cemetery, thirty-five-year-old Katherine Pfeiffer stood motionless. One hand touched the headstone in front of her; the other clutched the delicate fingers of her five-year-old son, Calvin. He tugged and pulled at times, distracted by this and that, but he'd yet to complain, even if he didn't understand what they were really doing there.

Kate kept her eyes on the marker in front of her. The name *Marcus Pfeiffer* was carved into the granite shape, along with the dates of his birth and death. An epitaph read, *Love Always.*

Kate's mind reeled. *Could it really be a whole year since that terrible, awful day?* A year since he'd been found murdered on her kitchen floor on a night she'd chosen to work far too late.

Kate Pfeiffer was a special agent with the FBI. She was supposed to be strong and brave and unemotional. But all she remembered from that time was her knees giving out with the shock of her discovery. She recalled the desperate efforts to revive him and lashing out at the police as they pulled her away from the scene while they gathered evidence. She remembered being short of breath and throwing up and endless crying.

What she didn't remember was how she got through it.

She figured it was her son who'd made it possible. Thinking of him, she found a way to pull herself together. She'd been told that children fed off the emotions of their parents. She didn't want him feeding off such pain.

She ran her fingers across her husband's name, then pointed to a spot on the wet grass. "Put the flowers there."

Calvin let go of her hand and placed a small bouquet against the gravestone.

"Why do we come here?" Calvin asked.

"To visit your dad," she said.

"But Daddy's not here."

"No," she said. "This is just a place where we remember him. He's up in heaven now."

Her son looked up at her, making that face that only young children can make. The one that said they understood the words being spoken but had no idea what any of it meant.

"When is he coming back?"

"Oh, sweetheart," Kate said, squeezing his hand tightly. "He's not coming back. It doesn't work that way."

"But I want him to come back."

She crouched down beside him, inched the zipper on his coat up a bit to keep the chill off him, and forced a smile. "I know you do," she said. "So do I. If we're both real good, one day we'll go see him there."

Calvin looked around, as if he could spot heaven somewhere, as if it might be a place nearby, like the rehab center where his father had worked, a place they'd been to dozens of times.

"But I want to go now," he said.

She pulled him close and held him tighter than she'd really intended to. He didn't know what he was saying, of course, but the thought of losing him and the images it put in her mind were more than she could really bear.

"Don't say that," she whispered, brushing his hair back. "You need to stay here with me. Otherwise, Mommy will be all alone."

"But sometimes you leave me all alone," he said.

She sighed. "Sometimes Mommy has to go do things," she explained. "Sometimes I have to go catch the bad people. But I always leave you with Nana, and I promise I'll always come back for you. No matter what."

Calvin nodded, wrinkled his face, and then sneezed. The last thing either of them needed was to catch a cold.

She looked back at her husband's grave. *I miss you. It's so hard without you. I don't know if I'm doing the right thing anymore. And I don't have anyone to ask or talk to.*

For the first time in her life, Kate understood why the living could be angry with the dead. The sense of abandonment was so strong there were moments when it overrode all reason.

She choked back the tears that were forming and took a breath. "I'm sorry," she whispered. "I know you didn't want to go, either."

No matter how long she stared or how many times she came to this place, the one-sided conversation was always the same. There were no answers. There was no sense of absolution. Only silence.

"Come on, Cal," she said. "Nana's baking cookies."

He nodded sadly.

Leaving was always painful. But the fact was, she had a job to do. A job she did better than most. And even though part of her wanted to quit and be done with it, part of her was defiant.

Every time she considered it, an angry voice rose up inside, insisting that she never quit. Not until she was too old to go on, or until they made her step down, or until she'd cracked every case the Bureau thought it would never break. Not until she'd somehow paid the criminal world back for everything they'd taken from her and her son.

It was a dark, lonely road. But it was the path she'd chosen to keep. And for now, it lead to New York and a homicide that just might be related to a case she'd been working for a very long time.

Chapter 4

AN HOUR later, Kate found herself sitting in the window seat of the Amtrak *Acela* as it raced from Washington to New York. Her partner Billy Ray Massimo sat across from her, his attention buried in the *USA Today*.

The trip to New York was an odd one. They were following up a new lead, one that might or might not have been connected to their current case—a string of nineteen murders in several states, the last eleven in the Boston area.

All the victims had died the same way, throats slashed, jugular veins torn open. Autopsies showed the victims had been drained of most of their blood, yet there was never much spilled at the scene.

The incident in New York was different. The victim was a young woman at an after-hours party. Her throat had been partially sliced, and she'd somehow escaped death. A shootout in the parking lot followed and then a near riot as everyone fled the scene.

It didn't sound much like the Boston murders to her, but they wouldn't know for sure until they got there. In the meantime, Kate stared out the window as the scenery flew past in a blur: trees one minute, an open field or commercial area the next, abruptly followed by the walls of a dark tunnel that seemed to spring upon them with the suddenness of a lightning strike.

Her own thoughts were playing a similar game. The details of their case raced around in her head, accompanied by the confidence that they would solve it at some point and then engulfed by the sudden dose of reality that some cases were never solved, including her husband's.

She looked across to Billy Ray. "Haven't you finished that yet?"

He lowered the paper. "You want a section?"

"No, I want talk about the case."

Billy Ray gave her a slight smirk and then folded the paper and put it away. "What's there to talk about?" he asked. "I thought we'd beaten everything to death by now."

There was no malice in Billy Ray's voice, only humor and his sweet Southern accent.

"Have we come to a conclusion?"

"No."

"Then there must be more to discuss."

He sighed. "I guess this comes with having an partner who's OCD."

"Your damn right it does," she said. "And I've been obsessing over two different things this whole ride up. Back and forth like a tennis match. This case, then my husband's case, and then back to this again."

"Kate," he said, shaking his head as if he knew where this was going.

"What if they're related?"

"Related?" Billy Ray said. The sound of exasperation was hard to cover. "The MOs are completely different. Marcus was stabbed."

"People had been disappearing from the shelter he ran," she said. "People he insisted were on the right track to sobriety. Recovering one day, and then, suddenly, they were gone."

"That's what happens in rehab, Kate. People fall off the wagon. They disappear. First, they go on a binge, and then they're too ashamed to come back. They move on. If they're lucky, they find a new place and get straight again and hope and pray it sticks this time."

There was something in Billy's tone that told her he knew this firsthand somehow.

"Mark thought they were being lured away," she said. "A month after he died, the Virginia State Police found two of them. Their throats had been cut."

"Had their blood been drained?"

"The coroner couldn't tell," she said.

Billy Ray exhaled and looked away. When he turned back, he had a different expression on his face, more like a parent trying to get through to a stubborn child.

"I didn't know Mark all that well," he said. "But he seemed like a terrific person. He worked with people the rest of the world would rather just forget about. He gave them hope. You can't imagine how much respect I have for that. But everything about his death says it was a botched robbery. Someone broke into your house, and he surprised them."

She took a deep breath. She understood what he was saying. She'd been considering this thought for hours now. But if the New York thing was connected to their case—if it was a break or a change in the MO—then there might be other breaks in the pattern.

"Mark knew something," she said firmly. "Maybe he knew what this guy looked like, or where he could be found, or who he was hanging out with. He called me. He said he had something to tell me."

"You have no idea what he was going to tell you, Kate. Maybe he was going to tell you that someone had just given him a big donation so he could open another halfway house or that someone from the house had gotten on their feet and gotten a job and started a new life."

All that was true. Those were the kind of things Mark had reveled in. He loved to share good news, whether it was big or small.

"I should have come home."

"Mark wasn't defenseless. He wasn't a child."

"Nor was he a federal agent taught to shoot and kill," she said.

"Which somehow makes it your fault again?" Billy Ray asked. "How many times are we going to get on this merry-go-round?"

Kate looked out the window. There wasn't much to see. The train had begun to slow. It was rounding a long curve and heading east. Buildings blocked the view to either side.

Maybe he was right. She just didn't know anymore. She didn't know what was worse—losing someone to a random incident or losing him or her to some grand conspiracy. She guessed it was all the same. The pain came from losing; it didn't matter how.

She looked back to Billy Ray. "You should be a shrink instead of an agent," she said. "You'd make a hell of a lot more money."

He chuckled and smiled. "And disappoint the old man? You know he's got me charted to the Senate in ten years. Shrinks don't get to be senators."

She laughed. Around them, other passengers began getting their things together. They were a few minutes from the station. The train continued on. It coasted into another tunnel and began the long, dark ride under the city to the waiting platforms of Penn Station.

—⟋⟍—

Forty minutes later, after grabbing a rental car and heading north through the city, Kate and Billy Ray stood in front of a stained concrete loading dock in front of the abandoned Hammersmith Mills factory. White outlines marked the spots where two armed bouncers had been found dead. Large swaths of dried blood showed how violently they'd died.

Here and there, little chalk circles marked the final resting places of nineteen different shell casings. Long, straight chalk lines traced bullet paths away from where the dead men had fallen. Orange chalk indicated shots from one victim's .357 revolver. Blue chalk tracked shots from the Tech 9. From the look of things, they'd gone down with guns blazing.

"These guys went out like the seventh cavalry," Billy Ray said.

Kate couldn't disagree with that.

"We found nineteen casings," a stocky New York City detective named McMullan explained. "And the .357 had a single live round left inside to go along with five spent shells in the cylinder, so we have to assume it was fired five times.

"Twenty-four rounds," she said.

He nodded. "So far, we've dug bullet fragments out of two cars and a truck across the street from here. Total of twelve. Based on the shell types, we were able to determine who fired what. Those are the lines you see on the ground. The rest of the slugs haven't been recovered yet."

Kate scanned the lines. It looked like both men had been up against the loading bay doors of the factory when they opened fire.

"They hit anyone?" she asked. "'Cause I don't see another outline."

McMullen shook his head.

"You're telling me they fired twenty-four shots in a space the size of a two-car garage and hit nothing?"

"That's exactly what I'm tellin' you," McMullen said.

Billy Ray offered a possible explanation. "I've seen a few gang shootings where the two sides sprayed bullets in every direction, but no one hit a damn thing because they were all taking cover or running at the time."

"Sure," McMullen said. "I've seen that too. Except, out here, we have no return fire. This was a one-sided gunfight, but somehow, the guys with the guns ended up losing."

Kate noticed that most of the orange lines and most of the blue lines converged at a single point, like they'd been fired at a stationary target, catching it in a cross fire. The point was inside the fencing. The target couldn't have been a car.

"You found no blood?" she asked, just to be sure.

"Only theirs," he said, pointing to the chalk outlines.

"And they died how?"

"Their throats were ripped out."

Billy Ray looked surprised. "What?"

"Don't you FBI types hear too good?" McMullen snapped. "I said their throats were ripped out. Larynxes, voice boxes, and everything else in there—gone."

"Which means…" she began.

"Someone killed these bastards with their bare hands."

"While they were blazing away with their guns?"

"That's what the evidence shows."

Silence fell over them. Kate looked around, wondering how it could have gone down that way. McMullen stood with his hands in his pockets and his eyebrows up, rocking back and forth as the truth soaked in.

Finally, Billy Ray shook his head. "No way," he said. "You've got something wrong here."

Kate didn't like what she was seeing, either. "Maybe they had armor on," she offered. "Like those guys who robbed the bank in California a few years back. The ones who took on thirty cops, till the cops broke into a rifle store to get more firepower."

"Yeah, I remember that," McMullen said scratching his head. "Those guys were walking tanks. They looked like robots from outer space. According to the witnesses here, this was one guy, and he was all decked out in civilian clothes. Looked like John Travolta in *Saturday Night Fever*. Last I checked, shiny polyester ain't bulletproof."

"You've witnesses to confirm that?"

"A whole roomful of 'em," McMullen insisted. "And none of them say anything about a guy in armor or even a vest. Besides, if the perp was wearing a vest, we'd find compressed slugs that hit him, mushroomed, and fell off."

He pointed to the chalk lines once again and came back to his conclusion. "These guys weren't drilling shots uselessly into an armored assailant; they were missing."

Kate couldn't see how that was possible from such close range, but she couldn't come up with any other answer.

"What else you got?"

"We believe there was a third victim."

"Where?"

McMullen pointed to a circle on the ground. "We found a Glock over there," he said. "Most of the witnesses said there were three guys at this door when they came in—two black guys and one white guy. The white guy seems to be missing."

"Could the Glock belong to the assailant?" Billy Ray asked.

"Possibly," McMullan said, shrugging, "except it was never fired. Would you get in a war like this and never pull the trigger and then leave your gun on the ground when you left?"

McMullen was right; that made no sense. The Glock seemed more likely to be the third bouncer's gun. "What are the chances you'll get a hit on the prints?"

McMullan tilted his head to the side as if he was calculating. "Considering the quality of people at a rave like this, I'd say damn near a hundred percent. Most of these guys have enjoyed the hospitality of the New York State penal system at one time or another. We should have a name in a day or two."

Kate guessed that McMullan was right, but she wondered what good it would do beyond telling them who the third victim was.

She studied the scene again, walking around it, looking at it from the victims' perspectives. None of it made any sense to her. The .357 shells were aimed fairly consistently. Shots from the Tech 9 had fanned the whole lot. At the rate a gun like the Tech 9 dispensed bullets, the whole thing couldn't have taken more than a few seconds. But how in the hell they'd managed to hit nothing and then been killed at arm's length was beyond her.

"Any motive?"

McMullen eased toward the door. "Our first thought was robbery. Maybe someone got greedy. The problem is, nobody touched the cash."

"What about the drugs?"

"My guys impounded enough dope to fill a couple of suitcases. This wasn't a theft. Even these poor bastards died with the door money on 'em. I'm talkin' thousands."

Kate looked at Billy Ray. He shook his head. Neither of them had any answers.

"So it wasn't a hit, it wasn't a turf war, and it wasn't a theft," she said. "What the hell was it?"

McMullan shrugged. He looked tired and a little ragged, probably sick of being on the scene already. "I don't know," he said, waving them toward the open doors. "But come with me. I'll show you the weird part."

As McMullen went under the police tape and entered the building, Billy Ray exchanged glances with Kate.

"The weird part?" he said.

"I'd have thought this was the weird part," she replied.

She ducked under the tape and stepped into the expansive warehouse. Shade and light fell down from above, mixing on the floor in strange patterns.

McMullen pointed to an opening in the ceiling. It was a busted-out skylight. Glass littered the floor beneath it.

"I've been here for the better part of twelve hours," McMullen said. "I've interviewed hookers who promised to take care of me if I let them go and trust funders who tried to bribe me or threaten me with their big-time lawyers. I've talked to junkies and thugs and a few businessmen who were pissing their pants about even giving me their names. Everybody has a different story about why they were here and what they thought was really going on in this place. But on this"—he nodded toward the busted skylight—"on this one point, every single one of them says the same damn thing."

"Which is?"

"He fell."

"Who fell?" Billy Ray asked.

"The assailant," McMullan explained. "He crashed through the skylight with a big knife sticking out of his ribs, dropped to concrete floor, and landed flat on his face. They all thought he was dead. Then he got up, ripped the knife out of his side, and ran into the crowd. At least five people saw him leave through this entrance. That's when the shooting started."

Kate now understood why no one had bothered trying to explain the incident over the phone or even talk about it until she and Billy Ray were on the scene.

"That's a hell of a fall," Billy Ray noted. "The guy had to be on something."

"Sure," McMullen said. "But even if he was on some designer drug that makes you insane and unable to feel pain, that fall would have killed ninety-nine out of a hundred people. Yet this guy gets up and walks away."

Kate couldn't even imagine the hundredth person surviving. "What was he doing on the roof in the first place?"

"That's where he took the girl," McMullan said. "The one whose throat he cut."

Suddenly, Kate remembered why they were here. "We're going to need to talk to her," she said.

"Sure," McMullen said. "You can find her at Belleview in protective custody. But good luck getting anything out of her. Whatever she was on, she doesn't remember a damn thing."

Kate looked at Billy Ray. "Maybe her mind will clear up by the time we get there."

"Yeah, that always happens," McMullen said sarcastically.

Kate sighed. Looking over the entire scene, she felt lost. The initial call had given her hope that they might be on to something, especially when they'd heard that a victim had survived, but the details were baffling.

It felt odd. It felt wrong. All the other crimes were so clean and quiet. This one was loud and chaotic and messy. She had no way of explaining what had happened in the abandoned factory, but whatever had gone down, she didn't think it was connected to the Boston crimes.

When Billy Ray spoke, he sounded like he was thinking along the same lines. "So all this happens," he said, "and all we know is that some crazy, doped-up freak managed to kill a couple of armed thugs and run away. Is that it?"

"We do know one other thing," McMullan said.

"Which is?" Kate asked.

McMullan looked back up toward the broken skylight in the ceiling, and Kate's gaze followed.

"As psychotic and dangerous as this guy was, somebody managed to stick a twelve-inch blade in his gut and throw him through that skylight. And it wasn't our drugged-out, hundred-and-five-pound little girl, I can promise you that."

Kate squinted at the broken metal frame high above. McMullen was right. Something else had gone down on that roof—something bad—and the young woman had been just a small part of it.

Chapter 5

Boston, Massachusetts

ON THE twenty-ninth floor of a building owned by his company, Timeless Exports Imports, Drake Castillion sat calmly, gazing across his desk. Broad shouldered, but tall enough to appear lean, he had black eyes; thick, wavy hair that looked black in the low light but was actually deep brown in color; and a gaunt face that appeared both wise and aristocratic.

His hands clasped loosely in front of him, he rested his elbows on his black marble desk and gazed across its flecked surface at a man named Victor Losini.

As Drake watched, Losini's gaze darted around the windowless office, studying the ancient artwork and long-forgotten relics Drake had collected. Despite being a former member of Interpol and running one of the best-known investigation firms in the world, Victor Losini seemed nervous.

A pair of elevator doors opened behind Losini; the office, along with the rest of the floor, was accessible only through them. A striking woman in a gray business suit came in. She was tall and thin, with long legs and cinnamon-colored skin.

Drake watched as Losini looked her up and down.

"The report you wanted," she said, placing a file on Drake's desk.

"Thank you, Vivian," Drake said.

She nodded, walked back to the elevator, and stepped inside. As the doors closed, Losini's gaze lingered.

"I sense you'd like to be on that elevator yourself," Drake said.

"With her?" Losini said. "Sure."

"Or even without her," Drake replied.

"I don't follow you."

"You intend to turn me down," Drake said.

Losini sighed and then got down to business. "I know the other agencies you've used to look for this man," he said. "They're top-notch outfits. If they couldn't find him, it's because he's not out there."

"They failed me, Mr. Losini. One of them betrayed me by taking my money and not even bothering to look. I sense you'll do better."

"With all due respect," Losini replied, "I know five years at the rates those guys charge can't run you less than ten million dollars. I know my agency will charge you fifty thousand a week to do the same. It's your money, that's true, and you say money is no object, but I've worked for plenty of rich guys who said the same thing. Sooner or later, money becomes an object. Sooner or later, you realize you're just wasting your time. "

Losini looked proud of himself, his wit and wisdom bright and quick in his own mind. Drake stood, drawing up to his full six-foot-three height. Losini seemed a bit startled.

"Come with me," Drake said as he walked to a door on the right-hand side of the room. "I'll teach you something about the true nature of time."

Losini stood up cautiously as Drake swiped a card through the reader on the door and unlocked it.

Drake opened the door and held it, waving Losini forward.

"Where are we going?"

"To my inner sanctum of sorts," Drake said.

Losini looked suspicious.

"My company owns the building," Drake explained. "Business is conducted down below, but my private residence is up here, from the twenty-seventh floor to the roof."

"I'm not sure that's going to change anything."

Drake offered a cunning grin. "Surely the other agencies told you how reclusive I am. Aren't you the least bit curious to see what they never did?"

Losini hesitated, and then his confidence returned. "If you insist."

Drake pulled the door wide and ducked into the hall. Losini followed. They walked past a small fountain in a dark hallway of gray-and-black granite. Only recessed fluorescent lights lit the corridor.

"Why is it so dim in here?"

"I have a condition," Drake said. "Light bothers my eyes."

"I see."

They came out into a more spacious room, one with a view that took in all of Boston. The city was lit up for the night, and the moon rode high above.

Losini stared, duly impressed. The lights gave the city a pristine facade, as if it were a virgin metropolis. But beauty and the truth were seldom the same thing. And Losini's eyes, Drake noticed, were drawn to the lesser of the two.

"Over here," he said.

In the center of this great room was a large pendulum swung on a fifty-foot cable. Up above, somewhere hidden in the rafters, it attached to a bearing made of polished, frictionless titanium. Three stories below, a twenty-pound sphere made of solid brass swished repetitively across a map of the world patterned in silver and onyx. It moved back and forth in long, smooth strokes. In the silence, each pass could just be heard, like a whisper.

"Do you know what this is, Mr. Losini?"

"A pendulum of some kind."

"Not just any pendulum," Drake explained. "A Foucault pendulum, although this one is far older than the man for whom they're named. I purchased it to remind me of life's great truth: Time is more valuable and precious than any other commodity. Time makes all things possible."

"I'm really not sure what you're driving at," Losini said.

Drake decided to explain. "The man who designed this pendulum died in a revolt against the Roman Empire in the year 483, fourteen hundred years before Foucault demonstrated the principle of these machines and explained how they work. This pendulum was lost, buried in the rubble of a city, and then found again in 1938. Before it could be fully excavated, the men working on it were killed by the Nazi party for their political activities, and the pendulum was buried again, this time in a warehouse in Berlin.

"Hitler is said to have wanted it for the Reichstag. But before he could mount it anywhere, he was overrun by the Allies and chose to kill himself like the coward that he was. Fifty years later, it came to me, and now, finally, it swings freely."

"And that tells me…what?"

"The designer is gone," Drake said. "The discoverers are gone. Hitler and his third Reich are gone. But the pendulum itself lives on. Time has made the machine more powerful than its creator, even its usurper."

Losini looked at the pendulum one more time. As abstract as the concept was, he seemed to grasp it. "Once it gets pushed, it keeps on going," he said, "slowly turning in the circle over your map of the world down there."

"The other way around," Drake said, correcting him. "The pendulum swings in one place, unwilling to change. The world revolves around it."

Losini nodded and seemed to understand what Drake was saying. "Neat trick," he said, "but even if the world revolves around that hunk of steel, it's not going to bend its will to you or me. I can't find a man who doesn't exist. And the guy you're looking for is either dead or locked up in some third world prison, where they don't keep records or submit to inspections. And that makes him as good as gone."

Drake shook his head. "I assure you he's not dead, Mr. Losini. And as for a prison…I doubt there's one on this earth that could hold him."

Losini's gaze narrowed. His interest seemed peaked at last. He was feeling his roots. The lawman with a criminal to hunt whom Drake had just elevated above him and his kind.

Drake only wished he'd tried that tactic earlier. "Let's stop kidding ourselves," he said. "You could have turned me down over the phone when I told you this would be an extremely difficult task. You could have called or sent an e-mail canceling our meeting after the other agencies told you they'd tried and failed. But you didn't do either. You came in person. There must be a reason. I think it's that you believe in yourself—as all men should. You believe you can do the impossible and succeed where they failed."

Losini hesitated.

"Am I wrong?"

Losini cleared his throat. "There is one option neither of them tried," he admitted.

"A new method?"

"Facial recognition technology. Not exactly new, but getting better all the time. You gave me a picture. It looks kind of old, but you insist it's relatively recent, so we can use it. I have friends at Interpol and in Homeland Security. I can get them to code this guy's features into their network, put a John Doe tag on him, and give him a high-level threat category, the one they use to watch for terrorists. He pops up anywhere on the grid, and we'll get a notification."

"Cameras," Drake said.

Losini nodded. "You told me he travels, never stays in one place very long. There are cameras everywhere now, especially around transportation hubs. Unless he's riding a horse or paddling a canoe, he'll show up sooner or later."

Drake digested this. "Why wouldn't the other agencies have offered this service?"

"Because it's illegal," Losini replied bluntly. "Because they don't know the people I do, and they wouldn't have the guts to grease the skids the way I'm willing to, even if they did share my contacts."

"Can you actually do what you propose?"

Losini nodded without blinking. "Anyone gets caught, and there's going to be hell to pay, but with enough money and promises, I think I can convince them to spread the net."

"How effective is that kind of search?"

"Far better than anyone thinks or really wants to know. Big Brother is already watching, you can count on that."

Drake took in the information. There were risks, but it was worth it. "How much?"

"I'll need a million to spread around," Losini said without batting an eye. "And that's just to get the doors open. A couple million to follow and ten million for putting my company at risk."

Drake nodded. "You'll have it."

Losini appeared surprised. Perhaps he'd expected an argument or a negotiation. Things Drake had no time for. "Any other questions?

"Yeah," Losini said. "Why is this guy is so important to you? Did he steal your wife or kill somebody or something like that?"

Drake spoke in a flat tone. "He's killed many people in his time. None that you would know or care about, trust me."

Losini's face soured. "I don't do private vengeance. Not even for your kind of money."

"He was a soldier once," Drake explained. "There were wars. They left him…disturbed."

"I need more than that," Losini insisted. "I need to understand your interest."

"It's very simple," Drake said. "I have wealth, power, influence…But despite all this, despite everything I possess, I'm alone on this desolate rock of a world. The man in the photo, the man you'll be looking for, is the closest thing to family that I've ever had."

Losini took that in, perhaps wondering if there was any significance. "And when I find him?"

"Contact my office," Drake said coldly. "And leave the rest to me."

Chapter 6

New York City, Columbia University

IDA WASHINGTON used the strength in her arms and the power in her shoulders to force her wheelchair forward and over an obstruction that blocked her path. As she bumped down on the other side, she noticed the offending item was a beige-colored textbook from one of the classes she taught.

She shrugged. Moving around her cramped little office at Columbia University required a combination of dexterity, arm strength, and the occasional willingness to four-wheel it over things. Students often wondered about the state of their term papers once they were returned. Did the tattered edges mean Professor Washington had read it over several times? Were tire tracks the equivalent of a gold star or a sign she thought very little of the work?

Truth was, they were just a result of too much stuff and too little space.

A decade of inhabiting the same office led to clutter in most professors' lives. Ida was no different. Surrounding her were stacks of unfinished research, keepsakes, and a collection of rare books, many of which had been around far longer than her fifty-nine years.

They gathered dust, mostly. The only thing that didn't was a picture of her and her mother taken when she was a little girl. They were standing on the old wooden porch in front of the small house she'd grown up in.

In addition to the books, shelves on each wall were stocked with artifacts from around the world. At times, they seemed like relics from another life, as if they belonged to a former tenant who'd left them behind when he or she moved on.

In a way, that was true. Ida had collected these things before her accident. Before a fall in Guatemala had damaged her spine and rendered her legs all but useless. She'd ended up in a wheelchair. She hadn't set foot outside New York since.

She didn't need to—the Internet and a network of friends and contacts brought the world to her.

Instead of fading away, Ida had continued to work, raising her profile even higher than before. In many ways, she was now considered *the* leading expert on ancient documents and forgotten religions.

She'd petitioned many nations, organizations, and historical societies to give up documents and relics they held secret. She was so familiar with the Freedom of Information Act and similar rules from around the world that she'd been asked to author a book on digging up information. She'd agreed to write it, but only if someone would publish it under the title *Being a Pain in the Ass.*

So far, there were no takers.

Didn't matter. She knew the value of persistence. It's what got things done. At the moment, she was practicing what she preached. After years of pushing and cajoling and begging, she believed she was closing in on a secret, one that was long hidden by the Catholic Church and other religious organizations.

She wheeled herself up to her desk and moved the computer mouse. The monitor came on, displaying fragments of an old document, parts of which had been found in different places. It read like a holy order, like a call to arms.

A contact within the church had authenticated it in confidence as part of a larger text and the root of a much bigger story. Her friend had promised to explain what he could, while insisting there were things he could not tell her. She understood that too. In her line of work, you took what you could get.

She checked the time: nearly 1:00 a.m. in New York, 7:00 a.m. in Rome. With a type of excitement and nervousness she could scarcely remember, she reached for the phone and dialed a European number.

The call went through and began ringing.

"Come on, Father Hershel," she whispered to herself.

Despite living in New York for years, she retained a hint of her Southern accent. Georgia had been her childhood home. Only college had brought her north.

A click on the line told her the receiver had been picked up. She waited to hear Father Hershel's cheery hello, but no one spoke.

"Hello?" she said. "Father Hershel?"

A discordant male voice jarred her. "I'm afraid Father Hershel is not available."

"Is he not in yet?" she said. "I didn't realize how early it was—"

"I'm quite sure you know what time it is, Ms. Washington."

That the man on the other end of the line knew her name was a little uncomfortable for her.

"Who am I talking with?" she asked firmly.

"I'm Father Dante Masiangleo," the man said. "Father Hershel has been transferred to another position. How can I be of assistance?"

Ida was speechless. No small feat. She didn't know this Masiangelo person. Father Hershel had never mentioned him, not even as someone who might have a problem with the truth Ida was searching for.

"Where has Father Hershel been moved to? And why?"

"He will no longer take your calls, Ms. Washington. You've played on his kindness and manipulated him, but Father Hershel is aware of your intentions and does not wish to let you discredit the Church."

"I'm only seeking information," she said. "I hardly see how revealing the truth could be an attempt to discredit."

"You are in possession of mere fragments of a document," he said. "Viewing such a small portion of the whole can result in misunderstanding. Drawing of conclusions that bear no relation to reality. This is how it would discredit us."

"That's why I want to know the rest of it," she said. "When you keep things hidden, people have no choice but to draw their own conclusions."

"I can only tell you that what you possess was never supposed to see the light of day," he replied, "or to be viewed by the outside world. It was part of an internal discussion relating to a point of theology."

"It talks about war," she said.

"A spiritual war," he insisted.

"You don't need soldiers or swords for a spiritual war," she countered. "The fragment references the bringing of weapons to a zealot's army."

"Metaphors, I assure you."

"Come on, Father. Do you really expect me to believe that?"

The priest sighed. "Does the document you have not speak of demons?"

The document was written in ancient Latin, and the translation was odd and difficult. It read like a confirmation of fears, that something not of this world had entered it and now dwelled among the people. The church called them the Fallen. It claimed they were demons sent to destroy humanity and undermine the Lord.

"It does," she admitted.

"And pray tell me," he asked, "what good might swords be against such creatures?"

"Well, I don't know," she said, sensing his logic. "That's another reason I want to see the rest of this letter."

"I'm afraid that won't be possible," he said. "No other record of it exists."

Ida heard crackling and clicks on the line. She guessed the call was being recorded. Her sense of paranoia ticked up, but aside from excommunicating people, the church didn't have much power to intimidate these days. And considering she was a Southern Baptist who hadn't even been to her own church for years, that didn't concern her.

"Well, I'm not done looking yet," she told him. "So I guess we'll see about that."

"Certainly," he replied. "Should you happen upon anything of note, we would enjoy making it part of our collection."

"I'm sure you would," she replied. "Good day, Father Masiangleo."

"Good day, Ms. Washington."

A click on the line told her he'd hung up. She did the same, turning off her computer and grabbing her coat, wondering the whole time how she might locate Father Hershel.

By the time she'd rolled her wheelchair out of the office, she was smiling. Father Masiangelo had given her something without realizing it. His offhand comment about making such a note part of their collection told her two things: one, they kept such documents (not a big secret, really), and two, even the church believed that other fragments or better-preserved copies might still exist somewhere.

She rolled through the main corridor and reached the exit of the large building. As she put her key in the security door, she had the strangest feeling of being watched.

She looked around. No one was there at this hour.

"Come on, Ida," she said to herself. "Wait till you really find something before you start getting paranoid."

She turned the key, hit the silver button with the wheelchair logo on it, and waited while the door opened. As she rolled down the ramp, she thought about getting a cab, but she was only seven blocks from home. At this time of night, it might take thirty minutes for a handicap-accessible cab to arrive. And even then, it was awkward with the chair. By that time, she could have been home drinking chamomile tea and getting ready for bed.

She rolled across the campus like she'd done a thousand times before. The familiar sights and places should have comforted her, even in the dark. But they didn't, and the odd feeling of being watched returned. She stopped to look around again.

She saw nothing. No one. But the hair on the back of her neck rose up, and Ida decided to get herself home ASAP.

She began moving again, heading out onto Amsterdam Avenue and heading down to 107th Street. Halfway down the block, she heard footsteps on the pavement behind her. Or at least she thought she did.

She rolled faster and faster. Her heart was pounding. She saw no one, but she didn't care. She just wanted to get home.

Her arms were strong from years of pushing the chair, and once it got going, she could move pretty quickly. Heading down the sidewalk with a slight descending grade, she was traveling so rapidly that she felt a little out of control.

As she reached a gap between the buildings, a group of students came around a corner. She crashed into them, sending one of them sprawling. She heard a bottle smash and a muffled curse.

Hands grabbed her chair and stopped it.

"I'm sorry," she said to the young man on the ground.

He looked up at her, dazed. His friend held her wheelchair tight, gripping one wheel and one armrest. She noticed his hands were tattooed. The words HATE and FEAR were spelled out on his knuckles.

The man she'd knocked down was lying in a stain of liquid and shattered glass. She recognized the charcoal scent of whiskey.

He stood up and threw the neck of the shattered bottle away. "What's your problem, bitch?"

His face was harder and older than she'd expected. So was the man who still held her chair. It took only a second for Ida to realize these weren't students at Columbia and only a second more to realize she was in a great deal of trouble.

Chapter 7

THE KIND of terror only felt by the powerless gripped Ida Washington.

"You think you own the street," one of them said to her.

"Just let me go," she said. "It was an accident."

"You cause an accident, you got to pay," the guy holding her chair said.

"I'm sorry," she repeated. "I'll buy you a new bottle of liquor, if you want."

"You gonna buy more than that," the punk insisted.

In a blink, he grabbed her and yanked her out of the chair. She went to scream, but he clamped his hand down over her mouth. Her carried her like a rag doll and slammed her to the ground behind a dumpster that smelled of urine, sour milk, and trash.

She reached up and scratched his face, clawing for his eyes.

He pulled back, cursed, and slugged her in retaliation. The blow knocked her woozy.

Through a haze, she saw her chair being flung into the wall across from her and one of the thugs pulling her purse from the ground. He rifled through it, throwing stuff out.

"What's she donating to the cause?" the man on top of her called out.

"Man, this old hag ain't got more than five dollars in here." He pointed to a trio of small rings on Ida's fingers. "She's got some jewelry, Shakes. Cut it off her."

The man holding her down, the one who had been called "Shakes," pulled out a knife, but Ida was already slipping the rings off her hand.

She threw them at the thugs.

"Easy with the goods, Grandma."

Ida squirmed, but the man kept his weight on her. "She got any plastic?"

"Oh yeah," the man with her purse said.

"What's your pin?"

Ida was trembling. She knew they would probably kill her once they had what they wanted. She'd seen their faces. Their tattoos. They'd be easy too easy to identify.

"Make her talk," one of them yelled.

The man on top of her slapped her and then grabbed her face violently. "Tell me your damn pin!"

He released his hand enough to let her talk. "Nineteen fifty-two," she whispered almost inaudibly.

"What?"

"One…nine…five…Help!" she screamed. "Somebody please—"

Another blow knocked her groggy.

"Hey, man," one of the guys said. "She's seen our faces. She can ID us to the cops."

"Not if she's dead," Shakes said.

He pulled out a snub-nosed .38 revolver and cocked the hammer, then stopped and looked back down the alleyway as if something had distracted him.

Ida turned her eyes and tried to focus. She saw a man standing there. He was a silhouette, lit up by the streetlights on Amsterdam Avenue.

"Move along, jack-off," one of the guys said. He pulled out a knife and made sure it was visible.

The man under the streetlight didn't react one way or another. He just stood there. To Ida, his image seemed blurred. He looked like an angel, she thought, a dark angel. Somehow, the vision gave her strength.

With Shakes distracted, she jammed her hand into his neck. He rocked backward, and his hand came off her mouth.

She screamed for half a second before Shakes clamped his hand back onto her face. She saw the gun swinging her way as if to pistol whip her across the temple. But before he struck, his weight came off her, and he was flung away into the far wall.

The sound of shooting boomed through the alleyway. She saw a knife slash forward, followed by more flashes from the barrel of the .38. A long blade caught the light as it slashed through the air.

One of the thugs crumbled to the ground, doubling over and clutching at his stomach. The second man screamed and fell back, his neck slashed and gushing blood.

Shakes grabbed for a knife, having emptied the revolver. But the man in the dark coat caught his arm and stopped it cold. He held it for a second and then brought the katana-like weapon down hard and fast. It hit Shakes in front of his elbow and took off half of his arm.

Shakes screamed and fell to his knees, clutching at the bloody stump.

Ida saw the curved blade rise up in the stranger's hands.

"No!" she shouted.

The stranger hesitated. He held the sword high as if to decapitate Shakes right there in the alley.

Shakes began to move. Somehow, he made it to his feet and stumbled off, cradling what was left of his arm, headed down the alley to God knows where.

As he left, Ida tried to focus on the figure dressed in black who'd just saved her. He lowered the sword and wiped it clean. As he turned toward her, his short blond hair caught the light, and his eyes seemed almost iridescent in the dark.

He was speaking to himself, but Ida could not make out what he was saying, it sounded like Latin. He sheathed his sword. It hid perfectly under his long charcoal-colored coat. Then he bent down beside her.

"It was you," she said. "You were following me?"

She stared at his face. He couldn't have been more than thirty, but there were miles of pain in that face. And his eyes…They seemed so bright in the darkness, like a cat's eyes reflecting the moonlight.

"Who are you?" she asked.

"You know who I am," he replied in a cold voice. "I'm one of the Fallen."

Chapter 8

IDA WASHINGTON woke up in her office. She was lying fully clothed on a couch where she often napped. Her mind reeled with bizarre thoughts. Men with swords, thugs attacking her. As she studied the familiar surroundings, the images began to fade.

"Thank God it was a dream," she said to herself.

She pulled herself up to a sitting position and felt another dizzy spell. She put a hand to her head and then pulled it back instantly. He face was bruised and tender. A welt on her cheekbone was raised where she'd been struck.

It wasn't a dream.

The handle on the front door moved and the door opened. In came the man who'd rescued her. The man with the sword who'd slashed and hacked the thugs who'd attacked her. She should have felt thankful, but she mostly felt afraid.

"Who are you?" she demanded before he'd fully entered the room.

He closed the door. "We've been over that."

"What are you doing here?"

"Bringing you ice," he said, holding up a wet towel with ice cubes wrapped inside. "For your face."

He handed it to her, and she placed it gently against her cheek, thankful for the cooling sensation.

"Thank you," she said. "And thank you for saving me. But why didn't you bring me to a hospital or a police station?"

He leaned against the wall. "Those places are problematic for me."

She guessed a sword-wielding maniac would not be welcome in either spot. "I have to call the police," she said, heaving herself off the couch and onto her chair.

"No."

"You killed two men in an alley."

"Their bodies are gone," he said. "No one will ever miss them."

"What about the guy who lost an arm?"

"He won't live long with an arm like that. And if he does, he won't remember anything," the man assured her. "I erased it from his mind."

She cocked her head to the side. "You *erased it from his mind*?" she repeated. "I don't know what your deal is, but you're obviously crazy. If you think—"

He glared at her. "You know exactly what my deal is, Ida Washington. I'm one of the Fallen. The very group whose identity you're searching for."

The words shocked her, but she was well aware that he could have searched her office while she was unconscious. "So you're a demon?" she said incredulously.

"The church would tell you that," he insisted.

"I see. And what do you call yourself?"

"My name is Christian," he said. "But I've had many names over the years."

"Over the years?" she said. "You can't be more than thirty-five."

He looked her in the eye. "I'm a lot older than that. I was a Roman soldier—a captain of the legion—when I was attacked and fell from grace. My throat was slit wide open by a man who called himself Drakos. As I lay dying, I heard an offer of life extended to me and I took it. In that moment, I became one of the Fallen, what others call demons, or creatures of the night, or the Nosferatu."

She began to shake her head. "Unless I missed it, you don't have a scar."

"It healed."

"Oh, I see. And yet, you have marks on your hands and arms?"

"The transformation heals all existing wounds," he explained. "All sickness ends when one crosses into the void. But once the metamorphosis is complete, the process stops. Injuries after that remain forever. This burn on my arm came at the hands of the Inquisition four hundred years ago."

"The Inquisition?" Ida pursed her lips and tilted her head. She knew better than to argue with a delusional person, but she couldn't help herself. "I suppose this means you're all immortal."

"Not immortal. We die by the thousands. Most by our own hand. But we don't age."

"You really expect me to believe all this?"

"Mythology tells you we exist," he said. "There are stories and legends of us in every culture on earth—demons, spirits of the dead that still walk among men, stealers of life. There's a reason for that."

"Yeah, there's a very good reason," she said. "It's because people are crazy."

He didn't react, didn't smile or laugh or scowl like she might have expected him to.

She sighed and shook her head softly. "Look, I thank you once again for saving my life. But I can't help you, sonny. You're not the first person I've met living a delusion. This city's full of 'em. I guess you're doing better than most, because you don't have tinfoil on your head, but that doesn't make any of this real. I'm afraid you're in the wrong building. You don't need a history professor; you need psychiatric care."

He stared at her.

"Listen to yourself," she continued. "You twist the story to make it fit the circumstances and the questions that come your way. You change it up or add a wrinkle every time I ask you something. I honestly don't know how you people keep it all straight."

His black eyes focused on her, and she began to feel dizzy once again.

"You're looking for the truth," he said coldly. "For an explanation of what you saw as a child. A blaze of blue-white flame that left nothing but ash."

Her heart skipped a beat. "What did you say?"

"I can see it in your mind," he said. "You climbed from your bed because you heard a commotion, and you looked out your window. You saw a man in chains being dragged into the woods by three other men in long coats. But it wasn't a lynching. The man in the chains was white, as pale as bone. The men who took him wore black, the long coats of the Ignis Purgata. You followed them. You watched as they chained him to a tree. You screamed as they drove a spike through his heart, and you cried as the tree burst into flames—blue-white flames that haunt your dreams even today. The next morning, you went back there and stirred the ashes with a long stick. Everyone insisted that lightning had hit the tree, but you knew better."

She was shocked. Stunned into silence. A feeling of vertigo swept over her. He was telling her things she had never shared with another living soul. Describing images she'd fought to bury for years, memories she'd tried all her life to deny.

"You can't know that," she said. "Nobody knows that."

"You know it."

In desperate need for something to restore her sense of balance, she gazed at the photo on her desk with the familiar image of her and her mother on a flat wooden porch. The color had slowly faded from the print. After all these years, it looked more like a black-and-white photo that had been touched up than a vibrant color print. Just like her memories.

She thought back to the burning tree and the pale man chained to it. She remembered his eyes, flashing in the night before they stabbed him. She could still hear his scream. She recalled her mother telling her the tree had been hit by lightning. But she also remembered following the men with the black coats and trying to stay out of the moonlight. The skies had been clear all night.

She looked up to the man who'd saved her. His eyes had been so bright in the darkness of the alley, but they were black in the sparsely lit office.

"I don't want to believe this," she said.

"But you do," he insisted.

Yes, she did. A new wave of fear swept over her. "It's said your kind steal souls from the living."

"Mostly, they just kill and murder for pleasure," he replied.

"Just so you know," she said, "this whole building is under video surveillance. Anything happens to me, they're going to come looking for you."

"I'm not going to harm you," he said. "I spilled enough innocent blood while I was human to make me sick of it all. I just need your help."

Despite the conflict and fear in her heart, an overwhelming sense of pity began to fill her. Whether the man was deranged or somehow telling the truth, whether her own mind was playing tricks on her or not, she figured the only way to get him out of that office was to tell him whatever he wanted to know.

"What is it you want from me?"

"You've found traces of my history," he said. "I want to know what they are. The truth about my past. The origin of this curse. I could take it from you by force, but that's not my way."

She thought for a moment and then nodded. She'd give him what he asked for and pray that he left once he had it. Settling into her wheelchair, she moved herself to the desk and reached for a thick book on the top of a stack on the right-hand side.

"This," she said, pulling the book from the stack and dropping it on the desk with a heavy thud, "is all I've been able to find."

Chapter 9

CHRISTIAN WATCHED as Ida opened her large book of notes. He sensed she was still nervous but had accepted what he'd said as the truth. "Thank you for helping me."

She looked sad, drained, but relieved. "I suppose it's the least I could do. You did save my life."

He nodded.

"Might make it easier if you tell me what you know about your own beginning."

Part of him didn't want to speak. His own memories were a vault sealed shut for centuries. But it was necessary.

"I was a Roman captain," he said finally. "My name was Tiberius then. I'd spent ten years in the legion by the time we ended up in Germania, near the Black Forest. Our leaders were fools. The commander of our legion continued to attack even as the numbers and terrain went against us. He wanted glory. He wanted fame in Rome. We paid for it with our blood."

"Amazing how little has changed in two thousand years," she said.

"Eventually, I couldn't let him order the men to useless deaths anymore. As the men retreated, I moved against him. Others defended him. They were comrades. I killed them to get at him, and then I ran him through."

She sat quietly.

"I knew word of what I'd done would eventually reach Rome and I would be killed or put in the Coliseum as an example for anyone who might defy the wishes of the powerful. I feared for my parents, for my sisters. So I left and headed for the wilderness, intending to fight the Visigoths on my own until they slew me."

"What happened?" she asked. "Was it one of them?"

"No," he replied. "They'd had enough of us and were pulling back themselves. The field was left to the vultures and the dead. I decided to head north and see what was beyond the river. I assumed I would encounter some of the Goths sooner or later. I was fairly certain I wouldn't see the sunrise again, but before I made it across the field, I was attacked. What I now know is one of the most powerful Nosferatu threw me to the ground and slit my throat. His name was Drakos. He offered to save me from the wound he'd inflicted."

"By transforming you," she guessed.

He nodded, thinking about that far-off night. "I ran from him the next day," he said, "when my strength had recovered. I heard him calling after me. Heard his voice in my mind. He insisted I would seek him out sooner or later. He said those who are turned always come back to their masters."

"Did you?"

"I swore to myself I wouldn't," he told her. "And for seventeen years, I wandered. But there was so much I couldn't understand. Why do parts of this curse seem to make us stronger, while others make us weak? I can strike with the speed of a cobra. I have the strength of ten men. The ability to see into hearts and minds. To see through the night like a bird of prey. Yet, in the sunlight, I stumble like a drunk who can't find his feet? At the sight of a cross, my eyes begin to fail, and my ears ring with pain."

"I've read this," she said. "I wouldn't have believed it was anything but superstition. Not sure I believe it now."

Christian understood. "I ran into others who'd been turned. Some of them had formed into clans, but they had no desire for civilization. They lingered on the borders of our world, in the wilderness and the lawless places, hunting in packs. Everyplace where one found war and death, the Nosferatu could be found feeding on the living in anonymity."

Ida was watching him closely. Her eyes were wide, drinking in what he was saying. She was a scholar of history, learning a part that few knew. "So you went to this Drakos for answers?"

Christian nodded. "I found him in the remnants of a Roman city as the empire was crumbling. He explained that the others were scavengers, no better than vultures or rats. He insisted that he had a higher goal—the restoration of order. He told me he was once a member of the legion like I had been. He recalled a time when all the world trembled before Roman footsteps. He insisted it could be like that again. But only if we had an army of our own."

"To fight the Church," she noted. "So is that what began this war?"

Christian shook his head. "No. It had been going on for centuries. Maybe even forever. Undeclared and one-sided. Drake was determined to fight back. He wanted soldiers and warriors, like me. He wanted an army of Nosferatu that would refrain from the addiction and weakness that came with stealing life from others.

"We traveled together for centuries, slowly building up a group he called the Brethren. It wasn't easy. To find one who would resist the addiction of the blood, you had to turn a hundred. Even those who fought it for years might succumb at any moment."

"Sounds like a slow process," she said. "But then, I suppose your friend Drakos has all the time he needs."

Christian nodded. "One day, he'll unleash what he's been preparing. In the meantime, he stays hidden."

"But you no longer hide with him," she noted.

"We had a falling out," he explained.

"Over what?"

"He destroyed someone I loved."

"It's been written that your kind feels nothing like love. Only hatred and pain and greed," she replied.

"It's complicated," he said. "There are exceptions. There are a few of your kind with the gift to reach through the void and light our souls. I found one who could touch mine. Drake betrayed her to the Inquisition as a witch."

She stared at him quietly. He decided he'd said enough.

"At any rate, he never gave you what you wanted," she guessed.

"With Drake, it was always half truths. He gave me a few answers but never the most important one—where had we come from, why were we like this. Maybe he didn't have it; maybe he didn't know. But I believe the answers are out there. And the only group that seems to know more about us than we do is the Church. If they have the truth, perhaps there's a way to end this."

They sat quietly for a moment.

He'd told her the truth about himself, and she hadn't scoffed or judged him or shut down because it was too much to take in. He sensed a type of strength he'd encountered in few others.

"I'm not sure what to think," she said. "If you're making this up, it's one hell of a story. Either way, I'll tell you what I know."

She turned to a section near the middle of the thick journal. "Last summer, I found reference to a group of men, once priests, who gave up their vows to rid the earth of the scourge in the fifth century. They went by boat to Malta to destroy that which should not have come into being. They were never heard from again."

Christian thought back. "I've never heard of any Nosferatu setting foot on Malta. It was always a fortress of the Church. Are you sure these men went there?"

She turned the page. "Yes, though I don't think they stayed there. I found only one other reference to them. It called them crusaders of the light, but if they were crusaders in the strictest sense, they were going the wrong way. Out from Malta and into Spain and France."

He wondered if Malta had been the original base of the Ignis Purgata. Certainly, the soldiers from there were known for their strength and zeal.

"If there's nothing else referencing them, I can't see how that helps me."

"Relax, sonny," she said. "I'm just getting warmed up."

He gave some ground. "By all means."

"A few months later, I found part of a scroll in a French library that was once owned by Louis the Fifteenth. It made references to the Fallen. Louis was begging the Church for help to eradicate the infestation. I'm pretty sure they're talking about you and your kind. Now, it might be a leap, but if the French reference is connected with the Maltese one, and this 'coming into being' stuff, it tells me that you're probably right. The Church knows where you came from, or at least they think they do."

"Go on," he said.

"I worked backward from there," she said. "Eventually, I found reference to a fourth-century journal from an Egyptian monk of the Coptic Church. It is said to contain a group of letters sent to the office of the Holy Father, St. Julius the First, who was the Pope from 337 to 352. According to tradition, they were returned with a scathing rebuke, but kept in the monastery because all papal communications were considered sacred."

"What do they say?"

She shook her head. "Their text isn't described in detail, but the papers are known as the 'pleadings of the corrupter,' not the one who takes men's souls, but the one who changes them."

Christian sat up taller.

"Mean something to you?"

"Our own myth," he said. "When people don't know the answers, they guess, they make up stories. In that way, the Nosferatu are no different. The term *corruptor* refers to the one who began our lineage. Our legend—if you want to call it that—talked always of an original corruptor. The head of the pyramid. A dark Adam who had already fallen at the moment of creation. To me, it never seemed any more likely to be real than the Garden of Eden itself."

"Well," she said, "from the look of things, you share that myth with the Catholic Church."

Somehow, that didn't surprise him. "What happened to these letters?"

"As I understand it, they were held in Egypt for a long time. Protected within the monastery, even treasured. Sixteen hundred years later, World War Two arrived. Rommel and the Afrika Corps were about to overrun Egypt. Fearing the letters would be destroyed, they were moved."

"Where?"

"To the belly of the beast," she said. "Germany."

His eyebrows went up.

"At the time, things looked bleak," she pointed out. "France, with the largest army in all of Europe, had crumbled before the Nazi onslaught in six weeks. England was being bombed into rubble. It seemed likely that Hitler would win the whole war in a matter of months. With that in mind, these papers were sent to Germany for safekeeping."

"Makes sense," he said.

She nodded. "Three years later, with the tables now fully turned and the Allies obliterating Germany from the air, a communiqué was received in Washington through an emissary of the Catholic Church. It begged President Roosevelt to spare Cologne Cathedral at almost any cost. It claimed there were items hidden there that were crucial to the world's heritage—and even perhaps its spiritual survival."

"Spiritual survival?"

She nodded. "One day later, orders came down simultaneously from FDR and Winston Churchill to their respective military commanders, directing them to avoid hitting the cathedral at any cost. As I understand it, a few bombs did hit the structure by accident. But by the end of the war, when the rest of the city was smoldering in ruins, the cathedral stood relatively untouched."

Christian took a deep breath. He'd been in Germany in 1945. He'd even been in Cologne. Could he really have been that close to the answers and not known it?

"You think the items they were trying to protect were the letters from this Egyptian monk?"

She placed her notes down. "I can't be sure," she said. "Who knows what treasures the Church has hidden? But most are just that—treasures, artifacts, inert remnants of the world's past. Whatever this communiqué referred to, it was forward-looking, something that the church believed would affect the *future*."

Christian had never considered that. "A prophetic document?"

She nodded.

"You think it could be related to the Fallen?"

She smiled. The kindly smile of an older aunt. "The real question is, do you?"

Christian felt like he was grasping at straws, but what else did he have to hold on to. He wasn't sure what he'd find there, but he knew, somehow, he had to find a way into the cathedral in Cologne, a place his kind never went.

Chapter 10

KATE PFEIFFER sat at a computer desk in a neatly organized office that had once been the spare bedroom in her house. She ignored the pile of mail to her left and the Christmas decorations that were still hanging a couple of months after they should have been taken down.

Home for twenty-four hours, she'd had dinner, played with her son, and even washed dishes with her mom, enjoying a moment of the regular world for a change. But as soon as Calvin went to bed, Kate had retired to her office and begun checking e-mails, looking for any kind of update on the case.

A message from Billy Ray looked promising. She clicked the link and waited as a YouTube video began to play.

At first, all she could see was a dark, jumpy image with lots of noise. A few seconds later, she realized the noise was club music and the grainy image was a picture of people moving on a dance floor.

Suddenly, the image became shaky again. A crash of glass overrode the sound of the music, and the camera jerked around, catching something for a split second as it dropped from above and disappeared into the crowd.

"Did you see that?" a voice said. "Some dude just fell through the roof."

Muffled noises and random curses came next and then nothing but the backs of people's heads as the amateur cameraman tried to hold the phone up high enough to see over the crowd.

"He's dead," someone said. "He's got to be."

SHADOWS OF THE MIDNIGHT SUN

A murmur went through the crowd, and then a lurid, piercing scream rang out. Even on the bad audio of the phone, it gave Kate chills. The crowd began to push back, bumping and jostling the cameraman/phone operator.

A new set of screams rang out, and the crowd parted. A figure appeared, running across the floor with what looked like a knife in his hand.

"You seeing this?"

"That guy came through the roof."

"This is off the hook!"

The figure with the knife disappeared. Moments later, gunfire rang out. A room-wide panic hit, and the video ended.

She looked back at the note Billy Ray had posted on the e-mail: *Our suspect on YouTube.*

The action looked exactly like what had been described by the eyewitness accounts, though they would have to do some work to prove it. She watched it again, trying to get a look at the suspect's face. There was something odd about the way he moved. When pausing the video and going frame by frame, the short video was even stranger. The suspect was blurry even as those around him appeared relatively clear.

She put it down to the strobe lights and the chaotic movement of the crowd and the cheap camera-phone. But it was definitely bizarre.

The door to her office opened and Kate turned.

Her mother stood there.

"I thought you'd gone home," Kate said.

"I wonder if we could talk."

Kate didn't want to talk right now. She wanted to go through the video one more time, maybe ten more times if necessary. She wanted to call Billy Ray and have him get the video over to the techs who could take it apart and enhance it.

"I don't know how much longer I can do this," her mother said, cutting off any attempt to postpone the argument.

"Do what, Mother?"

"Watch you run around the world and ignore your son."

Kate rolled her eyes. "Oh please, let's not have this argument tonight."

"If I weren't here, you'd have to be," her mom said. "I'm enabling you, and one day, you're going to hate me for it."

Kate could feel the anger rising up inside her. She kept quiet, the only technique she'd learned that could keep this from becoming a full-fledged shouting match.

"He's already lost his father," her mom said, firing the most painful bullet in her arsenal. "Do you really want him to grow up without you?"

"That's not fair," she said. "I'm doing the best I can. I have a job to do, an important job."

"More important than raising your son?"

"Stop it!" Kate snapped.

"Lower your voice."

The fury was uncontrollable now. "Don't come in here and pick a fight with me and then tell me to lower my damn voice. Calvin doesn't have a father because someone murdered him. It wasn't an accident, it wasn't some unfortunate circumstance—it was murder. My job is to find people who do the same thing to other families, and stop them. And I'm damn good at it."

"I'm not saying you're not good at it," her mother pleaded, "just that maybe someone else might be better suited for the job."

"Thanks for reminding me."

Her mom huffed as if her statement was not meant to sound the way it did. "You know what I mean; maybe you should let someone else take the reins for a while."

Kate shook her head. She almost launched into a tirade about how all her mom ever did was bake cookies and work for the PTA, and how could she possibly understand anything above such a trivial level? But she didn't want to hurt her mother. She just wanted support and understanding—two things that never seemed to come.

"What do I have to say to get through to you?" she pleaded. "This is my career. After what happened to Mark, how can you not understand why it's so important to me?"

Her mother didn't respond. In her passive-aggressive way, she just moved to a new subject rather than answer a question that would require some honesty. "I know they offered you a desk job. You could take it, and at least you'd be in town."

A desk job. It sounds like purgatory.

She glanced back at the screen and the frozen image of the half-visible suspect running out of the building. Guys like this were out there, dangerous and hidden. She damn well wasn't going to sit at a desk and look for tax evaders or embezzlers while violent killers were running around.

"You weren't here when Mark died," her mother added. "That's not your fault. But you are choosing not to be here while Cal grows up."

Kate felt like she might break in half, like she was being attacked from all sides for doing the best she could. Why the hell couldn't anyone see that?

"I cannot do this right now," she said. "If you don't want to watch Cal, that's fine. Just let me know. I'll find someone else, but I'm not having this discussion for the hundredth time. Not tonight."

Her mom didn't respond, she just folded her arms across her chest, walked out, and slammed the door.

Kate shook her head and tried to let her feelings settle. She felt trapped. No matter how hard she worked, she was letting somebody down—Calvin, her mother, the Bureau.

Was it really possible to run so hard for so long, only to keep falling farther and farther behind?

The computer pinged once again as another message from Billy Ray broke her trance.

Bad news: Two more victims found. Looks like we're going to Boston in the morning.

Chapter 11

Mountains of Northern Croatia

THE AGING 4x4 climbed a rutted dirt road that cut through the hilly mountain country. In places, the vehicle splashed through the mud left by melting slush, but as it climbed ever higher, the track became frozen permafrost, as hard as concrete, though nowhere near as smooth.

High above the road, a heavy sky threatened to dump more snow on the mountain pass, adding to the seven inches that had accumulated during the night. So far, nothing more than flurries had come, but as the day wore on, that was expected to change.

Inside the vehicle, sitting in the passenger seat, Simon Lathatch considered the weather. The snowfall the night before had been a blessing; another blizzard this evening would be a curse.

"The lord giveth, and the lord taketh away," he said quietly.

Simon Lathatch was a man of average height, but broad shouldered and solid through and through. At sixty-one, he was also ten years older than anyone in his position had ever been, and he carried the scars and weathered features to show for it.

His face was the color of burlap and not much smoother. His right hand showed burn marks and was withered and only partially useful after a confrontation that had ripped half the muscle off his forearm and left him with extensive nerve damage. He could feel nothing with his fingers. But he had survived.

His driver turned toward him as the SUV lurched through another rough section.

"We're almost there," the young man assured him. "Another mile."

The driver's name was Aldo. There was such zeal in his young face. At that age, one could see only victories ahead and the glory of God.

"I would like to go with you," Aldo added. "I believe I'm ready."

Simon smiled benignly. He spoke with a Swiss tone in his voice that sounded like German, softened by the French. "No one is ready, my son. But if you are to follow the path, you must take your first step at some point."

"I'm not afraid," the driver said proudly.

Simon's smile faded. He looked away. He knew what waited for them, what his men had captured. "You should be."

A few minutes later, they came upon a flat section of the road. Up ahead, two men wearing black oil coats that resembled American dusters stood on the side of the road. They had with them four horses.

Aldo guided the SUV up beside them and stopped. Simon stepped out and shook hands with the horsemen. One of them handed him a heavy duster similar to the ones they wore.

They were now above seven thousand feet, and the air was crisp, the temperature well below freezing; the scenery was white snow cover and drifts pressed up against a forest of evergreens. The flurries were becoming steadier.

"Where is Henrick?" Simon asked.

"He stayed with the prisoner," the lead horseman said. "He felt it would be dangerous to leave only the Venatores to watch him."

"The hunters will be fine," Simon replied, quite sure that Henrick, his second-in-command, had other reasons for not meeting him at the road.

Simon mounted up. The two horsemen and Aldo did the same. "How far?"

"Three miles," one of the horsemen said. "At an abandoned farmhouse."

Simon nodded. "Lead on."

The horsemen turned their steeds and moved off, disappearing into the forest, with Simon and Aldo following. Thirty minutes later, they came into a clearing, a sloping pasture of open ground that had once been tilled. The storm had turned it into a field of white. Hoofprints in the snow from the horsemen's outbound journey were only smooth depressions now.

On the far side, the remnants of a stone farmhouse waited. It wasn't much more than a burned-out derelict. It had only three stone walls, and a pile of rubble where the fourth had fallen down. A few heavy wooden beams crossed the remaining part of the structure. Wet and rotting in the snow, they were also charred and blackened from some long-ago fire.

The four men rode up to the farmhouse and dismounted.

Simon and Aldo entered the ruins. A fire crackled in one corner. It was mostly red embers, but it created enough heat to melt the snow around it and added a hint of warmth and color to this bitterly cold land.

Two men sat around it, eating some type of canned rations like soldiers. They stood as Simon entered.

Simon raised his hand. "Sit," he told them. "Eat. You've earned the rest."

A third man came in from the opposite side of the ruined farmhouse—Henrick Vanderwall.

Powerfully built and taller than the others in the room, Vanderwall had a Norwegian look about him, with a mane of straw-colored hair, pale-blue eyes, and a face blessed with high cheekbones and a strong jaw. He was only forty and showed little of the wear and tear that Simon Lathatch had built up over the years.

"God has brought you here safely," the tall Norwegian said.

"God and Aldo," Simon replied, smiling. "He should be a driver on the Formula One circuit instead of here with us."

Aldo smiled at the compliment.

"You have a prisoner," Simon confirmed.

Henrick nodded and pointed to the two men who sat eating.

"The hunters chased him throughout the night. Six hours without pause. God gave us providence by bringing the storm early. Even an abomination such as this one cannot hide its tracks in the freshly fallen snow."

Simon had thought as much on the way up.

"Come," Henrick said sharply. "I'll take you to the demon."

Henrick did not wait but turned away and stepped back out through a gap in the old stone wall.

Simon nodded to Aldo, and together, they followed Henrick and his purposeful strides.

"We caught it in the fields to the south," Henrick said, his breath streaming ice vapors as he spoke.

"Strange that it ran from you without a fight," Simon noted.

"It did fight," Henrick assured him. "One of the men was killed, along with his horse."

He pointed to two mounds in the snow. Simon's heart grew heavy at the loss of another soldier.

"We snared it by the neck and brought it down."

"Palladium ropes," Simon guessed.

Henrick nodded. "As you know, it's the only tool we have to sap their strength."

For reasons not understood, the rare metal affected the demons, somehow diluting their great power. Chains made of Palladium were used to hold them. Whips and lassos with thin strands of palladium in the twine were proven weapons against them.

Henrick waved an open hand toward a thick tree at the edge of the forest. From this side, the bands of several large chains wrapped around it could be seen. Four chains—two making horizontal lines around the tree, two crisscrossed in an "X."

As Simon got closer, he heard sounds of anguish. He noticed the heavy-gauge chains had begun to cut into the tree as the creature on the other side strained to tear itself free.

Two more of Henrick's hunters guarded the tree. They stood twenty feet back from it, holding long pikes at the ready. Their horses stood tied a few yards behind them, their eyes covered by metal blinds. Still, they appeared nervous.

"You see how they keep their distance?" Simon mentioned to Aldo. "You see their vigilance?"

Aldo nodded.

"The horses sense the difference between the living and the dead," he said. "All animals do, far more easily than us. Proximity brings danger, even for the pure of heart. We must guard ourselves carefully from this point on."

Aldo nodded, and despite the cold, he wiped a thin sheen of sweat from his brow.

They walked around the tree, making a wide turn that kept them ten feet from it. Chained to it was a shirtless man, thin and shivering. Several strange tattoos on his body looked like patterns of ancient writing. He hung forward, held up by the chains. His head drooped, and a mop of long black hair hid his face.

Aldo was surprised and underwhelmed. "Are we sure this isn't just—"

Simon held up a hand, silencing Aldo.

Despite years of training in the order, despite being selected only from the brightest, the purest, and the most zealous believers, this was the moment that defined many who wanted to join the Venatores of the Ignis Purgata, the Hunters of the Purifying Fire.

Simon wished he could explain to Aldo what he was about witness, but he knew better than to try. Sometimes one must be shown the truth instead of told it. He stepped forward, steeling himself and confronting the demon.

"Your time on this earth is coming to an end," he said. "Do you've anything you wish to confess?"

"I don't know what you're talking about," the man said, sounding Slavic but speaking English. "Why are you doing this? I've only stolen drugs and some money. I've done nothing else."

"We don't care about the things you've taken," Simon said, edging closer. "We care for the lives and the souls you've damned to hell. Tell me, Nosferatu, how many mortals have you infected in your time?"

The man shook his head, never looking up. "What are you saying? I don't know these words."

"What clan are you with?" Simon asked, studying the tattoos. "Where is your lair?"

"I don't know what you mean," the chained man said. "I've just—"

"You are an abomination," Simon said, cutting him off harshly. "A demon from the void. You have no rights here, and you will soon be sent into darkness and fire long prepared for your kind."

"For God sakes, you must be insane," the man mumbled. "I haven't done anything!"

"Maybe we are mistaken," Aldo said.

It was Henrick who snapped at this. "Silence!"

"But it's daylight," Aldo said.

"The clouds are thick," Simon explained. He kept his attention on the man in front of him. He did not dare let his concentration waver, not at this range.

"You've been chained to this tree through the bitter cold of night. No clothes, no food, no fire, and yet, you live. The tree you're tied to turns black from your very presence. Explain this to me."

The mop of hair shook; still, the head didn't come up. "I don't know what you're talking about. I'm freezing."

Simon spoke to Henrick without taking his eyes off the demon. "Have you used the prism, to confirm our belief?"

Henrick nodded. "This one is strong. He still controls his body. Even through the prism's spyglass, we cannot yet be certain. But we know what he is. Any living man would have frozen to death in the night."

Henrick's assumptions bothered Simon for two reasons.

To begin with, he found them dangerous. While he believed what they were looking at was not a man, there were requirements before acting. The death of a human by mistake could not be taken back.

But perhaps more important, if the creature in front of them could hold its human form for so long, even in such bitter cold, even when viewed through the lens of the ancient prism, then Simon feared it was more powerful than they'd first suspected.

"You've slaughtered people in this land for a century," he said.

The man shook his head.

Simon unbuttoned the top button on his coat. "You've fed off the dying and hidden yourself beneath the cloak of constant wars. But I tell you now, you've stayed too long, demon. The wars here are finished, and without them to hide your bloodlust, your predations have made the presence of your clan known."

He unbuttoned the second and third button on his coat and then the forth, allowing it to fall open. He sensed the anger building in the demon. There were no more denials. Only silence and growing rage.

The stringy muscles of the demon began to flex, and he pulled taught against the chain. The limp hands clinched slowly into fists, and the chains shifted, cutting deeper into the tree as if it were made of something softer than solid pine.

But the hunters had chosen well. The tree was far too thick and too filled with life for the demon to destroy it. The cold had weakened it. The effort of maintaining its shell and appearance had drained it, and a being such as this could not break the chains of palladium.

"You will tell us the location of your clan," Simon demanded.

No answer came back.

"I will find them whether you help us or not."

Still, the creature remained silent, but it shifted and moved further. It seemed to be priming for something.

Behind him, Simon heard the horses shuffle. They snorted nervously. One reared up.

"Very well," Simon said, realizing the creature would not speak. He reached into his coat. From it he pulled the head of a four-bladed spear. He attached it to a long steel shaft handed to him by Henrick.

Suddenly, the demon lunged at Simon. Bared teeth flashed, displaying two-inch-long fangs dripping with venom.

The chains snapped taught. Behind them, the horses reared and neighed as the demon released a call that sounded like a hiss and the growl of a wildcat, all at the same time.

Aldo jumped backward, slipping and landing on the ground. Even the guards with the sharpened pikes took a step away. Only Simon and Henrick stood unmoved.

The thing strained to reach Simon, its head snaking back and forth. "You will set me free," it hissed, looking into Simon's eyes.

Simon did not flinch. He stared back at it.

It quickly turned to the others, realizing which were the weaker of its enemies, avoiding Henrick and focusing on Aldo, who was lying in the snow, staring up in shock.

"Kill the rest and loosen the chains," it whispered.

Simon did not move. He needed to see how Aldo would respond to the will of the demon. It was a necessary test if he were to become one of the Venatores.

Kill them and loosen the chains.

This time the words were inaudible, heard only in the minds of the men gathered around. Aldo began to stand, an act that told Simon he was hearing the words, letting them into his mind. The creature repeated its call, and as Aldo got to his feet, he began reaching into his coat for his own weapon.

Simon couldn't take his eyes off the dangerous creature now. It was exerting all its will.

Aldo pulled out a sidearm, a weapon normally forbidden to the Cleansing Fire for many reasons, but in this dangerous country, that rule had been relaxed for a driver.

I will grant you power and glory.

The hunters were frozen, unable to move. Simon was locked in a battle of wills, fighting to control his own mind and to stay focused on his task.

Aldo took a step forward.

"Stop him, Henrick!"

The creature moved from side to side, the chains sliding around the tree like coiling snakes. Aldo began raising his weapon.

Kill them and set me free!

"Henrick!"

Simon heard a heavy thud as Henrick tackled Aldo and held him down.

The creature reacted, howling and focusing back on Simon now with all its malevolent will.

"Hypocrite," the thing shouted. "Murderer! Others will come for you. There is one greater than all of you. He will destroy you and drink your blood!"

As the demon raged, Simon held up the spear. "This is the Staff of Constantine's servant," he said. "Consecrated in the Battle of the Milvian Bridge. Blessed by the Church and empowered by God. It has cast a thousand demons more powerful than you into hell, and tonight it will end your bloodlust."

The creature's eyes fell to the spear. It pulled back, slamming itself against the tree as if it recognized the instrument of destruction.

"There is no salvation for your kind," Simon explained. "Only flames and darkness await you."

The creature pressed its back into the tree.

Simon was undeterred. He thrust the spear forward. It punctured the center of the demon's chest, and the thing arched its back and howled in agony. A wave of light flashed through its body, and a shock wave went forth in all directions, crossing the landscape, stirring the fallen snow, and echoing back off distant outcroppings of rock and stone.

At the same moment, both the demon and the tree behind it burst into flames. The creature writhed as the fire engulfed it and the blue-white tongues of heat snaked their way around the trunk.

Eventually, the demon's movements began to subside, and finally, it fell limp, hanging in the chains, nothing more than a burning corpse.

Simon withdrew the staff and stood back. The bark crackled and popped as the fire began to take hold. Flames licked upward along the trunk and into the tree limbs above. By morning, there would be nothing left but a pile of ash.

Convinced the abomination had been destroyed, Simon finally turned. He saw Henrick still holding Aldo to the ground. Blood ran deep into the snow.

"What have you done?"

Henrick withdrew a small dagger from Aldo's back and climbed off him.

"Are you mad?" Simon shouted, dropping down beside the young man.

"I had no choice," Henrick said. "His mind was taken."

Simon rolled Aldo over. The young man stared upward blankly. The wound was in his side, perhaps through a lung. Not fatal. Not if they got him help. He waved the hunters over.

"Take him inside. See to him. We will need to leave immediately."

"There could be other demons around," Henrick said.

"There may well be," Simon agreed. "But your actions have made it impossible for us to search."

"You would let them escape?"

Simon had once admired Henrick's dedication, but it bordered on obsession.

"Aldo was not your only mistake made tonight," he told Henrick. "This is not a clan leader. It's nothing more than one of the *infirmus*. A bottom-feeder. You've revealed our presence to destroy a scavenger."

Henrick's jaw tightened. "I disagree. You saw its power. How do you explain it so easily taking the mind of your driver? The echo of its destruction?"

Simon didn't like the real answer, but he could not deny it. This demon was a bottom-feeder, he knew that, but it was also stronger, far stronger, than it should have been. He glanced up at the storm building above them.

"Their power grows," Simon explained ruefully. "Even among the weakest."

"You believe this?"

Simon nodded. He had long suspected it, but he was now all but certain. At each step over the last year, he'd seen the evidence. He'd seen the signs. There could be only one explanation.

"The dark time of the prophecy is almost upon us, Henrick. For them— and for us—the reckoning will soon begin."

Chapter 12

Cologne, Germany

WAVES OF sound washed over the crowd at the iconic opera house at the center of Cologne known as Haus Gürzenich. The music rose like colored light and lingered like jasmine and rose.

For reasons Christian could never know, music had a way of breaking through and reaching his kind. As the rhythms swirled around him, it brought a momentary release from the prison of a disconnected existence, especially in large crowds. Perhaps it was because each patron in a great hall like this experienced the same waves of energy and sound, the same rise and fall of the instruments as they built to a crescendo.

Perhaps the alignment of thoughts and emotions brought on by the music transcended both time and space. Like a shared dance. Or maybe it was just his imagination, but as he sat and absorbed the beauty emanating from the stage, the music somehow touched his dead soul.

As the symphony finished and an ovation rose up, Christian opened his eyes. Caught up in the moment, he'd lost track of why he'd come to the concert hall in the first place. That reason was now leaving the building somewhere.

He glanced around quickly, caught sight of a diminutive man who was headed for the exit, and followed.

A moment later, he was out on the plaza. The night air was cold, just above freezing. The overcast sky caught the lights of the city, changing the dull color of the clouds to a washed-out orange glow. A short distance away, a pair of sleek trains passed in opposite directions on the Hohenzollernbrucke Bridge.

In the other direction, the great spires of Cologne Cathedral towered into the night. Lit up from below, majestic and slightly greenish in tint, the great structure loomed over the city like a watchman, its gothic facade hiding secrets that few but the highest members of the Church would know.

One who might was Morgan Faust, the man Christian now followed. Faust was officially listed as a caretaker, but his education proved him to be a man of letters, a scholar who held doctorates in theology, history, and Latin. A passion for classical music seemed another obsession, and after Christian had learned that Faust would attend the symphony tonight, he'd decided to join him at a distance.

He tracked Faust along the promenade that ran in front of the river. The man seemed drawn and thin, even at five foot four. He wore a dark-charcoal overcoat with a wool scarf and leather gloves to fight off the cold. His hair and beard were gray, and he walked with a slight hitch in his gait.

He traveled slowly, not a man in a hurry. He probably had few cares in the world at this point. But his route was odd. His path was taking him away from the cathedral.

Christian wondered where he was headed.

Faust continued along the promenade and turned away from the river. Four blocks later, he turned down another lane, and then he stopped in front of an old bookstore. The store was well lit, but it didn't appear to be open. No one was moving around inside.

Faust knocked once and then twice more. A figure opened the door a crack, glanced up and down the street, and then let Faust in. A second later, the door closed, and the outside lights went dim.

Christian waited a few minutes and then moved forward. He put his hand to the door and listened.

He heard voices inside. *An argument*, he thought. *No, just a negotiation.*

"We had an understanding," Faust said. "Five hundred euros. Which is too much to begin with."

"That was the price," the shopkeeper replied. "But not anymore. I have another offer. A collector willing to pay three times that. Besides, I thought you were buying for the Church, not your personal assortment. With the Church, there are reasons to give a discount. But what can you do for me?"

It sounded as if the man was mocking Faust.

"You had an agreement with me, Ulrich," Faust said. "A man should keep his word."

"Good luck finding that these days."

With the two men arguing, Christian sensed his chance. He turned the handle and pushed the door open, breaking the lock. Stepping through, he closed it behind him. A thin infrared beam stretched across the front foyer, perhaps to notify the owner when customers entered. Christian placed his hand in the beam. It passed right through, as if he weren't there.

Still, it would sense his clothes. He stepped over it and into the back room.

The two men turned in shock.

"The store is closed," the shopkeeper blurted out, stepping from behind the table. "You'll have to come back tomorrow if you want something."

"Sit down," Christian ordered, staring into the shopkeeper's eyes.

The man stopped in his tracks. He took a step backward and sat. His face went blank; he stared forward as if looking off into the far distance or perhaps into an abyss.

Christian turned his attention to Dr. Faust.

The wiry little man stepped backward, bumping awkwardly into a bookshelf. His hands were trembling; he kept his gaze deliberately from Christian's face, looking at the floor.

"You are Nosferatu," Faust whispered.

"I've been called that many times," Christian said. "But that's not who I am."

"Why have you come here? I've done nothing to you."

Christian nodded and stepped toward him. "You've done no harm to me, this is true."

"Then leave me," Faust said. "I will not speak of you. I will tell no one of this encounter. The Church will not send out the hunters."

"The Ignis Purgata already know of my existence," Christian said. "They will hunt me whether you speak of this night or not."

Faust looked at the bookstore owner, who remained catatonic.

Christian considered what he'd seen in the shopkeeper's mind. "He's cheating you," he told Faust, having sensed the owner's thoughts. "He has no other buyer."

Faust continued to look anywhere but at Christian. "He knows me too well. He knows how much I love the old books. At least it's only money. You fleece people's souls."

The accusation hit a chord in Christian that he fought to resist, for he had done his damage over the years. In truth, he was surprised that Faust had the guts to accuse him, considering the fear that seemed to grip him. An inner strength must have filled him. His hand had gone to the crucifix around his neck. He held it tight.

Christian paused. There were mysteries of his kind that baffled him to this day. The pain his kind felt upon the sight of a crucifix was a phenomenon that he could not explain. He would have liked to believe it was superstition, but he had felt it intensely at times, like blinding light cast into eyes that had grown used to the dark.

For now, Faust gripped the crucifix, covering it, holding it tight.

"Leave me, Nosferatu," Faust said, looking up. "Or I will force you to."

Faust made a mistake of meeting Christian's gaze. Christian stared coldly, his lifeless black eyes invading Faust's mind. He could read Faust's thoughts, not every word or construct, but enough to know the story of his contemplations.

Likewise, Faust could now feel Christian's thoughts, if he dared look into the darkness that was to be found there.

"What do you want?" Faust whispered.

"Answers," Christian said. "Forever, I've been seeking answers. Some of which your church has hidden away."

Faust's hand slid off the crucifix; it dropped back under the neckline of his shirt. "The knowledge I have is not meant for you."

"Who has the right to make that judgment?"

Faust was silent.

"You are a learned man," Christian added, "a man who does not accept what he is told without making up his own mind. If you were in my position, you would also quest for the truth."

"Truth…"

"*Veritas*," Christian said.

"*Veritas*," Faust repeated.

Faust was completely mesmerized now. Not catatonic like the shopkeeper, but thinking, feeling, connecting with Christian. It was slightly possible that he could have torn himself away and Christian would have been forced to take what he needed from Faust's mind by force, but the man's guard had come down. He was no longer in fear of Christian; he was interested, curious.

"You understand what I seek?"

"The origin of your curse," Faust said.

"But you don't know it," Christian said, reading Faust's thoughts.

"I know where the answer might lie," Faust said. "Below the western spire of the cathedral lies a circular vault. It can only be reached via a small hidden staircase. One way in, one way out. The vault itself is fireproof, and there are cameras that will see you. The letters of old lie within it. I am the caretaker of these sacred items; I know what rests inside, though I have never seen them myself."

Christian nodded. "There are combinations, locks, passwords. You will give them to me."

Faust nodded. As the numbers and codes flashed into Faust's mind, they also imprinted themselves on Christian's. But hearing Faust's thoughts, Christian realized there was another layer of security he could not penetrate without Faust being present.

"Finish your business and meet me at the cathedral," Christian said.

"I'm not due back until tomorrow night," Faust said.

"Then tomorrow night we shall meet. Until then, you will forget about me."

Faust nodded, and Christian turned to go. He put his hand on the door, but a whisper from Faust stopped him from opening it.

"He wanted to die," Faust said.

Christian turned. Faust wasn't even looking at him; he was just staring into the distance. The words were a reverberation of the last thoughts in Faust's mind before the bond was broken, as if he were talking in his sleep. Most likely Faust wouldn't even remember speaking them.

"He could no longer hear the music," Faust muttered. "He could no longer perform. He could no longer converse with others or enjoy their company. He was forced to live alone, as if he'd been banished. He wrote to his brothers of suicide…"

It took a moment for Christian to realize that Faust was speaking about the composer Beethoven, who'd become deaf at the very height of his career. The book Faust had been intent on purchasing contained some of Beethoven's letters, though not the famous Heiligenstadt Testament that told of his desire to die.

"He chose to live," Faust said finally. "Not for himself, but for the sake of the gift, for what he could give to the world. Even though he could no longer hear the music, others could. So he composed and he lived for them."

Christian studied Faust and considered the words he'd unknowingly spoken. He wondered if the caretaker had glimpsed the pain Christian tried so hard to hide. If Faust had seen past the veil when their minds were connected and become aware of the many times Christian had contemplated suicide. And if so was he trying to soothe that pain, or was it just a reaction, an act as unconscious and unintentional as talking in one's sleep.

Christian couldn't be sure, but whatever triggered it, the words reached him more deeply than he would have believed possible.

He glanced at the shopkeeper and then back at Faust.

Offer him two hundred euros. For that, he'll give you what you seek.

Faust sat down, and Christian turned and left the bookstore.

Chapter 13

Vatican City

SIMON LATHATCH sat at a five-hundred-year-old desk in an office that had belonged to the Ignis Purgata for centuries. The cold and damp of the rainy spring day had seeped into the poorly heated room and into Simon's old bones. Standing at the entrance was Aldo, his driver, his friend.

Simon stood and ushered him through the door. "Come in, Aldo. I'm glad to see you're feeling better."

Aldo shut the door and made his way to the other side of the large conference table. He moved oddly now, with a limp. He spoke with a stutter. "I'm…I'm…I'm sorry I failed you."

Simon had made many mistakes in his day, but this one hit home. He'd never been sure if Aldo was truly made of the stuff their order required. Most of the hunters were hard men—strong, yes, but more willful than Aldo, who was always eager to please.

Aldo was faithful and God-fearing, but too kind and understanding, too willing to believe there was good even where evil reigned: traits that did not mix well in a war with the demons.

Simon helped Aldo to sit and then took a chair beside him. "No, my son. It is I who has failed you. I should have trusted my instincts. You were not ready. Perhaps, in another time, you would have been, but not now, not in these days. Things are in motion now which make this time different than all the days of our past."

"I...I...don't understand," Aldo said.

"Had that demon been as it should have been, weakened and drained, you would have been safe. It would have been a small first step for you, and you would have taken it with ease. But you could never have been ready for the assault he directed at you."

"But it was...it was..." Aldo stopped and tried to clear his mind and make his tongue obey his thoughts. "It was so strong." He spat out the words, forcing them from his mouth.

Simon nodded sadly. "Far stronger than it should have been."

"How?"

Simon took a deep breath. "You will not understand all I say, but since it has affected you, I will try to explain. All things in this world are balanced by their opposites. Day with night, heat with cold. Flood and drought. A time approaches when new light will appear in the darkness. As it grows brighter and stronger, it threatens the source of the evil we fight. But as things are balanced, the demons also gain new strength in this time. They are all growing stronger, and they will continue to do so until the greatest of opportunities and the greatest of all perils share a single moment, when the demons will either be extinguished or reign supreme."

"But...surely good always trumps...evil."

"One day it shall," Simon agreed. "But even John's Revelation tells us of a thousand years of darkness."

Aldo nodded. "I...understand. I'm ready to...ready to...rejoin the fight."

Simon smiled like a proud father, but a hint of sadness could be seen. He put a hand on Aldo's shoulder. "Aldo, my brave son," he said, "I'm afraid the fight is over for you. The Church will have greater use for you elsewhere."

"But I have...earned my place," Aldo stated with emphasis.

"The conditions under which one is allowed in the order are very clear. None can be controlled. Once possession has taken place, expulsion from the order is mandatory. I have no choice. It is our law for fifteen hundred years."

Aldo looked crestfallen, his zeal and desire to be part of the order now cutting at his own heart like knives.

"I have…something else of value," he said quietly.

"You've much of value," Simon assured him.

"You don't understand," Aldo managed. "I can…hear them."

Simon looked up, studying Aldo more keenly. "What do you mean?"

"Their voices," Aldo said. "Or their thoughts. I hear them thinking. At first, it was too much. Like a crowd in a room. But it's less now. Sometimes… It is clear to me. Sometimes I can hear just one."

Simon felt ill. For a moment, he did not speak, trying to discern the right course of action. Aldo's mind had been wounded far worse than he'd thought.

The fiery destruction of the Fallen was believed to be the beginning of their eternal damnation in hellfire. At times in the past, demons put to death in this way were known to have called out in many voices, male and female, old and young. It was thought to be an echo of the souls they'd stolen, the humans they'd turned and made part of their clans, the minds they'd invaded.

It seemed as if this echo had somehow imprinted itself on Aldo, perhaps because he had been connected with the creature when Simon destroyed it.

"Have you told anyone of this?"

"No one," Aldo said. "Not even…the doctors."

Simon took a great breath. "That's for the best. These are merely echoes, Aldo. They will fade in time. But this is precisely why you must be expelled. Such effects are dangerous to our mission."

Aldo looked down at the ground. "I…I don't think they're echoes. I think they're real."

"Of course you do, my son." Never in the long war had Simon felt such abiding sadness. His mistake had damaged the truest of souls, perhaps irreparably. He had no choice.

"Aldo Gruvaleu," he said, "I release you from your duties today, the seventeenth of April. Tomorrow you will journey to the Monastery at Lake Maggiore on the border of Switzerland. It is a place of peace and great teaching. There, you will heal. And this will be forgotten. The echoes will fade, and you'll begin a new life in the service of the Lord."

Aldo blinked, and then, finally, sadly, he nodded.

"In a way, I wish I could join you," Simon insisted. "It has been many years since my path was not dominated by the great struggle."

Both men stood. Simon walked Aldo to the door and they embraced. As Aldo reached for the door handle, a question rose up in Simon's mind.

"How many of them do you hear?" he asked.

Aldo turned, looking back at Simon oddly, as if he hadn't really understood the question.

"How many voices?" Simon repeated.

Aldo blinked several times before finally responding. "All of them," he said calmly.

It was not possible, Simon thought. And now he was certain the voices were just echoes. They had to be.

CHAPTER 14

Boston, Massachusetts

KATE STEPPED from the passenger seat of a gray SUV and onto the cracked blacktop. The seldom-used street near the South Boston waterfront was slowly decaying, crumbling with time into little chunks of rubble.

It was 9:00 a.m. The sun was burning off the morning cloud cover as a crane lifted an orange stretcher from the water's edge. It raised the stretcher high enough to carry it over a rusted fence and brought it back toward the street, where several squad cars were parked with their lights going.

Boston PD was on-site, including their coroner and a forensics team. They'd cordoned off the area and done a preliminary exam before hauling up the body.

As the stretcher continued its slow journey, Kate and Billy Ray walked up to the group, showed their badges, and went through a round of introductions.

A detective named Tanner seemed to be in charge.

"What do we know?"

Tanner looked at his notes. "Female," he said. "Mid-twenties. Obviously no ID. No distinguishing marks, not even a small tattoo or a piercing."

"Was her throat cut?" Kate asked.

"It looks that way," Tanner said. "But not slashed."

The crane brought the stretcher out over the street, lowering it gently. Two uniformed officers reached out and guided it in for a soft landing.

Once it was down, one of them released the hook and gave the thumbs-up. The crane reeled in the cable.

Kate and Billy Ray stepped forward. A quick scan told her the dead woman would soon be confirmed as the latest victim.

Like each of the others, this body showed no signs of trauma other than a clean slice across the left jugular vein. On the other bodies, the cut was so clean that, where the skin and tissue pressed together, it almost disappeared, but in this case, the artery appeared open, distended and ragged.

As they studied the body, one of the cops began to look a little green.

Kate glanced at him. His was a kid. Smooth face, eager eyes. He couldn't have been on the force for more than a year or two, not a lot of experience or seniority. He should have been on a third watch beat somewhere, writing tickets and handing out DUIs. She wondered what the hell he was doing at a murder scene. Maybe he was covering for someone.

"You gonna be all right?"

He looked like he would either throw up or faint. Her money was on him puking.

"I, um…"

"Because if you throw up on the victim, you're going to screw up any evidence that might still be there."

He nodded, stepped back a little, and seemed to get it together.

She turned back to the body and pointed toward the jugular with a pen, careful not to touch it.

"What do you think?"

"The cut's a little ragged," Billy Ray said. "Not as clean as the others."

"No," she said. "Someone was in a hurry. Maybe that's a break."

She stared at the poor woman. Her facial features were Hispanic, her hair and eyebrows dark, her brown eyes staring lifelessly. But her skin tone was awfully pale, even for someone who'd been in the water. Kate figured she knew the reason for that.

"Exsanguinated," she said while putting her sunglasses on. "Just like the others."

"Yeah, that's what the coroner thinks too," Tanner said.

Across from them, the young cop looked like he was about to lose it.

"Tanner, you want to get this kid out of here?" she suggested.

"Go take a breather," Tanner said to the rookie. "Send Jenkins over."

As the young cop moved off, Billy Ray pointed to the woman's hands. Neither her palms nor her forearms showed any bruising or scratching.

"No defense wounds," he said. "Must have happened quick."

Kate was looking at her hands as well. Billy Ray was right, but there was something more. Her nails were perfect. Freshly manicured. Most of the other victims had been more run-down, stragglers from the edge of society just trying to hold on. Those nails told Kate this woman came from a different section of town.

"All these victims," Tanner said, agitated, "no sign that any of them resisted. They must have been drugged."

"All the tox screens have come back clean," Kate said. "No indication the kidneys or liver were trying to process any toxins. No sign of a bruising from a needle prick on any of the bodies. And no trace of any agents in the spinal cord or brain fluid."

That wasn't quite true; two of the victims had alcohol in their stomachs, but not enough to cause a blackout condition, especially as it hadn't been absorbed yet.

"I don't see any sign of restraints," Tanner noted, pointing to the woman's unmarked wrists. "It's more like they were sleeping when it happened."

"Yeah, but even then, we'd see some sign of trauma, some sign of activity until they bled out," Kate said. "Besides, even if that doesn't explain it, who has access to all these people in their sleep?"

Tanner shook his head. Billy Ray did the same. They'd been asking this question for months.

As Kate scanned the body for anything that would lead them somewhere, Officer Jenkins came up to replace the rookie who'd left.

He took one look at the body and his face changed. "What the hell…?"

Kate turned. "Are all your officers like this?"

Tanner shook his head and turned to Jenkins, who, instead of looking queasy, began to look angry.

"What's wrong?" Tanner asked.

Jenkins set his jaw. "I know this woman, Detective. She works with my wife at the brokerage. She's a stock trader or something."

"Are you sure?" Kate asked.

"I've seen her a dozen times or more," Jenkins said. "I'm sure."

Kate looked over at Billy Ray. He nodded. It was a terrible moment for Officer Jenkins, but for the first time since they'd taken the case, Kate felt they'd finally caught a break.

Chapter 15

FORTY-EIGHT HOURS after his meeting with Faust, Christian Hannover once again walked the streets of Cologne. With the workweek under way, the city was much quieter. As the midnight hour passed, the streets were all but deserted.

Moving through the cold and dark, Christian approached the soaring spires of Cologne Cathedral. He passed its main entrance, well aware of the ringing in his head that had already begun.

For a moment, he wondered about his sanity. His kind didn't enter churches, let alone a cathedral. They steered clear of them, even during the predations of the Middle Ages, during the plagues of Europe when men were at their weakest.

If he were caught inside, Christian would stand little chance of surviving. His strength would be sapped by the power of the sanctuary; his mind would be clouded. The Ignis Purgata would take him with ease.

In the distant past, the Order of the Purifying Fire had been known to use the sensation brought on by proximity to a church as a weapon against the Nosferatu. They called it the Cruciatus, which meant "the Torment."

They would drag a suspected Nosferatu before a church or into it and chain them there until the pain became too great to bear. Once the Nosferatu admitted all they knew, their destruction soon followed. From what he understood, it did not take long.

And yet, he could not turn back now. Not when the answers he'd sought for all these centuries might lie within his grasp.

He turned down a side alley, walking next to the structure until he came to a small door. It was a service entrance, a caretaker's door and heavily barred. A small light hung just above the door, illuminating the cobblestone street.

He moved past it and into the shadows, waiting there until the diminutive shape of Morgan Faust appeared.

Faust moved slowly, walking through the darkness until he emerged into the faint light from that small lamp. He stopped at the door.

"Use the key," Christian whispered.

Faust pulled out his keys and unlocked the door. He stepped inside, reached for a flashing alarm panel, and typed in a code. The flashing ceased.

Christian moved forward, took a deep breath, and forced himself to walk inside.

Although they were only in an anteroom near the back of the church, the ringing in his ears grew worse, and a wave of tension swept over his body. He closed the door behind him and forced himself to go forward. He would see this through.

Faust turned toward him at the sound of the door shutting. "Who are you?" he said, as if noticing Christian for the first time. "You're not supposed to be here."

"Take me to the vault," Christian said.

Faust blinked a couple of times and then led Christian into the church proper. Their footsteps echoed off the stone floor as they reached the central aisle.

Christian paused. The lines around him ran vertically, the arches and supports curving toward the sky. The narrow windows accentuated the effect, as if the whole structure itself were stretching toward heaven.

Christian remembered a time when the cathedral was being built. Despite the pain it inflicted on him, he could not help but feel its designers had done tremendous work.

As he stood admiring the architecture, a wave of tension crept up through his neck, and a spike of pain began to resonate in his side. He steadied himself against it, but other effects could not be countered. The ringing in his ears was becoming a painful, high-pitched tone, and though the church was dimly lit, Christian's pupils constricted as if in the presence of blinding light.

He moved forward, stumbling like a man in a blinding snowstorm. He found Faust with his hand. "Where's the vault?"

"Below us," Faust said. "Fifty feet below."

"Lead me there, Dr. Faust."

Faust approached a door, which led to a cramped room like a broom closet. He opened a small panel in the wall, revealing a hidden keypad. He typed in a code. A false wall slowly moved aside, and a stairwell appeared, narrow and spiraling.

Faust took the stairs and started down. Christian followed. His strength was faltering fast. He hoped being below the structure would relieve some of his pain.

He descended the stairs, following his mesmerized guide. The steps circled twice. On the third revolution, Faust's shoes touched the bottom. Christian stepped onto the flat stone floor a second later.

Another door beckoned. The cold steel of its construction shimmered in the dull light. Christian found he could see slightly better at this depth.

"Please do the honors," Christian said.

Faust stepped to the keypad and typed in his code. One of two red lights on the side of the steel door switched to green.

Next, he pressed his eye to a retinal scanning device. Moments later, the second light switched to green, and the locks in the vault's door unlatched one by one. When the last one released, the steel door opened and swung toward him without a sound.

Lights in the darkened room began to brighten slowly. The inside of the vault was circular. Two dozen sealed cabinets made of some high-tech, bulletproof acrylic lined the walls.

It would take days to go through all of them.

He turned to Faust. "You know what I'm looking for."

Faust didn't hesitate or even reply. He moved past Christian and stopped beside the third case. He tapped a code into the electronic lock, and the smoked-glass faceplate went clear and then slid to one side.

"These materials reference your kind," Faust said.

Faust handed him a document sealed in layer of plastic to protect it from the ravages of time. It was written on ancient paper, the ink faded and uneven, the words in Latin.

Christian remembered a time when those words were his first language. He read them only with great effort now. The document spoke of a purge of suspected Nosferatu in a village in Tuscany.

Another document claimed to understand the odd writing that the Nosferatu had developed to delineate themselves, as some of their groups had attempted to form a hierarchy.

The letter indicated great fear among the church that some form of unity was imminent among the infighting Nosferatu. But they were wrong. It had never worked. Clans ran for a while and then fractured. The bloodlust and the animal instinct inherent in the members always proved too great. Only those who resisted the lure of blood stood a chance to survive. If there was any danger to the Church, it came from Drake's Brethren.

Christian studied the document for a moment, noting how much of it was incorrect. It made him wonder if the Church knew all he thought it knew.

He looked at the caretaker. "I search for my origin, Faust. Show me what you know. The earliest documents relating to my kind. The ones from Egypt."

Faust dragged his hand across the sealed files and stopped, pulling another document. This one was protected behind thin sheets of clear Kevlar, each page kept separately. Christian had the impression that it was of great importance.

The parchment was dated Anno Domini 337, twelve years after the Nicene Council had finished deciding on the canon of the Christian Bible. It was a letter from a deacon in Alexandria named Cyril and meant to be delivered to the Pope in Rome, St. Julius I. But if Christian was reading it correctly, it had been sent back at the direction of the Pope, along with a scornful rebuke by a bishop named Timerius.

Part of the letter had been destroyed by fire, but what Christian read left his mind spinning.

It can only be a trick of the Dark One that you come to us with this request for mercy. The one you speak of has become a demon, and there is no cure to that plague. It is no mere possession, either, for no demon would have the power to remain within a mortal shell where we made effort to cast it out. And we have tried. Thus, we conclude this is not possession, but a transformation. The afflicted one is not controlled by other forces; he is an agent of darkness himself.

As such, he is no longer human and thus cannot receive the mercy he requests. Make no mistake, you've been approached by a dark spirit in the form of man, but do not be fooled. It is not a man. We fear he is not the only one, but the beginning of a plague.

If therefore they cannot be cleansed and also cannot be liberated, then we are faced with only one path of dealing with them. They must be destroyed.

Because of this, it has been decided that an army of warriors, holy and pure, will be raised. They will be created to rid the earth of this scourge.

We know that different gifts are given to each of God's children; some must be healers and others soldiers. You are to gather the purest soldiers of our faith and instruct them in the ways of the Church and the dangers they will face. Only those with the strongest zeal and the stoutest hearts must be selected. Above all, this must remain a secret, known only to the highest members of the council.

The order shall be known as the Ignis Purgata, the Cleansing Fire, the Fire of Purification. You will hunt the Dark One who has come to you at once. None shall stand before you.

As Christian read the document, a sick feeling coursed through his heart. He'd spent most of his life in hiding, avoiding the Church's death squads. He understood what they believed and why. But to face persecution and death for the equivalent of contracting a plague seemed as evil to Christian as the curse itself. And yet, if he'd read the document right, this did not have to be the path.

It can only be a trick of the Dark One that you come to us with this request for mercy.

Christian could barely imagine one of his kind getting close enough to the Church to ask for clemency. But then again, this was a long time back, before the Church in Rome had risen to unquestioned dominance in Europe, before the endless war between the Church and the Nosferatu had even begun. The date listed was decades before he'd even been born. Perhaps things had been different in those days. Perhaps policies had not yet settled.

"What do you know about this?" he asked.

"The contents are unknown to me," Faust said. "I am forbidden to look at them."

"Are there more like this?"

"There is a letter from one of the Nosferatu to Cyril," Faust said. "He claimed to be the first."

"The first?"

Faust nodded. "It's rumored that his existence was miserable. He wanted forgiveness."

"Why?" Christian asked angrily. "There's mercy for all sinners, is there not? Mercy is given for the blasphemous and the thieves and the murderers. Why not for the Nosferatu? At least for one who sought it?"

"Mercy is only for humankind," Faust said. "Not for the fallen angels of perdition, nor for the demons or their minions. Nor for the Nosferatu."

"Show me the letter," Christian demanded, growing angry.

Faust moved to another case, sliding the door open and gently leafing through the materials. He pulled out another document. Like the first, this letter was partially burned.

Faust handed it to Christian. "The pleadings of the damned."

Christian studied it. It was on coarse paper, written in a much rougher hand than the papal letter. It read like a confession.

I have lived as a rodent these three hundred years. A rat in the sewers. I have hidden from the light. It has taken the essence of life away from me and left me as a ghost that wanders the endless darkness. But it has brought about the desire of my soul to beg your forgiveness. Perhaps that is why it was placed upon me.

You know of me, others have spoken of me, now I reveal myself to you.

I was a soldier in the legion serving in Judea under Pontious Pilot, our governor. Yes, Pilot, who washed his hands of your Lord's pain and crucifixion and handed him to us.

It was I who took the lash to Jeshua, the one you call Christ. It was I who scourged him until blood ran on the stones like water. Fear spread through me as my hand rose, for I began to feel he was more than a man, but to crush the fear, I swung the lash harder and harder. To destroy the doubt in my mind, I tried to punish its source. I wished to break him. I wished to prove this Jew was mortal. When I was finished, I could not believe he still lived. He looked at me from a mask of blood, and I froze.

On the day of the Crucifixion, I watched as his hands and feet were pierced. The sun grew dark, and I fell. When I awoke, it was night. I was alone. And I could feel the draining of my soul.

Three hundred years now, I have existed in darkness only. God has cursed me for my acts. I cannot live, but I do not age. I feel no pleasure or peace or even the sweetness of life, unless I take it so briefly from another. In torment and fear, I beseech you, Cyril. I know of whom you serve. I beg of forgiveness. I ask for your intercession. It is said your Pope, your Holy Father, holds the keys to Heaven and Earth. If this be truth, he can forgive me, and it shall be forgiven. And then I can die and find peace.

I am known to you as the deceiver or the corruptor, but I sign my true name.

Drakos, member of the legion.

A wave of shock barreled through Christian.

Drakos, member of the legion.

For a long moment, he could not move. Could it be true? Could it possibly be true?

Drakos, the corruptor, the deceiver. The one who had taught him to fear the Church above all else. Could he have been the one?

In the years Christian had spent searching for the truth, Drakos had been both a guide and roadblock. He'd shown Christian many things, teaching him about his power and his vulnerability. But on other subjects, his explanations were vague. He claimed that certain lines of thought were not valid or worth looking into. He claimed to have searched in vain for the originator, the dark Adam some believed in. He claimed not to know the reasons the Church had taken to hunting the Nosferatu with such mercilessness.

All these were lies. Drakos, the corruptor. Drakos, the deceiver. The clarity hit Christian like a blast of arctic wind.

Among all the tortured denizens of the dark, Drake was the only one Christian had ever feared. He'd always thought that fear came from the manner of their meeting, from the fact that Drake had found him and slit his throat on that Roman battlefield, imprinting on him his power, or some portion of it. Perhaps because Drake had then prevented his death—*saved* was not a word Christian chose to use—it had left him with a sense of mastery. All who were turned felt this way toward their creators. But if Drake was the first…

"You know this letter to be authentic?" he asked Faust.

Faust spoke. "Every item in this vault is authentic. That is why this place was spared in the Great War."

Christian knew he welded great power, but he had never known why. Now he thought he had an answer. Drake was the first; from him, all the Nosferatu sprang like a pyramid. Those at the bottom were little more than scavengers, far down the lineage, but if Drake was the first, then Christian took his power directly from the Nosferatu king.

"The Church rejected his plea," Christian said, thinking aloud. "He crawled for three hundred years and then found the strength to ask forgiveness, and they rejected his plea and stirred the hatred in his heart."

Christian turned back to Faust. "What else is in here?"

"The rest will not concern you," Faust said. "Edicts, accountings, reports of your kind, and the linage of those who led the Ignis Purgata—none of that would help you."

Faust was speaking differently, no longer entranced. And with the noise of the church inside his head, Christian could not concentrate sharply enough to reach him again.

"You've helped me for reasons other than coercion," Christian said.

"I fear you," Faust said. "Where could I run that you would not find me? Some who have encountered your kind have been left catatonic, others made slaves or turned to darkness."

"I will not harm you," Christian said. "I'm not like the others."

Faust seemed to consider that for a moment. "So what are you, then?" he asked.

Christian paused. He had no answer for that. "I was told there were documents of prophecy here."

Faust stared back, able to look Christian in the eye now. "There are," he said.

"Where?"

Faust froze and made no sound, but Christian heard a voice whispering anyway.

You've come a long way to find what I would have shown you in time.

The voice spoke inside his head. The words came from elsewhere, from a presence that must have been nearby. Only one voice could reach inside his head like that. Only one mind on this earth had the power to do it.

Drake.

Chapter 16

CHRISTIAN HANDED the protected sheet of parchment to Faust. The wiry man began to shake.

Drake's voice spoke inside Christian's head. *What a strange place to find you after all these years.*

The words came through clearly, Drake had to be nearby, just outside the cathedral somewhere. Christian closed his eyes, trying to blank his mind and block the invading consciousness.

Have you forgotten what they do to us? Have you forgotten what they did to your beloved Elsa?

Christian winced in pain. It was no good. Those who were turned always heard their corruptors. Their minds were briefly joined during the transformation.

Beside Christian, Faust gulped at nothing. He moved to put the document back in its slot, trembling uncontrollably.

"His is the name of horror," Faust said. "We know what he does, what he's capable of!"

"Maybe you should have forgiven him," Christian said, fighting to control his own thoughts, well aware that Faust had nothing to do with what the Church had done seventeen hundred years ago.

I offer you what they would not give us, Drake's voice taunted. *I offer you absolution. Just return to me. Join me once again, and I will forgive your transgressions and all those of the Brethren you've dispatched.*

Christian moved about the tiny vault, trying to figure out what to do. He went to the stairs. Faust followed, sealing the treasury of records behind them.

Christian began to climb the spiral staircase. He slowed as he neared the top, confronted with the blinding pain once again.

As he re-entered the church proper, Christian put a hand on the wall to steady himself. He stared down the long, narrow nave toward the altar. All he could see was light—blinding light. All he could feel was pain—blinding pain.

At least he understood now. This was punishment—never again to be part of the light.

In a strange way, it helped him at this moment. The blinding pain made Christian feel weak, but it also seemed to dampen the power of Drake's voice. Christian could still hear the corruptor's thoughts, but they did not reach him with the same power, and at least Christian knew that his mind was his own.

Perhaps because of this, Drake somehow turned his thoughts toward Faust.

So, you have a friend with you, he said. *Come to me, little man. Your knowledge shall be of great use.*

Faust looked woozy, as if entering a daze.

Christian grabbed him. "Don't listen."

"He'll turn me," Faust said.

"Not in here, he won't."

Faust continued to shake. It seemed as if Drake might overwhelm the small caretaker's thoughts at any moment.

"Go to the altar," Christian said. "Even Drakos can't reach you there."

Faust did not move.

Christian shook him. "Go!" he shouted. "I can't help you anymore, but I won't have you damned because of me."

Faust began to move off and then stopped, turning back toward Christian. "The prophecy you asked about, I know only rumors of it."

"Tell me," Christian asked, fighting against the agony he felt.

Drake's voice came crashing through. *Do not speak!*

Faust fell to his knees, as if fighting to hold up a tremendous weight. He put one hand to his head. He struggled to get the words out. "It is said a time will come when the sentence ends. Perhaps two thousand years punishment is enough."

It had been nearly two thousand years for Drake, Christian thought. "What are you saying?"

Faust began shaking. Drake was trying to block him from speaking.

"Forgiveness for the Nosferatu is not—"

Faust doubled over, calling out in pain. Drake was crushing him. Burning his mind.

Christian dropped beside Faust and grabbed him by the shoulders. "What forgiveness?"

Christian could barely see, but his presence and his own will seemed to shield Faust from Drake, if only a little.

"Forgiveness is not denied forever," Faust managed. "A messenger will arrive. An angel that brings mercy."

Christian's heart pounded from the tension, from the torment of the Cruciatus, but above all else, from what he was hearing. A glimmer of hope he had never heard whispered before.

"What are you saying?" he shouted to Faust.

"An angel for the Fallen. The prophecy says it will come."

"How will I know it? How can I find it?"

Drake's will bore down on them both like a weight that crushed the breath from its victims.

"You…will see…shadows," Faust managed.

"What shadows?" he asked. "We live in the dark."

"Shadows…" Faust said. "Beneath…the Midnight…Sun."

With all his mental energy, Christian tried to throw off Drake. *Leave us!*

It was not enough. Drake's voice returned, breaking through once more, crashing over them in a crescendo.

No more words!

Faust screamed in pain and stiffened as if convulsing. He fell over, shaking, and his eyes rolled up in his head. Christian picked him up and carried him toward the altar.

The blinding light cut through his mind like knives; the noise rang in his head like pounding bells. He struggled forward, dropping to his knees as it reached an intolerable level.

From there, he shoved Faust forward, sliding him along the floor and into the rail upon which the priest would offer Holy Communion.

Faust lay there, unmoving, but he would be safe.

In agony, Christian turned and crawled away. As he distanced himself from the altar, the pain faded, but as it did, Drake's voice returned.

You can't stay in there forever.

Drake was right. Christian was growing weaker with every moment. If he collapsed, either the death squads would find him or Drake would find a human to come in and take him.

Christian staggered to his feet, gazing along the aisle toward the rear doors of the church. The length of the nave seemed endless. He stumbled along it, grabbing hold of a pew and steadying himself. He edged his way to the far wall, his head clearing a bit more with each step away from the altar.

He gazed at the great doors at the back of the cathedral, then glanced over to the side entrance. Where was Drake? Even he could not be every-where at once.

Gathering his strength, Christian headed for the great doors at the back. He ripped two long pieces of wrought iron from an elaborate display on the wall. He would use them as staves, his only weapon.

He picked up the pace, fell to one knee just before reaching the exit, and then rose again, busting through the doors and out onto the front steps of the cathedral.

A tall, broad-shouldered figure stood in the darkness on the far side of the street. He wore a long gray coat that fell around him like a cloak. He stared at Christian without moving.

"Hello, old friend," Drake said. "It's been a long time."

Chapter 17

AT 2:00 in the morning, the streets were dark and deserted. A slight breeze ruffled Drake's gray coat. It opened slightly, revealing the glint of a sword Christian had learned to fear, a curved samurai blade forged by a master in ancient Japan. None made since was its equal.

Drake seemed content not to raise it just yet. "You don't look quite yourself."

Either Drake was gloating at Christian's weakened condition or it was his idea of a joke. Like Drake, Christian looked exactly as he had seventeen hundred years ago.

A second figure came from the shadows, his shaved head and cruel eyes looking the same as they had been when Christian last saw him in the sixteenth century. He was not as tall or strong in the shoulders as Drake, but he was Christian's equal in stature. The sight of him turned Christian's stomach.

"You remember Lagos," Drake said.

Indeed, Christian remembered Lagos, a murderer long before Drake turned him. "The executioner," Christian whispered. "One day, I'll kill him for what he's done."

Drake nodded, taking it in. Lagos didn't react; he knew better than to steal his master's thunder.

For whatever reason, Drake still hadn't moved. Christian found himself thankful for the delay. Now that he was outside the church, his strength was slowly beginning to return.

When Drake eventually took a step forward, Christian raised the two staves he'd gathered in the cathedral. He began to wield them, whirling them around in the style of an Indonesian stick fighter.

He took his stance with a half turn, one stick high across his shoulder, the other pointed opposite and low across his waist.

"A new style for you," Drake noted.

"Come closer," Christian urged. "I believe you'll find it painfully effective."

"You believe…" Drake began to laugh. "That's your problem, my friend. You don't believe anything. You never have. Not since the day I met you. Not since you grasped for power and killed the commandant of the legion and then fell into fear over what you'd done. You should have seized the reins instead of crawling away to die."

Christian's mind briefly traveled back to the moment of their meeting.

"You were lost then," Drake continued, "and you're lost now. Come back to the Brethren. I will give you purpose once again."

Drake must have been insane if he thought Christian would ever rejoin his cause after all he'd done.

"You lied to me all those years ago," Christian pointed out. "'No road back to the light,' you said. But you're wrong. A change is coming. A chance for mercy."

"There is no forgiveness," Drake said. "Not for us. Not for them. We will fight to the death—the Church and the Nosferatu. Only one entity can survive."

"And what could possibly make you think it will be our side?" Christian asked. "The curse fell upon our souls. We're the ones dammed by it."

"No," Drake said, beginning to move forward, sword held point down. "You see things backward. We have been given power to punish them—for their arrogance."

"You're more delusional than I thought."

110

"Am I?" Drake said. "You've seen what I asked of them. Don't you understand? Do you think I hid in the sewers and the caves for three centuries and then decided to fight? No. I had no power until they denied me mercy. I was a worm in the earth until they rejected me!"

He was bellowing now, raging against the past and not thinking. Christian felt his own strength growing, but in a full fury, Drake would be unstoppable.

"What are you saying?"

"The law of unintended consequences. They gave me this power by their own selfishness. Everything has balance and an opposite. Their arrogance disturbed this balance. We are chosen to restore it."

Drake continued to approach. Lagos shadowed him like a wingman. They were no more than twenty feet from Christian now. The time for talk was ending. Christian tensed for a furious and, most likely, hopeless battle.

"I will no longer beg," Drake spat. "I will eclipse them. And they will beg for mercy from *me*."

"And the angel of forgiveness?" Christian asked.

"I've been waiting for a thousand years to see it," Drake said. "And when it comes, I will destroy it."

Christian's mind whirled. He felt almost as dizzy as he had in the church, but for different reasons. *Drake has known of the angel for a thousand years? How? And why would he want to destroy it?*

Christian banished the confusion and questions in his head; he had no time to consider the possibilities, no time to be distracted. But even as he cleared his mind, a thought came forth with such power that he could not keep it to himself.

"I won't let you! Not after all you've done to the world."

"Then you'll die!"

Drake lunged and swung the samurai blade. Christian stepped back and countered as the blade sliced the air in front of him. He feinted with his left hand and swung the other pike in his right on a sharp, descending arc, hoping to cave in Drake's head. It whipped through the air in a blur, coming down from above. But Drake pirouetted to the side, and the pike missed his head by inches, catching the front of his coat and slicing the fabric with its jagged edge.

Drake took a step back, evaluating the attempt. "My tailor will be very unhappy with you," he said calmly. And then he raised his sword and stepped forward. He snapped his arms, and the polished blade flashed once again.

Christian avoided the first slash, but a second almost caught him. He parried it with the makeshift spike in his hand and was forced back even farther. Drake continued the assault, whirling the blade like a master.

Blow after blow came Christian's way as the onslaught grew. He could hardly keep up with it. He parried one thrust, then dodged and stepped back, and then parried again.

Drake's blade caught one of the pikes square on. It took the top half with it, decapitating the length of metal as if it were a rotten stick. Before Christian could react, Drake's blade came back toward him on a downward arc.

Christian dove away and rolled. Coming up, he flung the remnants of the first stave at Drake like he was throwing a knife. Drake swatted it away like a baseball player fouling off a pitch.

"Is that the best you can do?" Drake asked, looking at Christian's remaining makeshift weapon.

Christian said nothing. He felt as if Drake were toying with him.

"I told you once, if not a thousand times," Drake said, "never walk in the open without arms. They will come for us—in their own words—'like thieves in the night.'"

With that, Drake unleashed another barrage. He pressed forward unmercifully. Christian found himself being pushed back into the darker recesses of the alley, beside the church where he'd met Faust at the caretaker's door.

He continued to retreat, avoiding Drake's blade and deflecting it with glancing blows when he could. If Drake swung hard and dead on, Christian would have to sacrifice the last pike to protect himself. He would then be defenseless.

His only hope was to wound Drake, or even throw him off-balance enough for a chance to run.

Instead, he backed into a solid brick wall.

Drake stopped his approach. His wolfish eyes gleamed almost green in the darkness.

"Last chance," Drake whispered. "Life or death?"

Christian shook his head, well aware that he was about to die, quite certain that the fires of hell awaited him. He'd felt them claw at him once before. A warning. A premonition, perhaps. He would soon know the truth, what lay beyond the great void.

"We're already dead," he said calmly.

He gripped the pike and tensed, preparing to plunge it into Drake's heart in a death embrace, even as Drake's sword came down on him.

"So blind," Drake said, sounding disappointed. And then, surprisingly, Drake turned and began to walk away. He'd taken three steps when he whispered, "Take him."

Only now did Christian become aware of the figures on either side of him—one to the left and one to the right. With all his attention focused on Drake, he'd been unable to sense them lurking in the darkness.

Drones—Drake's most loyal henchmen. He gave them great physical power, but stripped and burned their minds down to a childlike state. Little if any of their own thoughts still existed; they lived now only to do Drake's bidding.

The snap of a palladium whip sounded from his right, a weapon normally reserved for the Ignis Purgata. The last pike was ripped from Christian's hand. At the same time, another whip snapped in from the left, wrapping around his leg and yanking it out from under him.

Christian dropped face-first, hitting the ground with a jarring impact. He managed to get his hands on the whip and pull it free from the first drone's grip.

Even as he did, the other drone leapt onto his back, looping a forearm around Christian's throat and bending his head back.

To a human, the drones would look like men, large and perhaps menacing in an indescribable way, but through Christian's eyes, they were monstrous creatures of bone and fang.

As Christian struggled to breathe, he reared back, slamming the second drone into the stone wall behind them, cracking the bricks and pushing some out of place. The drone howled but did not let go.

Its partner approached in a hunched position, swinging a chain with a spiked ball on the end, something like a morning star from the Middle Ages. Based on the heavy gloves the drone wore, the weapon was probably made out of palladium as well.

The chain flew in. Christian blocked it with his free hand, and it wrapped quickly around his arm, burning him like molten steel. The pain was excruciating, but this was his chance and he knew it.

Summoning all his strength, Christian ripped the chain from the drone's hand and then slammed himself backward once again, crashing through the wall. Bricks, mortar, and dust fell in a rumbling cloud. Christian and the drone that had tried to choke him ended up in a storeroom of the rear building.

Rolling free of the drone's grasp, Christian found himself next to an ancient wooden support beam. He slammed his hand into the beam, splintering the corner. Chaff and long slivers of wood flew everywhere, along with a two-foot daggerlike shard.

Christian dove for it, grabbed the splintered piece of wood, and rolled over, just as the drone leapt for him. With a jerk of his arm, Christian thrust the shard upward, plunging it into the beast's abdomen.

The creature howled in pain and staggered backward. It fell, shaking uncontrollably. The wooden spike caught fire, and then the drone's entire body flared as its death dance began.

The second of Drake's hideous creations pushed through the gaping hole in the wall, but paused at the sight of its brother burning.

Christian swung the barbed morning star in a haymaker fashion. The bulk of it caught the creature in the temple, snapping its head to the side.

The bony skull caved in, and the thing's neck cracked as it fell in a heap. In seconds, it was ablaze like its brother.

With flames jumping from the dead creatures to the walls and ceiling of the aged building, Christian knew he had to get out. He pushed through the jagged gap in the brick wall and saw Lagos charging with a machete in his hand.

Christina flung the palladium chain at his legs. It wrapped around them like a bolo, pulling Lagos's feet out from under him. He fell, lunging forward, stretching out like a diver.

Christian didn't wait.

He raced down the alley and out across the plaza and toward the river. He sensed Drake following as he jumped over a fence and onto the promenade. Ahead lay the bridge. A train was moving out of the station and picking up speed. That was the answer, if it didn't kill him in the process.

Christian raced toward the tracks and leapt, grabbing a metal bar on the last car and holding on as the train throttled up.

The train was soon racing across the bridge. Christian felt the presence of Drake and Lagos being left behind. Before the distance became too great, he heard Drake's voice one last time.

Run all you want, my friend. But the war is upon us. Soon you'll have no choice but to return to my side, for you'll have nowhere else to turn.

Chapter 18

Vatican City

IN THE early morning hours of a rainy day, Simon Lathatch walked the halls of the Vatican's inner buildings, accompanied by a bishop named Messini.

Anton Messini was the ordained leader of the Ignis Purgata. He did not fight or take part in the physical actions of the war against the Nosferatu. His post was a spiritual one, caring for the souls of the hunters.

It was a post well needed. The men of the order lived in conflict, both physical and mental. As servants of the Church, peace was their goal. But as the endless war filled their lives with death and pain and horrors that human eyes were never meant to see, they grew colder and harder in response. If they failed to act with determination and violence, the scourge of the Nosferatu would engulf the world. But if they lost their way and forgot the peace of the Lord, they might lose their very souls.

Simon had known Messini for decades. For the last twenty years, he'd been the sword of justice at Messini's beck and call.

"My heart grieves for your driver," Messini said as the two men walked slowly, hands clasped behind their backs.

"He will recover," Simon insisted. "And he's free now."

"I sense that you're not altogether displeased."

"The burden is heavy," Simon explained. "Aldo's soul was filled with light. He should not have to endure the darkness that lies ahead."

Messini nodded thoughtfully. "I remember a day when yours was filled with joy as well."

"A long time ago," Simon replied.

"You might have been better off if I'd never chosen you."

Simon had often considered how his life would have been had he never known of the Fallen and the war against them.

"The darkness had already come to my village," he said. "Having seen its cruel face in the eyes of the dead, how could I turn away?"

The two men walked on, respectful to each other, but there was tension in the air. Simon knew the reason, a conversation he'd dreaded for the past several years.

"Perhaps it's time you allowed yourself to look to brighter places," Messini said.

Simon stopped. He turned and looked up at his friend and mentor.

"You've carried the burden long enough," Messini elaborated. "Your service to the Church has been unparalleled. The sacrifices you've made, all that you've given up—these things have not been taken for granted."

Simon turned to the window. His thoughts drifted like the mist outside. His life had been simple once. The pleasures of a parish priest usually were. Marriages of blushing young couples. Baptisms for their children. Sermons for the flock. Even the funerals of those who'd passed gave him a chance to speak of God's love.

What had he seen of love these past thirty years?

He stared at his withered hand, a causality of his experience. He thought of lost friends, thought of the Fallen damned to burn in hell. He had always hoped there would be another way.

"My job is not yet finished," he insisted, sounding much like Aldo had the day before.

"It's not wise to hold on past one's season," Messini advised.

"I understand that," Simon insisted. "And once again, I state for the record, my job is not complete. I will not be stepping down at this time."

"Be reasonable, Simon."

"It's not for my own purposes that I stay on," Simon explained. "The task at hand is too valuable to be left to children."

The bishop seemed unfazed by this answer. "Henrick Vanderwall is not a child. He's the most competent hunter the order has ever claimed."

Simon had great misgivings about Henrick, but there was more to it than that. "If things continue as they are, he will no doubt be the greatest hunter of us all. But I'm not sure it's God's glory he seeks. Nor do I believe things will continue as they have been. A change is upon us, Bishop. The time for hunting may soon be over."

Messini straightened, his eyes sharpened and focused on Simon like daggers. He was no longer the kindly older mentor, but a powerful figure prepared to put a subordinate in check. "I urge you to consider what you're saying, very carefully."

"I have," Simon replied. "I've prayed on this for a long time. And in case I'm wrong, Henrick should remain my second. But if you put him in charge at this point, he'll do more harm than good. He doesn't yet understand the significance of what's happening here."

"And just what do you think is happening, Simon?" There was great suspicion in Messini's tone.

Simon turned toward the window and stared once again into the mist outside. "I believe we stand at the edge of the Reckoning. The coming of the angel and the Midnight Sun."

Messini did not react. The prophecy Simon spoke of was a point of contention among the order. It had not been granted a proper seal of belief, but neither had it been rejected as heresy.

"We've been debating this prophecy for a thousand years," Messini said. "It divides us."

"You take no position?"

"I'm wary," Messini said. "Do not forget, it came to us from the lips of a demon in the first place. I do not trust in this legend the way you do."

Simon understood the resistance. "'As the moment draws near, their power shall grow, and the Church's strength shall wane and be divided.' We have seen the weakest among them becoming more powerful. Aldo's misfortune is only the latest proof of this."

Messini did not reply.

"It says, 'We shall face confusion as they find understanding,'" Simon added, pressing. "We are at odds over this very point. And yet, one of them has entered the cathedral in Cologne and accessed the records of their origin, records we have kept secret for millennia. He left a caretaker alive whom he could have destroyed. Upon leaving, he fought with Drakos himself. Never in history have we seen this."

"Simon—"

"How could it be anything but a sign?"

"You're reading too much into—"

"No," Simon replied more sharply than he'd intended. "Something has been shown to us—and for a reason. We blame them for all that has occurred. But we could have forgiven Drakos seventeen centuries ago. How many lives would have been spared had our ancestors chosen mercy instead of war?"

"Blasphemy," Messini snapped.

"Truth," Simon insisted. "We're not infallible. Millions have suffered because of that choice. Until we admit our sin, it will only continue. We should have forgiven him."

"You tread dangerously, my friend."

"Is that not the Church's function, its purpose? To show mercy? To save souls?"

"The Nosferatu have no souls."

"And yet, the Father sends them a healer."

Messini's eyes were locked on Simon. "I understand your argument, all of which hinges on this radical prophecy. Do you truly believe in it, Simon? Or is it just your hope that there might be peace after so much killing?"

"I believe this prophecy is valid," Simon replied firmly, "and that its fulfillment is nearly upon us."

Messini took a deep breath and held it, thinking. "And how would you handle it? How would you have *us* handle this? Assuming I agreed."

"I'm not sure," Simon replied, "but I feel the two in Cologne must know something. Perhaps they're searching for the angel already, to find this forgiveness they believe in."

"Or to destroy it."

Messini nodded. At least he seemed to be considering the possibility. "It has been said that this angel will be born blind, unaware of its nature. Its arrival offers two paths—darkness and light, destruction and salvation."

Simon nodded. "If this is so, then we must find the angel before the Nosferatu discover it."

Messini rubbed his temple, the strain showing in his face. He sighed and walked over to Simon, staring out through the window and into the gloom as if the answer might be found there. "You make it no easier for me."

"I'm sorry, old friend."

"Not necessary," Messini said. "We must ensure that darkness does not prevail, either in the world or in our own hearts. If you're right, if by some chance this prophecy is true, then we must reach the angel before the Nosferatu find him."

"But where do we look?" Simon asked. He'd suspected for years that the Church had some secrets even he had no access to.

Messini did not hesitate. "The prophecy tells us he will be found 'across the sea, in the port city, whose heart is French, whose blood is mixed, where God and pagans are praised together. Her people cried out, unanswered in the night, drowned by nature and endless sorrows.'"

Simon considered the clues, but Messini didn't make him guess. "We believe it speaks of America," he said, "and the city of New Orleans."

"I will send the hunters to America," Simon promised.

"And you will remain in charge of the order," Messini added. "If this prophecy begins to unfold, you will continue at the helm. But if things are no less certain by the end of this year, you will step down."

Simon nodded his agreement. Either way, his time with the order was coming to an end.

Chapter 19

Compton, California

SMOG DRAPED Los Angeles in blanket of pollution, ozone, and carbon dioxide. During the day, it turned the sunlight into yellow haze. At night, it dropped into the city, burning the eyes and lungs of those who had to breathe it.

Leroy Atherton had endured it all his life. It wasn't a problem, it wasn't something he noticed—it was just the air. Same as the freeway outside his house was just the road. He'd never given much thought to either one, but lately, it felt like he was dying with every breath. At night, he'd have sworn that highway ran right through his living room.

A half mile from his house, the traffic on the 105 rumbled and roared and never, ever stopped. The endless sound of rubber against the road and the semis barreling past, even at 3:00 in morning, was relentless, like the beating of a drum.

Sweating and frustrated, Leroy rolled over and pulled the pillow against his head, trying to cover his ears, but the pillow was rough and it scratched his face. And the tiny apartment was a sweatbox, even in the spring.

He fought for sleep, tossing and turning, kicking the sheets. His T-shirt was drenched, and his dark face beaded up with sweat, no matter how many times he ran a towel across it.

He looked over at the nightstand to see the time, but the red digits of his clock were dark. He reached for the chain on the light and pulled it. Nothing happened.

He yanked it up and down half a dozen times to no avail. No power, no light, no fan. Only heat and sweat and darkness.

"Goddamned electric company," he swore.

He shoved the light back angrily, and it toppled off the nightstand and crashed to the bare floor. As it fell, the cord hooked the drawer in the nightstand, pulling it open a couple of inches. Inside, Leroy saw the butt of his nickel-plated .38 revolver.

He stared at it.

Why hadn't he used it when he had the chance? It was always there, inches from his grasp. All he had to do was grab it and pull the damn trigger.

He turned away, flipping over onto his side and trying once more to get some sleep. Out on the highway, a big rig downshifted, and the engine braking rumbled through the apartment, shaking the walls.

Leroy threw the sheet off and went to the window. He tried to pull it down, but it wouldn't budge.

He yanked on it and tried to force it, but his hand slipped and he sliced his palm on a tab of metal.

He pulled his hand back and then slammed his fist against the windowpane, cracking it.

"Goddamn you," he shouted, thundering another punch into the frame. "Goddamn you!"

The glass shattered and went everywhere, and Leroy sat back on the bed, his shoulders slumped, his hand bleeding, his body quivering with adrenaline. With the strap of his T-shirt, he wiped the sweat from his face. He had to get out of there, had to get out of that damn coffin of an apartment.

He stood and, without thinking about it much, grabbed the .38 and stuffed it in his pocket. He made his way to the front door, flung it open, and charged down the stairs.

He stopped on the ground floor. The light in the stairwell flickered, illuminating a red bicycle chained to a post. Leroy stared at the bike. His son's bike.

What did it matter anymore?

He lived in a crack neighborhood, in a crummy apartment with no electricity. He had eight dollars and a few dimes in his pocket. He had six shots in the .38. And he no longer had a son.

What did anything matter, unless he did something about it?

He turned from the bike and began to walk. Slowly, aimlessly, he wandered out onto the streets. Bare feet to the grime, dirt, and cement.

At first, he didn't know where he was going, but he kept walking. Soon enough, he began to realize he was headed in the right direction.

The time had come, he decided. There was nothing left for him in this place, so the time had come for revenge.

He pushed on. Two hours later, he'd covered five miles. His feet were bloody and blistered, his sweat-drenched shirt gone, thrown away in disgust. His eyes were as red as fire.

He found the house he was looking for—a dirty little box of a house with plywood where the front window should have been and a warped roof sinking under its own weight.

He pushed through the gate in the rusty chain-link fence and paused by a dead tree in the front lawn. A hundred yards away, a traffic light stood watch in the night. The street was quiet.

Leroy pulled out the .38, sliding his finger up next to the trigger. He took a breath and started forward.

"Time to pay," he whispered. "Time to pay for what you done to my boy."

He crossed the postage stamp of a lawn and reached the porch. He cocked the hammer on the gun, aimed at the lock, and pulled the trigger.

The gun sounded off, shattering the calm. Without waiting, Leroy slammed his two hundred–pound body against the door, splintering the wood frame and forcing the door wide open.

He rushed into the house with the gun ready. A woman's voice shouted. A dog barked continuously in the small kitchen. Leroy charged past a dilapidated couch toward a short hallway with two doors. He kicked in the right-hand door in time to see a teenager in skivvies grabbing a baseball bat.

He raised the gun, and the kid froze.

"You killed my son," Leroy yelled. "You goddamned worthless piece of crap, you killed my boy."

The teenager backed into a thin wall of old wood paneling.

Leroy lunged forward, slapped the bat out of the kid's arms, and grabbed the kid by the neck. He threw the skinny punk down onto the ratty mattress of a bed and stuck the gun in his face.

A woman stuck her head around the door.

"Get back!" Leroy shouted.

She ducked around the corner. "Oh God! Oh God!" she shrieked.

"I'll blow his head off. You come in here, and I'll blow his goddamned head right off."

The woman screamed, and the dog continued to bark, and the kid yelled to his mom.

"Get out of here, Momma. Just get out!"

The woman disappeared and shouted from somewhere in the hall. "Please don't shoot him. Oh God, please don't kill him!"

"Close the door!" Leroy shouted.

"Please!"

"Close the goddamned door!" As Leroy yelled, he felt his heart pounding, spit flying from his lips.

The woman shut the door, and Leroy turned back to the kid. He was thin, a lot skinnier than he'd been the last time Leroy saw him in a police lineup. The same day, a couple of cops told him there wasn't enough evidence to make an arrest.

"Not enough evidence, my ass," he said. "Enough for me!"

The kid was shaking, the scraggly, pathetic attempt at a mustache quivering on his upper lip. The room smelled of pot and cigarettes and stale beer. The mattress looked like it had been pulled out of a dumpster.

"Why?" Leroy shouted, jamming the gun back in punk kid's face. "Why?"

He didn't really expect an answer. He expected the kid to cuss at him, to tell him to go to hell, or to promise that his gang would pay the old man back. But the kid shook uncontrollably, staring at the gun and then Leroy's face.

"I'm sorry," he mumbled. "I'm so sorry...I didn't know."

"Didn't know what?"

"I didn't know him. They just told me to do it. He pissed someone off, and I had to do it."

Leroy's world spun. "You didn't even know who he was? You killed my son, and you didn't even know who he was?"

"They told me to," the kid whimpered. "I had to."

Leroy cocked the hammer again and pressed the barrel of the gun against the kid's forehead. The kid's mother cried in the hall, the dog wouldn't shut the hell up, and the teenager who'd killed his son shook and sobbed and closed his eyes.

Leroy clenched his jaw. His own body was shaking. He felt like he was going to throw up. He pressed the gun harder and harder, pressed it down so hard that the kid's head was forced back into the ratty pillow.

"Goddamn you!" he shouted.

He tried. Leroy tried with all his might to pull the trigger, but he couldn't do it.

He pushed himself off the boy and stumbled back, slamming into the wall. He tilted his head back and looked up at the ceiling, tears streaming down his face. He couldn't do it.

He couldn't do it.

His chest heaved and fell. His heart pounded so hard he thought it would explode. His head throbbed like he was having a stroke.

He pushed off the wall. The kid hadn't moved. He just lay there, shaking. Leroy turned and busted out the door into the hall. He raced past the sobbing woman, who'd slid down the wall and sat on the floor. He raced past the barking dog and out the front door.

And from there, he ran. Bloody feet and all, he ran as fast as he could.

He had no idea where he was going, but he couldn't run fast enough. Sobbing and gasping for air, he raced down the block. He threw the gun away and ran toward a fence and climbed it. He caught his foot at the top and fell forward. He tumbled down a sloped concrete bank and landed in a trickle of water and filth that led to the LA River.

About four feet wide and ten inches deep, the water ran in a narrow canal, half-filled with abandoned shopping carts, trash, and sand.

The sound of police sirens spurred him on, and Leroy managed to get up and get moving again. He ran along the river. Ran until his arms and legs flopped and flapped with little coordination. He stumbled again when his knee gave out, splashing down in the water and skinning his elbows on the concrete beneath it.

This time he stayed down.

He lay still, half his body in the water. It was probably contaminated, but as least it felt cold. It washed over him and numbed his body, washing off the sweat. He could hear it trickling past, even over the sound of trucks and cars and the police sirens in the distance that he felt certain were meant for him.

He cried quietly as his mind assaulted him for his failure. He'd watched that scrawny kid murder his own son in front of the apartment. He'd moved too slowly to do anything about it then, and now he couldn't even find a way to even the score. He couldn't kill him. He wanted to, he'd tried to, but he couldn't do it.

As he looked into the skinny kid's eyes, the kid seemed different than the killer Leroy had imagined him to be. He seemed lost and mistreated, wasting away and afraid. The kid even wanted forgiveness for what he'd done.

And for some reason, as he lay in the water, Leroy wanted the kid to be forgiven, wanted the child's mind to be healed. It didn't make sense to him, but that was what Leroy wanted more than anything else at that moment.

A stinging feeling in his hand got Leroy's attention. He looked at where the window had sliced it. The blood was trickling again, and the wound burned with a cold fire from the water soaking into it.

And then he saw something else, something that puzzled him. Across the palm of his hand, spreading out from the cut, his skin was changing color. It was turning a strange gray color, with a swirling pattern that spread like fire charring paper from the other side.

He pulled his hand from the river. Suddenly, his senses returned. Who knew what the hell was in that water?

He shook off his hand, rubbed it against his pant leg, and began to climb out of the stream.

He looked up the concrete embankment. A ten-foot crawl was all he needed. But his head was spinning, and he found he could hardly move.

He tried to set his feet and scramble up the slope, but he slipped and fell back into the trickle of the river. His head hit the concrete, and his world became blurry. Even the noise of the cars and sirens in the distance faded, until all he heard was the trickle of the water running beside him.

Unable to move, Leroy rested there, slowly passing out and unaware that the strange pattern on his skin had begun traveling up his arm and across the rest of his body.

Chapter 20

LEROY ATHERTON felt something covering his mouth, smothering him. He brought his hands up to move it, but someone grabbed them and forced them back down. His eyelids cracked open.

Through blurred vision, he saw a face above him—a woman in her thirties. Her dark hair was pulled back in a ponytail. She looked Hispanic, with dark eyes. She wore a blue shirt. Her lips were moving, but Leroy could hear no sound coming from them, like he was watching TV with the mute button on.

He reached for the thing on his face once again, but she pulled his hand back and slammed it down this time.

He began to hear something, a wailing noise, up and down, up and down. It felt like they were swaying side to side, like when the earthquake hit a few years back. It suddenly dawned on Leroy that he was in an ambulance with an oxygen mask strapped to his face. The woman above him was a paramedic.

"Blood pressure one ninety over one fifty-five," she said loudly.

She wasn't talking to him, but to someone else in the cramped space.

"He's burning up," she added. "Temp, one-oh-five. Heart rate, one seventy."

"One seventy?" another voice said.

She glanced at a monitor. "And rising."

Leroy had no idea what those numbers meant, but by the sound of her voice, it had to be bad.

Maybe he was dying. Maybe it would be better that way.

She looked over him again, blocking the lights in the roof behind her. He could see her better now. She was young and pretty, not a stitch of makeup on.

"We're almost there," she said, "just hang on a little longer."

The ambulance pulled into the bay at Pacific Hospital in Long Beach. It screeched to a halt as someone doused the siren. The back doors opened quickly, and Leroy was carried out on his stretcher and run into the emergency room.

His head lolled to the side, and he saw others in the waiting room as they passed. Some looked ill and gray, others held bloodstained towels to various wounds, all of them looked miserable.

He must have been worse, he thought, since they rolled him right past and into a trauma room.

The pretty EMT talked the whole way, rattling off terms and statistics to a nurse. And then she was gone.

A doctor appeared over him. He looked Indian to Leroy.

"What do we have here, people?"

"Found in a canal that leads to the LA River," the nurse said. "Possible overdose."

Another nurse was attaching leads to his chest.

"What's he on?"

Leroy shook his head. He didn't take any of that crap, but the doctor wasn't looking at him.

Something began to beep rapidly, loud and alarming.

"This can't this be right," the nurse said.

"What does it say?"

"Heart rate is over two hundred."

"Charge the paddles."

"But he's not in A-fib," the nurse replied.

The doctor seemed stunned. He looked at the monitor. "Tachycardia."

"Rhythm is normal."

"We have to slow it down," the doctor said. "Digitalis, ten cc's. Stand by with Tambocor, and get him on a drip of potassium chloride."

The doctor turned his attention to Leroy and pulled the oxygen mask away. "What drugs have you taken? I can't help you if I don't know what I'm dealing with."

"I don't do drugs."

"It's not the time to lie," the doctor said. "I'm not the cops."

The doctor looked scared. And suddenly, Leroy was scared. And some new alarm began to go off in the background.

The nurse stretched out his arm, looking for a vein, and then froze. "What the hell is this?" she said.

Leroy glanced over and saw that strange pattern again. It now covered his entire arm. It looked like spirals of light and dark, with swirls that radiated outward. In places, the pattern seemed to be moving and pulsating under the skin.

"You gotta help me," Leroy said. He reached for the doctor with his free hand.

"What drugs are you—"

Suddenly, his whole body arched in a seizure. Leroy couldn't see anymore. He only heard movement and felt pain.

A pair of hands pressed down on him, holding his arm in place while another set of hands began to wrap restraints around it.

"What's happening to his skin?" the nurse shouted.

"Just get that needle in him."

"But there's a pattern here," the nurse said. "It's changing."

"For God sakes, Nurse!"

Another seizure racked Leroy's body. He arched his back and felt his jaw clamp tight and his legs begin to shake. The nurse tried to restrain him, but Leroy threw her and the doctor aside, pushing them away from the bed. They crashed to the floor, along with a tray of scalpels and other medical supplies.

Leroy pulled his arm loose from the restraint, rolled off the bed, and ripped out the IV.

A pair of security guards appeared, and Leroy dashed the other way, crashing through the curtain and colliding with another gurney that was being wheeled down the hall. He hit the rolling stretcher so hard it tipped over. Leroy came down on top of it and on top of the young boy who'd been lying on it.

"I'm sorry," Leroy managed. "I'm so—"

He looked at the kid lying on the ground in the fetal position—a young black kid, no older than his son. His head had been shaved for surgery, an old scar on a different part of his scalp showing that this wasn't the first. The kid's eyes were closed, and dark circles that looked like bruises lay beneath them. He didn't seem to be breathing.

"Get away from him," one of the guards shouted.

Leroy didn't hear it. He kept staring at the child, thinking no one so young should die. He reached out for the kid, wanting to touch him, though he didn't know why. A snap of energy surged through his fingers like an electrical shock. A flutter of muscle spasms ran through the kid, the tiniest of shudders, unseen by anyone but Leroy.

Leroy looked on, stunned and dazed, until the security guards yanked him backward and slammed him onto the ground. This time they held him down and a needle went harshly into his leg. It shot liquid fire into his thigh, and Leroy went dizzy almost instantly. In seconds, the air seemed thick and hazy, and moments later, the world was gone.

Chapter 21

CHRISTIAN SLIPPED through the darkened halls at Columbia University long after everyone else had gone home. He approached Ida's office and noticed the door was ajar. A thin beam of light spilled out of the office and across the marble floor of the hall.

He pushed open the door and stepped inside. The place had been ransacked. He knew immediately by whom.

Ida sat in the middle of the mess, picking through broken keepsakes. Some type of clear acrylic award had been separated from its base. She flung it toward a trash can. It hit the wall with thud and dropped into the basket.

"Two points," she said, then suddenly realized he was there. She focused on him, and a look of anger resolved into a mild scowl. "You sure do know how to sneak around."

"Comes with the territory," he said.

"I suppose it does," she said, sifting through some more debris. "I was kind of hoping I'd never see you again."

"I came to warn you," he said.

"You're a little late," she said, looking around. "Can you believe this?"

He nodded. "The Ignis Purgata," he said. "You rattled their chain about Cologne. I showed up. They probably put two and two together."

She heaved a broken piece of an ancient pot toward the waste basket. "I really needed to clean this place up anyway. They just stopped me from procrastinating anymore."

She should have been in tears, but she was cracking jokes as she sorted through a lifetime of memories, now destroyed.

"Did you find what you were looking for over there?"

Christian crouched down and began to help with the cleanup. After a long silence, he spoke.

"Do you believe in angels?"

"Not really," she said. "But then again, my perspective on some things has begun to change since I met you. Is that what you discovered?"

"I found the truth about myself," he said, "that Drakos is the one from whom this curse began. I also heard of a prophecy. It spoke of a chance at redemption for the Fallen. The arrival of an angel of forgiveness. The caretaker said there were documents pertaining to this redemption in the Vatican."

Her eyes searched him. "You believe him?"

"I do."

Ida sighed. "I suppose a visit to the Vatican is out of the question?"

"Are you kidding?" he said. "The cathedral almost killed me."

"I was talking about me," she said.

He looked at her. "Oh, right. Well, I'm thinking you might not be on the guest list, either."

He lifted a bookcase back into position and found the picture of Ida and her mother beneath it. The glass was broken. He pulled out the last few pieces and handed her the photo and frame.

"Thank you," she said.

"I should thank you," he replied. "You've helped me onto a path I never thought existed."

"So what do you do now?" she asked. "How do you find an angel?"

"No idea," he said, "but I have to before Drake does."

He explained about the fight and how Drake had threatened to destroy the angel, how he'd been waiting a thousand years for the chance.

"So who told him about this forgiveness?"

"Not sure," Christian said. "Certainly, I never heard a word of it during our time together. But the caretaker mentioned something else. Something I have heard of."

"What would that be?"

Christian took the long way around to explain it. "Remember the one I told you about," he said, "the one I told you I loved?"

She nodded.

"Her name was Elsa," Christian said. "She had the gift of second sight. She could foretell events that were coming. Not small things, but big events. Moments of danger and ecstasy. The birth of a child to a couple who had yet to conceive, a fire in the village, the pain of life and death."

Christian realized his voice had trailed off as his mind went back to that distant time.

"Her and I were together. She had a way of reaching through the void and making me feel alive again. Human. I always knew it bothered Drake, but he never did more than warn me that it would cause me pain one day. That day came when the Inquisition arrived in Lisbon and someone gave them her name as a heretic and an even a witch. They caught her and set to burn her at the stake. I rescued her but moments too late. They burned her—burned her badly. She should have died."

Christian looked away, thinking of that dark night.

"It was Drake who gave her up to them," Ida guessed.

He nodded. "I didn't know at first. He claimed he would help save her, but he was late. I think he hoped she would die before we arrived."

"Why?"

"I've wondered all these years what Drake was so afraid of," he said. "Now I think I know. Several nights before the Inquisition came, I watched Elsa in the grips of a fever. She spoke in her sleep. Words that made no sense. I haven't thought of those words since. But the caretaker used them in the cathedral."

"What words?"

"The Midnight Sun."

Christian leaned against the wall, thinking. In all their time together, Christian had never seen Drake expend so much energy on so feeble an opponent as Faust. He'd done so through the power and noise of the cathedral, and even through Christian's vigorous attempt to block him.

He looked over at Elsa. "Twice in my life, I've heard someone talk of 'shadows beneath the Midnight Sun.' And twice, Drake has tried to destroy them."

"What does it mean?" Ida asked.

"I don't know," he said. "But Elsa might."

Ida cocked her head slightly. "She's still alive? The way you spoke, I'd have thought she'd died long ago."

Christian fought against a wave of guilt. "She would have been better off that way," he said. "But I turned her into something else."

"She's like you."

"Not exactly," he said. "She's a prisoner of my mistakes, my choices. Something I can never undo."

Ida sat silently. The words seemed to resonate with her. "We've all made mistakes," she said gently. "What matters most is what we do afterward."

"She hid herself away," Christian explained. "I promised to leave her alone, to never seek her out again."

Ida reached out and put her hand on his. "My, you're cold, sonny." She didn't let go. "But you must have a good heart. All who feel guilt do."

As he considered this, she continued.

"You see this picture?" she said. "This is the only picture I have of my mother. It was taken shortly after my father died and shortly before she took up with a man who drank too much and liked to hurt others when he was feeling bad. I always thought it was me. I wasn't his child. He made that clear. I felt like I was the cause my mother's pain. A few years later, I left. I promised Momma I would never come back. I thought it would be better for her. Wasn't long before she died."

"You wish you had."

"Every day of my life," she said, her voice cracking. "I thought I was the problem, but he beat her down worse after I left. No one there to see it. I know the kind of pain you feel. I know that, no matter what I say, nothing's gonna lift it from you any more than you can lift mine from me."

He understood what she was saying, but confusion swirled inside him. He felt like he'd rather die than break his word to Elsa and cause her more suffering. After all he'd done, the one honorable thing he could point to was keeping his vow. But now...

If a chance at redemption had come into the world, he couldn't allow Drake to destroy it or corrupt it. So many thousands had suffered from the curse without hope, including her. So many more would suffer if Drake succeeded.

"Strange as this sounds," Ida said, "we're not so different. We're both trapped in bodies we never asked for. Both handicapped and blessed in our own ways. Both hope someone out there can forgive us because we damn sure can't forgive ourselves."

"If you could go see your mother—"

"I'd do it in a heartbeat," she said. "I'd be sick to my stomach all the way there, but I'd go. There's so much I never got to say."

As she finished, Christian realized how much he'd begun to care for Ida. In some small way, it was similar to his feelings for Elsa, the kind of emotion the Nosferatu were not supposed to be capable of. And that brought a new torment to his mind. Ida wasn't safe here. She might not be safe anywhere.

"I've put you in harm's way," he said.

She wrinkled her brow as if the idea was ludicrous. "Sonny, I've dealt with worse than this," she said. "You should've been around in the sixties, when we were marching."

"I was around in the sixties," he reminded her.

"Right," she said. "Well, then you know what I mean. I'm doubting your friends from the Church will come back. This isn't the Dark Ages."

"It's not them I'm worried about."

"Drake," she said.

"He read my mind. He attacked the caretaker through a link I formed. I tried to block him, but I couldn't. I'm not sure if Drake saw your name or your face through my thoughts. But if he did, you won't be safe. I need to hide you."

She shook her head. "No thanks, sonny."

"He's not something you can deal with," Christian said. "You can't take this lightly."

She looked around her office and then over at the picture of her mother and her. "I've spent my whole life running, just like you. I'm not doing it anymore. If he shows up, then he shows up."

He wasn't going to win this argument and he knew it. He hoped Drake had been so preoccupied with his own quest that he hadn't become aware of Ida.

"I can't stay here and protect you."

She smiled at him once again. It was the warm, sad smile of someone who understood the reality of things, even if she wanted them to be different. "You go and do what you have to, sonny. You know where to find me if you need some help."

Chapter 22

KATE PFEIFFER and Billy Ray Massimo were back in Boston, cruising up I-95, heading for the skyscrapers downtown.

For the first time, Kate felt they were on to something more than just chasing the wind. Dumb luck had helped them out when Officer Jenkins recognized the victim, but it was the change in pattern, the increasing sloppiness of the crimes, that made it possible.

The latest victims were young women with friends and family and good jobs—facts that allowed them to recreate the victims' last steps. The last place they'd spent any money was a bar in Midtown called Chiraz.

Based on the time of death, Kate was certain the women had met the killer there or shortly afterward, perhaps in the parking lot or the alley behind the bar.

Video from a surveillance camera had shown them talking to a dozen people in the bar, but two in particular had stood out—a woman and a man who seemed to hover around them most of the night.

The man was unknown, but the woman had been identified. Her name was Vivian Dasher. She was an executive with Timeless Export and Imports, an old-money Boston company. Kate and Billy Ray had been informed that she worked most nights, dealing with foreign businesses on the Pacific Rim. They'd decided a surprise visit at her office was in order.

As they parked, Billy Ray glanced at her. "You think this is gonna lead to anything?"

"Let's hope so," she said.

They made their way into the building. A quick flash of their badges got them past the night guard and gave them access to the elevator, but when they emerged on the twenty-second floor, the receptionist wouldn't let them pass.

"Listen, honey," Kate said, "you may have your orders, but your bosses are going to drop you like a bad habit when we come back with a search warrant and turn this place upside down for a month. Do you understand what I'm talking about?"

The woman did not back off one little bit. "First of all, Mrs. Pfeiffer, they pay me twice what you make, so don't 'honey' me, I'm not some blonde bimbo who barely knows how to turn on my laptop. Second, this is a big firm. A lot of what we do is confidential, with a lot of lawyers involved, so your little badge and your threats don't scare me. I have very strict orders not to let anyone pass unless they have permission to be here, so if you want to—"

Kate never heard the rest of the speech. She'd seen a conference room door open across the way and saw Vivian Dasher walk out with another man beside her. Although Kate had only seen Ms. Dasher in the grainy video from the bar, she recognized her instantly.

"Ms. Dasher," she called, pushing past the receptionist's desk. "I'm Special Agent Kate Pfeiffer with the FBI. I need to speak with you."

Vivian stopped in her tracks, a cool, composed executive dumbfounded for a moment.

Kate had her badge out, her best *you're in trouble* voice going. A look of shock and surprise flashed over Ms. Dasher's face. But there was more to it than that. Instead of anger, she saw fear.

"I need to know what you were doing at a club called Chiraz last Thursday night," Kate pressed, "and who you were with."

Vivian Dasher didn't reply, but the man standing beside her did. The way he carried himself, he looked like he might be Vivian's boss or her father. He narrowed his gaze at Kate.

"Who are you again, and what is this all about?"

"Considering how loud I shout, I'm pretty sure you heard what I said," Kate replied.

"Yes," he said, his eyes narrowing on her. "I'm sure everyone on the floor heard. Which is what you wanted, correct?"

Kate was aggravated now. Whoever this guy was, he was a much cooler customer than Vivian. By running interference for her, he was giving her a chance to get over the shock that Kate was trying to induce.

"They're going to hear a lot more, unless we get a chance to talk to Ms. Dasher in private."

Kate knew she was on thin ice. Big shots like these could raise hell.

"How cunning of you," the man said, "disturbing my business to gain an audience."

"And you are?"

"Drake Castillion. I own this company."

"We're only following a lead," she replied. "If Ms. Dasher would like to talk to us outside, we'll disappear."

Vivian glanced at her boss. Kate noticed a slight tremble in her right hand. She was rattled.

"It's rather late," the man said. "No point in going outside in the dark. If Ms. Dasher wants to talk, we can talk in the conference room. At least then my people can get back to work instead of watching the sideshow."

Kate didn't like how this was playing out. "We don't need you there, Mr. Castillion."

"No," Vivian said. "I want someone there."

There was nothing Kate could do. If she backed off and came back later, they'd be lawyered up, and whatever part Ms. Dasher might have played in the murders would never be known.

"All right," she said. "Lead on."

Drake and Vivian turned in unison and walked back into the conference room from which they'd come.

Billy Ray moved up beside Kate. "You're out of your mind," he whispered.

"We're not going to get another shot at this," she said. "Come on."

They followed Drake and Vivian into the conference room and closed the door behind them. A polished cherrywood table dominated the center of the room. Ten chairs were arranged around it, with a larger chair at the head. Kate guessed that was Drake's chair, but for now, he and Vivian sat mid-table. Kate and Billy Ray sat opposite them, as if they were negotiating some deal.

Kate pulled out a digital recorder, placed it on the table, and switched it on. Another act she hoped would unnerve Ms. Dasher.

She stared at it and its little red power light.

Drake reached out and turned it off. "I don't think that will be necessary," he said.

"It's for your protection," Kate said.

Drake smiled. "I have a little more faith in my government than that."

Unfortunately, the calmer this Drake character seemed, the calmer Vivian was getting, and Kate needed the woman on edge if she was going to get anything out of her. She pulled out the victim's photos and shoved them across the table.

"These two women were last seen alive at the bar Chiraz, with you, Ms. Dasher. You and another man whom we haven't identified yet. At closing time, you all seemed real chummy. Forty-eight hours later, they're found dead. The coroner placed the time of death within eight hours of their leaving the bar. As near as we can tell, you were the last person to see them alive."

Vivian stared at the photos. She placed her shaking hand on one of them. "I…I remember them," she said. "We were drinking together. They knew who I was and—"

"You saying they came up to you?" Billy Ray asked.

"They wanted to work here," she said. "I gave them my card and told them to send me their résumés. It was just…I can't believe they're dead. How did it happen?"

"Throats slashed," Kate said bluntly. She kept the part about their blood being drained to herself.

Vivian looked away. It was a pretty good performance. But something was odd. Most suspects tended to look toward their lawyers as a way to get reassurance, and even though her boss was not her attorney, he sure was acting like one. Only, Vivian had yet to look at him, turning away every time.

Kate turned her attention toward Drake. He met her eyes and stared back. To her surprise, Kate found her attention wandering, her mind going blank.

"So why would these women want to work here?" The question came from Billy Ray.

Drake turned away, and Kate blinked several times to clear her head. *Weird*. She definitely needed to get more sleep.

"We're a very successful company," Drake said.

"And you work very strange hours."

Billy Ray looked at his watch. "It's nine o'clock in the evening, and you've got a whole floor filled with people. You and Ms. Dasher are still in the building."

"This company clears five hundred million dollars a year," Drake boasted. "Eighty percent of that comes in from overseas, in places that are sound asleep during what you government workers call business hours. As it happens, I just returned from Europe myself."

"Business or pleasure?" Billy Ray asked.

"Recruiting, actually."

Billy Ray backed off. But his salvo had given Kate some breathing room, and she felt her wits returning.

"Ms. Dasher," she began, "what if I told you the man you were seen with at the bar was a suspect in half a dozen other homicides. Could you tell me who he is and where we can find him?"

It was a lie, just to stir things up, but Vivian held quiet.

"If you don't speak," Kate added, "I'll have to consider you a suspect, a possible conspirator."

"I don't know him," she said.

"That's not what the video tells us," Billy Ray said.

"You bought him drinks all night," Kate added. "On your company card."

Under normal circumstances, Kate would have turned her glare toward the boss man right about now, just to see if he was aggravated or nervous, but for some reason, she didn't want to. She kept her eyes on Vivian.

Silence filled the room.

"Nothing to say?" Kate asked.

Vivian shook her head, and Kate chose to play her last card.

"I need you to come with us," she said, standing and pulling out a pair of cuffs.

Vivian's eyes grew wide. "What? This is ridiculous."

Billy Ray stood as well. His look said, *I hope you know what you're doing.*

"You were a person of interest when we came down here, and your unwillingness to talk makes you a suspect in my eyes. Now, please stand, turn around, and place your hands behind your back."

Kate was really on thin ice now, but she needed to push this until something broke, either the case or her career.

"Who the hell do you think you are?" Vivian shouted. The bitterness in her voice suggested a person used to always getting her way. She seemed like she might snap.

"Ms. Dasher, please turn around, or we will arrest you by force."

"You can't do this," Vivian replied. "You can't—"

A hand landed on Vivian's shoulder. Drake's hand. She calmed down instantly.

"You can't believe that I have anything to do with this?" she said. She was looking toward him for the first time, but her eyes were cast down, like a scolded hound.

"Of course not," he said. "But they are the FBI. Go with them. Don't talk to them. Don't try to explain. Not a word, understand? This is a power play, nothing more. We have lawyers who handle these kinds of situations and others who specialize in ruining careers. I'll have them all on the phone within the hour."

"Your lawyers keep late nights too?" Billy Ray said.

"No," Drake replied arrogantly. "They wake up when I call them."

Kate had heard it all before a hundred times. As if the Bureau wanted warm and fuzzy agents interested in giving a great customer service experience instead of solving crimes. Still, as Drake's eyes bore into her, she had an uneasy feeling.

She looked back at Vivian, who finally turned and allowed Kate to cuff her. A minute later, they were marching her out through the office to the astonishment of those working the floor. She wondered if it would do any good.

By the time they reached the elevator, the woman was no longer nervous; she was as cold as ice. Strange emotional flips were a dangerous sign in anyone, let alone a murder suspect. Standing in the elevator with her, Kate got a vibe that this woman was capable of anything. She began to feel they were on the right path.

Billy Ray pressed the button for the lobby floor, and the doors slowly closed. As the elevator dropped, a chill ran down Kate's spine. A thought seemed to form in her head spontaneously. It was like a whisper.

You're making a very big mistake.

She'd been thinking that was a possibility all night. But for reasons she couldn't explain, this thought seemed to come from somewhere else.

Chapter 23

CHRISTIAN STOOD at the edge of a brooding swamp on a rickety wooden dock. Out in the distance, the cypress trees sprouted from the green waters, standing guard over the deeper darkness with their drooping arms and Spanish moss.

The energy of life pulsed in the great swamp. It was vibrant and powerful and all encompassing. But something else lay out there, something brighter and sharper than the smooth energy of the trees and plants. It was waiting for him.

"You sho you want to go in there?" a cautious voice asked. "Nothing out there dats good fo' ya. Just water moccasins and gators. Some of them done growed big enough to eat ya whole."

An elderly Cajun man—part white, part black, part Seminole Indian—had led him down to the water's edge. He was scratching his belly through a pair of dirty overalls and a white T-shirt.

"I have business out there," Christian said.

"Business?" the Cajun man said, slipping a canoe into the water. "What the hell kinda business you got out there at dis time of night?"

Christian stared into the darkness. "The kind that's waited too long already."

The Cajun pulled the grease-stained cap off his head, ran his hand along his scalp, and then tucked the hat back down again. "Dey say an old witch live out dere. Dat any man who done see her, he ain't never been the same."

As the old Cajun spoke, he shook himself like a dog shaking off water. "Probably better to get eat up by a gator, I'd guess."

Christian didn't respond. His mind was on Elsa. She was out there; she was still alive. He could feel it. Had she become a witch, the very thing the Inquisition had accused her of? He couldn't imagine her kindness twisted in such a way, but time did strange things to damaged souls of this earth.

He climbed in the canoe, pushed off, and began paddling. The canoe was soon gliding through the still waters, splitting the surface and trailing a wake of silent ripples out behind it. As he reached the soaring trees, the canoe entered the mist. It drifted past his eyes in waves of white and gray. It reminded him of smoke, and he could almost taste the ashes on his tongue—ashes from a fire four hundred years past.

He paddled deeper and deeper into the wetlands until an hour had gone by. He could sense Elsa's presence and her pain more brightly with each passing moment.

Finally, he spotted an old shack built on stilts out in the distance. The wooden boards were gray-white in the moonlight. They reminded him of old bones. As he grew closer, he could see they were splitting and faded, broken in places and dark in sections where the rot had set in.

A wooden rocking chair sat motionless on the front porch. Bird droppings covered the sagging roof where a giant tree loomed over it, its wide arms and curtains of Spanish moss encircling and protecting the lonely structure.

The house was dark except for a single candle that burned and flickered through a small window. Christian paddled toward it, wondering what he would find inside after all these years.

He bumped up against the short dock that jutted from the weathered shack and climbed out of the canoe, tying the narrow bowline to a rusted cleat. As he walked toward the house, the floorboards creaked beneath his boots. By the time he made it to the porch, he sensed movement. He caught sight of a shape in the window. Fingers with long, curving nails touched the wick of the candle and put it out. A wisp of smoke hung in the air.

"You've no right to come here," a voice whispered. "You promised to leave me in peace."

The voice was familiar to him, but the tone was so different.

"I've broken every vow in my life except this one," he said. "I don't come here lightly."

A dark shape, half-lit by the moonlight, appeared just inside the doorway.

"Is it courage or fear that brings you to my door?"

"Both," he said. "But what do the reasons matter?"

"They always matter," the voice replied. "More than anything else. Will you never understand this?"

A new candle came to life, held in the curled and withered fingers of an old woman. The candlelight spilled upward, illuminating a face covered with the horrific scars of burned and melted flesh.

Christian's dead soul grieved for his love. He stared, his guilt a thousand times deeper than he ever could have imagined.

"Have you no decency?" she said.

"I see only that which I love."

For a second, her face softened. "The beauty is long gone."

Christian could feel the effect she'd always had on him. It burned almost as it once had—the feeling of love and light, but tainted by what he'd done.

Elsa had been burned at the stake by the murderers of the Inquisition. Christian had tried to rescue her with Drake's belated help, only to discover that Drake was the one who'd betrayed them, passing information to a murderer named Lagos, who held the position of high inquisitor.

During the battle to save her, Christian killed a dozen who had tried to stop him, but he reached Elsa too late. She was thrown on the fire and doused with oil. By the time Christian pulled her free, half her body had been charred.

"I know you hate me," he said. "And perhaps you should. I had no right to try turning you into what I am against your will. I was mad with pain. I couldn't bear to see you in agony, and I was too weak to let you go. If you had only accepted the gift—"

"The curse," she insisted. "Never lie to yourself. You know what it is. I was made to bring you to life. But instead, you tried to drag me into death."

She'd begged to die, but he'd stopped her pain by trying to transform her into one of the Nosferatu. She'd rejected his offer and thus became trapped as she was, burned and scared, aging slowly, but feeling with every second of her life.

"I'm sorry for what I did," he said once again. "If my death would heal you or change what happened, I would give it to you, even right here and now."

She shook her head. "Your death can purchase nothing, my love, for you are already dead. Only your life can change the world."

The candle flickered, as if sprits had now gathered around them, also waiting for the answers to come.

"I know what brought you here," she added. "Drake has returned to haunt you. You have discovered the truth about him—where he came from, who he is."

"I have," Christian said. "We fought in Cologne. I found records in the cathedral there. They speak of the curse, but the caretaker mentioned something else, something more important than the beginning. He said the punishment would end 'when shadows are seen beneath the Midnight Sun.' I heard you speak these same words in a dream, before Drake betrayed us and turned you over to Lagos and the inquisitors."

"Yes," she said. "Drake discovered them by searching your mind."

Christian knew this to be true. It only made it worse. "The caretaker spoke of an angel that brings forgiveness to the Nosferatu. Is that what you saw?"

"Not at first," she said. "But over time, the image became clearer to me."

"Drake intends to destroy this angel."

"Yes," she said. "He has been waiting an eternity to do so."

"Can he? Does he have the power?"

"It's difficult to say," she insisted. "It may depend on the manner of their meeting."

"I don't understand," he said. "You have the gift. Can't you tell me what will happen?"

She tried to smile, but the scars prevented it. She tried to explain. "The unseeing, like you, visualize the future as one thing, the way a blind man grasps a long, straight wall as the only path he knows—a line to be followed. But there are many futures, many paths. Each choice begets other choices, and the farther out one goes, the hazier things become."

She looked right at him, her pupils dilated in the dark, her eyes like black orbs in white porcelain. "There is no destiny for you or for any other," she explained. "There is no future that must be. Only the turning points. Only the possibilities. Each step is like a crossroads of its own. In one future, I was not supposed to be as I am, but once you made your choice, it could be no other way. In another, Drake was not supposed to have the power that he does. He was a miserable creature, a rat in the sewer, until he sought repentance. But when the Church refused to grant it, that was a sin of their own. Drake's powers stem from that moment, not from the original curse. He is the thorn in their side, which they can always feel but never see."

"But the prophecy tells of forgiveness."

"Yes," she said. "Another opportunity approaches. Another set of crossroads. What looms ahead is the end of the war between your kind and the Church, but the possibilities of victory and defeat come hand in hand. Only one will occur, and once it does, it will seem as if it were destined from the beginning."

His mind whirled, trying to follow her. He understood the concept, but he needed some way to use it for guidance.

"Drake betrayed us," he said, "because you had the vision of the Midnight Sun. He's afraid of it. I need to know why. Is it something that will kill him? The sun weakens us. Daylight in the night would give us no place to hide. Is that what you saw?"

She shook her head. "If it were so simple, what good would killing me have done? If you kill the rooster, the sun still rises."

"Then what, Elsa? Please."

She sighed and looked down before speaking. "If Drake took my life, you might have sensed it or felt it from him, but if the Inquisition murdered me, you'd walk in his dark crusade for all eternity. He is powerful, he is dangerous, but always remember, his greatest art is that of a deceiver, even of himself."

Christian remembered the fury in his heart as he attacked the executioners who'd cast the oil on her. If he could have, he'd have killed those men a thousand times over.

"I fear there isn't much time," he said.

"Far less than you know."

"So why not speak to me straight?" he asked, growing angry with her for the first time in his life.

"Because there is a price to be paid for the gift I hold."

"I'll pay it," he said. "Anything. Just tell me."

"It will fall on others," she said.

He paused. He didn't want to cause any more pain. He'd done enough of that. But he had to act. "I can't allow Drake to continue. Not when the stakes are this high."

She nodded, seeming pleased. "Then the fear does not control you completely," she said. "Give me your hand."

She reached out for him. As Christian grabbed her scared hand, a soft glow appeared around her. The mass of scars, the withered skin, and the straggly gray hair vanished, leaving only the young and beautiful woman he remembered. Her skin was perfect, her hair jet-black, her eyes beautiful and radiant. For a moment, he felt alive again. For a moment, he felt forgiven.

"Even the most powerful Nosferatu cannot know what will happen to their offspring," she began. "For Drake, a great surprise came when one of his chosen swore off all violence, even against the Church, even to defend himself. He was blessed for his virtue with the prophecy. He told Drake of it. And Drake murdered him."

"But why?"

"Drake was shunned," she reminded him. "And the shunned must protect themselves somehow. One way is to despise what is withheld from them, to reject that which rejects them. As you know, Drake no longer wants forgiveness. He begged for it once, and they threw it in his face. Now he wants revenge. That's why he builds his army."

Christian understood. "But if the Nosferatu are forgiven and released from the curse…"

"Drake loses his soldiers," she said. "And he is alone once again."

Christian could understand Drake's actions now. "But what of the Church? Why would the Church want to keep such a thing secret?"

"The prophecy came from one of your kind," she said. "They don't trust it. They fear it may be a trick to weaken their resolve, or worse yet, a trap of some kind. They will not rise to the angel's aid, though they might pretend to."

A breeze swept in and threatened to douse the candle. It flickered sideways, as if it would go out, much like the fragile hope Christian sensed on the horizon.

"I will stop Drake," he said. "But I need you to tell me how."

She gazed at him in silence, as if measuring him one last time. The moment seemed to draw itself out, suspended in time. Finally, she spoke.

"You are potent," she said, "the greatest of all the Nosferatu besides Drake himself, but you cannot destroy him with any power that he gave to you. If you fight fire with fire, you are the one who will get burned. You must find another way."

Christian felt lost in her words. He was more confused now than he had been before arriving.

"How?" he asked. "You must tell me."

Elsa shifted her gaze. Outside the door, the mist had grown thick.

"It's time for you to leave."

She let go of his hand, and her twisted form returned. His heart grieved once again.

She stood and moved to the porch. Christian had no choice but to follow her. She looked out over the still waters as if searching for something. When she finally spoke, she wasn't looking at him.

"It will begin with the Midnight Sun," she said. "And then you and the others shall hear a calling. The calling will test you and tempt you and try to break your will as nothing before ever has. But you must resist it until the sky goes dark again. If you chase the moment you seek, it will hide. But if you wait, if you lie quiet and still, it will come to you."

As she spoke this final riddle, Christian glanced toward the bayou in the direction of her gaze. A hooded figure stood in the shallow waters, a gray ghost up against the trees and darkness. No features could be seen, just a shape in a dark cloak. Like death itself.

Christian sensed Drake's presence, and his hand went to his sword. The figure vanished.

"What you see is a vision, nothing more," she said. "A fragment of the future passed to you through your bond with me."

"I feel danger for you."

"My end approaches," she said. "By your coming here, you have made it inevitable."

"No," he said, growing angry, sensing that Drake would somehow seek her out and torture her further. "I won't allow it."

"You cannot stop it," she said bluntly. "Not unless you wish to give up the future for all mankind."

He stared at her, thinking he would do that if necessary. He would trade everything, all of the world, to keep her safe, to undo what he'd done, but she would just hate him for it all the more.

"Now, leave me," she begged. "Leave me at long last to die in peace."

He reached for her hand, but she backed away into the shadows of the doorway and the candle went out.

For a moment, Christian did not move; he stood there as still as stone. He could hear no sound nor see any movement inside the house, as if she were already gone. Finally, he turned and made his way to the canoe. He climbed in, untied it, and pushed off.

As he guided the canoe across the water, he turned back once again, but the shack remained dark and Elsa was nowhere to be seen.

Chapter 24

Pacific Hospital, Los Angeles, California

LEROY ATHERTON woke up in a hospital bed. He was strapped down by tight nylon restraints. He could barely move his arms or legs. He felt disoriented and confused, and his throat was so dry it felt like it was closing up.

To Leroy's surprise, he wasn't alone. A white man he'd never seen before sat in a chair in the corner, watching over him.

The man wore a tweed sport coat and a V-neck sweater. A stethoscope lay draped over his shoulders.

"Welcome back to the living, Mr. Atherton. How do you feel?"

"Like I've been wandering in the desert."

"Are you angry?"

Leroy thought about that. "No," he said. Truth be told, he wasn't anything, not angry or sad or happy. He was just there. Blank and thirsty.

"Are you suicidal?"

"No."

"Good," the man said. "Then we can take these restraints off you."

He came over and began to undo the straps, massaging Leroy's wrists where the bands had left a mark. Next, he handed Leroy a cup of water. "For your thirst."

Leroy took the cup and drank from it. "Who are you?" he asked suspiciously.

"My name is Benjamin," the man said. "I've administered a drug that counteracted the sedative. I've done so because they're going to release you today."

"I guess you're a doctor, then," Leroy said.

"I'm a neurosurgeon."

That didn't sound good. "Is there something wrong with my brain?"

"Possibly," the doctor said. "I wouldn't know. I haven't examined you. Dr. Guidrey is your physician."

Leroy scrunched up his face. "I don't understand. What are you doing here, then?"

"What do you remember about the other night?" Benjamin asked.

Leroy had lived in Compton long enough not to trust anyone asking questions. "Are you a cop?"

"No, Mr. Atherton. I told you, I'm a doctor."

"But not my doctor," Leroy said suspiciously. "In fact, I ain't never seen you before, not even walking around."

Dr. Benjamin exhaled. "We're getting off on the wrong foot here," he said. "I'm not a policeman. I'm not a detective. I'm not concerned with anything you may or may not have done before you came through our doors. I only want to know what you remember about the other night, when you were brought into the ER."

Leroy processed this slowly. He wondered if the strangeness of this conversation had something to do with the medications he was on. Then he realized the strangeness was coming from Dr. Benjamin's side. "I don't remember much about that night."

"You got up from the emergency room table," Dr. Benjamin said. "You tried to run out. You knocked over a gurney with a patient of mine on it—a twelve-year-old boy named Emmanuel Pollard."

The moment came rushing back. "I'm sorry," Leroy said. "I was just trying to get away."

Dr. Benjamin frowned. "You put your hands on him, Mr. Atherton. You touched his face. Four witnesses saw it. The security camera recorded it."

"I…I wasn't myself," Leroy stammered. "I wasn't thinkin' straight. I just…" Leroy almost choked on a wave of emotion. He exhaled to let it out. "He reminded me of my son. Someone killed him six months ago."

Dr. Benjamin looked down. "I'm sorry to hear that."

It honestly sounded like the doctor was sorry, Leroy thought. But it also sounded like that wasn't what Dr. Benjamin wanted to talk about.

"I didn't mean to hurt that boy," Leroy insisted.

"You didn't hurt him," Dr. Benjamin said. "You couldn't have. He was already dead."

"Dead?"

The neurosurgeon nodded. "Brain-dead, anyway. He had a tumor. I tried to remove it. When we opened him up, it was much worse than we thought. His heart stopped three times on the table. The third time, it took five minutes to get the rhythm back. We had to close him up with half the tumor still lodged in his brain. It didn't matter. No brain functions returned."

"Oh God," Leroy whispered, shaking his head. "I'm so sorry."

"You shouldn't be," Benjamin said.

For the third or fourth time, Leroy didn't follow. "Why?"

"Because he's in the ICU now," Dr. Benjamin explained. "He has a long road ahead of him, but somehow, he's alive."

For the first time, Leroy smiled.

"He's talking," Dr. Benjamin added. "His reflexes are normal. His neurological responses are normal. His symptoms are gone. And so is the tumor that we couldn't get at."

Leroy felt a wave of happiness like he'd never felt in his life, except maybe the day his son was born. It seemed like he was dreaming, but it was real. "That's great" was about all he could say.

"It is," Benjamin said. "Though, it's not really possible."

Leroy tipped the Styrofoam cup up high, trying to get a last drop of water that was clinging to the bottom. "What do you mean it's not possible? If it happened, doesn't that make it possible?"

Dr. Benjamin smiled. He stood and took the cup from Leroy, refilling it and handing it back. As Leroy drank down the cool water, the neurosurgeon explained his position.

"I've been a doctor for thirty years, Mr. Atherton. I've seen a lot of hopeless, inoperable cases. I've seen people try anything and everything, from faith healing and herbal concoctions, to experimental drugs, and self-administered electroshock therapy. None if it works. They all want to believe it will, but it doesn't. When a patient is in his shape, there's nothing left to do. Tumors do not just disappear overnight. And brain-dead patients do not wake up and start talking."

Leroy blinked. "But he did, right? And you're sure he's okay, right?"

Benjamin nodded. "We've double- and triple-checked his brain with CT scans. The tumor is gone."

"So why are you looking at me like that?"

The doctor said nothing. He slipped his hands in his pockets and just stared. Finally, Leroy got it. Or at least he thought he did.

"You think I did something to him?"

Dr. Benjamin hesitated. "No," he said finally. "But part of me wants to believe you did. Part of me would like to think something of a miracle happened here last night."

Leroy didn't know what to say. He smiled. Dr. Benjamin smiled back, yellow teeth under a white mustache.

"Good luck, Mr. Atherton," Dr. Benjamin said, nodding a polite good-bye. "I'll tell the nurse you're ready to be discharged."

Leroy watched as the doctor made his way to the door. A question formed in his mind. "Where do I go?"

Dr. Benjamin turned.

"After I'm released?" Leroy added.

162

Now, it was the doctor who seemed confused by the simple question. He offered a simple answer. "Anywhere you want to, Mr. Atherton. Most people go home."

Leroy looked away. *Where does one go when they have no home?*

Chapter 25

Boston, Massachusetts

DRAKE STARED at the front door of the FBI building in downtown Boston from the backseat of a limo with dark tinted windows. A driver and one of Drake's drones sat up front.

The FBI's little intrusion was not his main concern. They could be a problem, but they could be dealt with. Vivian's deception was another story. It left him angry to a point of fury.

How could she have been so foolish? How, after all these years, had she gone wrong?

Drake had made many mistakes in his time, but Vivian was rapidly becoming one of his biggest. He would have killed her for it, but it would have raised too many flags. Besides, he needed her for the next step in the plan.

The doors to the building opened. One of Drake's lawyers led Vivian out of the building and down the steps. He brought her to the limo.

"Let her in," Drake said.

The driver got out of the limo, rounded the car, and opened the door for Vivian. The lawyer gave Drake a quick nod.

"She told them nothing," he said.

"Good."

The attorney moved off, but Vivian hesitated at the door, gripped with fear.

Drake sensed that she wanted to run, but he took control of her mind and forced her to climb into the vehicle. A moment later, they were heading toward I-95.

"Where?" Drake demanded.

"Where what?"

Drake turned to her. "Your brood of vipers—where do I find them?"

To Drake's utter surprise, she tried to close her mind to him. It only stirred the fires of his contempt. He began to force the information from her. Her face contorted as she tried to fight him.

"No!" she said.

Drake slapped her to the floor, picked her up, and then backhanded her across the face. His ring left a cut and an imprint on her cheek, a mark that would now scar her for life.

Vivian kept her mind shut, and Drake forced her against the door. He held her face in his hands and implored her to look at him.

"I gave you everything. I made you a queen, and this is how you repay me?"

"I can't...live...like this," she managed.

"You were forbidden to make others. You were forbidden to taste blood. You swore an oath."

Drake focused all his thoughts on her. "Where is your clan? Tell me!"

Her walls came down. And Drake saw it all: years of deception, a growing army of her own—even love, if it were possible. Of all things he would not allow, that feeling he despised the most.

His rage flared. He grabbed a chain that lay at his side and, with a short snap, lashed her with it. She turned to protect her face as Drake swung the chain again and it bit into her skin. Over and over again, he struck her, like he was lashing a slave or a mutineer on a ship.

Drake was an artist at bringing one to the doorstep of death and then backing off. After a dozen lashes, he stopped. He knew where the line was.

He looked toward the driver's compartment.

"Take us to Carlisle," he ordered.

The driver nodded.

Vivian was smart. She'd hidden the clan a long way out, in a rich community upstate, in a mansion with land and woods surrounding it. No one in that community would have a clue what lived down the road. They did their killing there, but their hunting and dumping in the city.

Thirty minutes into the drive, they pulled onto a newly blacktopped road cutting through a heavily wooded forest. The trees towered high. Even during the daytime, the sunlight rarely made an appearance here. Drake was impressed.

Vivian was broken, slumped on the floor, her clothes soaked with the strange rust-like blood of the Nosferatu. Drake pulled the entry code from her mind with ease. The limo passed through the steel gate, between twelve-foot walls of stone, and onto the driveway. The mansion at the far end loomed like a castle. It looked like it was closed up, as if the owners were away until summer.

Vivian's deception had been well done. Even Drake had never sensed it. The many times he'd searched her mind, she hadn't tried to block him or fight it, but somehow, she'd kept this place and her creations to herself. Because she'd given no resistance, he'd never even suspected.

It seemed odd how she could be so carful and carless at the same time. But Drake knew the answer. At first, the occasional victim was enough, but slowly, the addiction grew. Despite her caution, despite her intelligence, she became a slave to the fix, and soon, no amount of reason could keep her from the pursuit of her obsession.

Drake wrapped the chain around her neck and handed her off to his driver. "Bring her in. I want her to watch."

The drone nodded and pulled her out of the car.

As they entered the house, Drake pulled his sword. "Call them," he demanded.

Vivian—almost in a coma—did as ordered. But even then, Drake sensed she'd passed along a warning.

"Do you really think that will make a difference?"

He read her mind. Whatever respect she had once held toward him had been replaced by malice and hatred. It didn't matter. He would do what he had to do and then keep her under lock and key until she was needed again.

If her brood had run, it would have made things difficult, but the attachment they felt to their leader kept them close, foolishly so. Drake stepped forward into the vast living room. A door flew open.

A wiry-looking creature about Drake's height raced out and swung a blade at him. Drake parried, deflecting it. Another formerly human beast followed, coming up from the basement. He appeared much stronger. Perhaps he was Vivian's lover. Perhaps they had all been her lovers when life ran through their veins.

The two creatures charged Drake together. Drake kicked the smaller one away and spun. With one great swing of his sword, he cut the larger one in half. The body parts flew toward the wall, bursting into flames in the corner and setting the drapes on fire.

The next wave of attackers followed quickly as a third and fourth denizen of the lair charged and surrounded him. To a human, the fight would have seemed like a blur, but to Drake, these animals moved in slow motion. Child's play.

He clashed swords with the first, removing its arm, which hit the ground still grasping the weapon. Without hesitation, he ran his sword through the creature's heart.

Before Drake could pull his sword free, another charged him.

Drake stepped back and disarmed the creature, using a Far Eastern style of martial arts known as Shaolin, taught to him by the original master.

With the attacking creature's own sword in his hand, Drake impaled the thing multiple times. It was overkill, but it brought a sick feeling of satisfaction. The last strike went through the creature and into a wooden beam behind it. The creature burst into flames, pegged to the wall by the point of its own sword.

Drake scanned the room. The final member of Vivian's brood remained. It was weak and filled with fear, cowering in the corner of the room. He could feel anger building inside Vivian. She had empathy for this one. She thought of this one as the child of the clan.

"Spare his life," she said. "Make him your slave, but don't destroy him."

Drake turned to her. He'd seen this devotion in clans before. A desperate attempt to feel normal. It never lasted. He was surprised Vivian had given in to its temptation. Then again, she was young. Less than forty years in her shell. She would have seen her own folly had she been on earth as long as him.

By now, the mansion was ablaze, the fires raging all around them. They would have to leave soon.

"I will not kill it," he said.

She looked relieved.

"The drone will."

"No!" Vivian shouted.

Drake's driver let go of Vivian's chain and marched toward the cornered animal. Vivian let out an inhuman scream.

The drone dispatched the childlike creature to the next world, but as it did so, an enormous sword emerged from the smoke and flames. It pierced the drone's chest and lifted him upward. He too burst into flames as a monster of a being emerged from the smoke.

It stepped through the flames. At six foot seven and three hundred and forty pounds, it was a beast made of pure muscle, a goliath. In its human state, this huge menace would have been considered a freak show. Changed into a Nosferatu, it became a very dangerous creature.

The animal let out a battle cry, flinging the burning shape of the driver aside like a rag doll.

In its presence, Vivian found the courage to speak. "I'll see you in hell, Drakos."

With that, Drake heard her order the animal to kill him.

The giant advanced, but Drake did not move or raise his sword; he lowered it down until the tip hit the floor. The creature's advance began to slow. Finally, it stopped.

By now, flames had spread throughout the room, paint was boiling off the walls in places, and the smoke was so thick it was nearly impossible to see.

Drake concentrated on the giant. The huge sword dropped from its hand. Slowly, it began to kneel in front of its new master.

Vivian was in shock. "I command you!" she shouted. "I made you to kill him!"

The hulking figure strained as if trying to move, but neither its will nor Vivian's, or even both of them combined, were enough to break Drake's hold on her champion.

And then, with one swift cut, Drake took off its head.

As the latest eruption of flames billowed, Vivian collapsed to the floor. Drake turned and picked her up. He'd dealt with the problem, and no evidence would remain. More important, perhaps, Vivian would carry the scars of this lesson. She would never challenge him again.

With that in mind and his belief that the time of the angel was near, Drake carried her through the building. He stepped out the front doors, with the fire silhouetting his shape as if he had just emerged from the gates of hell itself.

Chapter 26

CHRISTIAN PADDLED back through the swamp in the deep hours of the night. Nocturnal birds seemed to flee their perches as he passed, cawing in the dark, warning others to stay away. Here and there, he saw glowing eyes reflecting the moonlight. Alligators watching him pass.

Some watched as if in a trance; others waited and then thrashed through the water to flee. One trailed along behind him, as if in formation. But even this one kept its distance.

The animals of this world were skittish in the presence of the Fallen. They recognized the Nosferatu as something different, something more—or perhaps less—than the living.

Christian turned to look at his escort. The alligator reduced its pace, drifting back, and then, with a powerful swipe of its tail, it turned and shot off into the dark water, heading back into the heart of the great swamp. He wondered if it was something Elsa had sent along to watch over his exit from the swamp.

Turning his eyes forward, Christian saw a lantern on the old Cajun's dock. Drawn to the yellow light, moths and other insects flickered. The old Cajun stood ten feet away, out of the swirling madness.

Christian bumped the dock and climbed out of the canoe. As he stepped onto the planks, the insects vanished into the night.

"You didn't have to wait up," Christian said.

"Couldn't sleep," the old man said. "Saw you in da dream world. Had to see you back here myself."

The Cajun looked past him out into the swamp and then toward the lantern where the swarming bugs had been a minute before. Christian could see that the old man had an idea something was wrong.

"You not from dis place, are you?" he said.

Christian thought of where this might go. "I was once."

The Cajun stepped back. "Please don't be hurtin' me, dark man. I done helped you. I let you go see da witch. I won't tell anyone. I won't talk about tonight."

"You have nothing to fear from me," Christian said. "Or from her. She's not a witch. She's just an old woman with a gift."

"What kind of gift?" he asked.

Christian thought long and hard. Elsa had many gifts, but one above all else. "Kindness," he said. "And love."

The old Cajun picked up the lantern, accidentally putting it out. In the pitch-dark of the moonless night, it became impossible to see. But then light began to spread across the dock, light from above. Soon there was a glow across the water, lighting up the whole swamp and the broad trunks of the trees, filling the canopy with light.

The Cajun dropped his cigar from his mouth in astonishment.

It came on without a sound. It looked like moonlight, only stronger. Pale and ghostly white, it was brighter than the brightest full moon Christian had ever seen, but the moon had been down for hours.

The old man looked around and then back down at the lantern, as if it were somehow the cause. He fiddled with the controls as Christian turned his eyes upward. It was difficult to see through the veil of the trees, but the light was definitely filtering through from the heavens.

Christian knew what he was seeing. The Midnight Sun had arrived.

"Dis mean something to you?" the old man asked.

Christian nodded. "It means the beginning of the end."

—⚏—

Two thousand miles away, Drake stood in the fortress-like space on the top floor of his building. The beaten and broken Vivian Dasher lay at his feet. In one hand, he held her chains. In the other, he held a long Roman dagger. It had meaning to him—meaning he couldn't avoid. He stared at it and then placed it into a wooden box and closed the lid.

Strangely, light began to fill the room, filtering in through the floor-to-ceiling windows. The light was pure like that from a helicopter spotlight, but Drake heard no sounds beyond the endless swish of his pendulum and Vivian's labored breathing. He stepped toward the windows.

High above, he saw a wispy pattern glowing brightly and spreading across the night sky in slow motion. It looked something like the starburst of a monstrous fireworks explosion. But there was no sound, and the light did not fade or fall.

"The Midnight Sun," he whispered.

From his vantage point, nothing was left to the imagination. In the night sky, a star was dying, but as it went through its death throes, it signaled the beginning of new life. The reckoning had arrived. Drake's wait was finally over.

The angel would soon appear. Drake would destroy it and then launch his war against the Church, with nothing to stop him.

—⚏—

Simon Lathatch sat at a desk in an old church in New Orleans. Dawn was still an hour away as he scratched notes into a small leather journal. The ink flowed dark and smooth into the old beaten book. It was the journal of the Ignis Purgata, kept by those who held his position. A book of triumphs and failures, of thoughts and conversations, a book of arguments made across time. Simon had kept and added to it since the day he'd assumed the leadership. When he retired, it would pass to his successor. Four others just like it were filled and bound with rubber bands on the shelf.

As he finished inscribing his latest thought, Simon's cell phone rang, jolting him.

He picked up the phone. It was Bishop Messini.

"Yes, Bishop," he said.

Simon expected bad news at such an hour. Instead, Messini spoke in excited tones.

"Go to your window, my friend. Look to the southern sky, if you can."

Simon had no window, but he had a set of stairs that led to the roof. He made his way up.

Upon reaching the roof, his eyes grew wide. The sky was ablaze with pure-white light.

"It's beautiful," he whispered.

"Your faith has been rewarded," Messini said. "The Midnight Sun proves you are on the right path. Now you must find a way to save us, to save us from ourselves, my friend."

CHAPTER 27

Carlisle, Massachusetts

NORTH OF Boston, the winter winds were long gone. Spring was beginning to show itself as Kate and Billy Ray turned up Rockland Road toward a house owned by Vivian Dasher. Her lawyer may have kept her from talking—and sprung her faster than anyone had expected—but he couldn't stop them from poking around in her business.

"You think we're gonna find anything here?" Billy Ray asked.

"It took all night to prove that Vivian owned this place," Kate said. "That tells me it's the kind of place you don't expect to get raided. I give us a fifty-fifty chance. Besides, there's nothing wrong with rattling her cage a little more."

As Kate spoke, something caught her attention, floating above the trees. "What's that?"

"Smoke," Billy Ray said.

A sick feeling formed in Kate's stomach. "Don't tell me."

They turned off Rockland onto a more residential street. A half mile down, fire trucks and emergency vehicles blocked the road.

"You've got to be kidding me," Kate said.

An officer stopped them, and Billy Ray rolled down his window.

"The road is closed due to a fire. You'll have to turn around."

Kate got out of the car.

"Excuse me, miss," the cop said.

"I'm with the FBI," Kate said. "We're here to serve a search warrant."

With that, she turned and began to walk. She moved up the country road while Billy Ray smoothed things over with the officer.

Pulling her badge from her pocket and waving it, the next line of cops let her by without a word. She made it past the edge of a stone wall and onto the mansion's grounds. The huge structure was a smoldering wreck. Black smoke continued to drift skyward from gaping holes in what had once been an expensive gabled roof. Muddy water flooded the grounds.

Firefighters were slowly removing their equipment from the shell that was once Vivian's house.

Kate stopped one of them. "What happened?"

"Three-alarm blaze," he said. "It was wicked bad, kept burning all night."

"Any survivors?"

The firefighter shook his head and moved off.

Kate advanced across the waterlogged ground. As she reached the front porch, the moment became surreal. Her stomach turned and twisted into knots. Any evidence that might have been found was surely gone now.

She spotted Vivian's lawyer talking with the fire commissioner. She marched over and gave him a blind-sided shove to the back.

He stumbled forward. "What the hell?"

"You think I don't know what happened here?" Kate shouted. "You think we can't get you for tampering in an investigation!"

Billy Ray grabbed Kate from behind, holding her back from doing any more damage.

Vivian's lawyer was named Whitestone. He was a high-society type, extremely expensive and well connected. He got to his feet, flicked some of the mud off his hand, and glared at her.

"I don't know what the hell you're talking about," he said. "I'm shocked by what I'm seeing in front of me. My only concern is for my client, wondering if she's has burned to death in there."

Kate pulled loose from Billy Ray. "You snake!" she yelled. "You told her. You let her know we were coming. She's not in there, and you know it!"

Whitestone picked up his briefcase and looked at Billy Ray, then back at Kate. "How could I have warned her? I just found out about this warrant two hours ago. The fire began late last night.

"What?"

"Last night," the fire commissioner said. "The first call came in around midnight."

"You really should learn to control yourself," Whitestone said. "Next time, you might actually hurt someone, and then your career will be over."

Whitestone began to walk off.

"Where is she?" Kate yelled after him.

"I don't know, Agent Pfeiffer," Whitestone replied.

Kate could not believe what she was seeing. She turned to the fire commissioner. "Did you find anything?"

"No bodies in the house, but a few super-hot spots that seem odd."

"Hot spots?" Kate said. "So it was arson."

"I didn't say that," the commissioner replied. "The hot spots are spread out in an odd pattern in what would have been the main living room. But there is no sign of an accelerant."

"That doesn't sound possible," Kate said.

"I agree," the commissioner said. "Something's not right about this scene. I really need some more time to study it before I can tell you anything."

"I want to see them," Kate demanded.

"I'll show you."

The commissioner headed toward the house. Kate started to follow but stopped when Billy Ray grabbed her.

"Hey, what is the matter with you? Have you lost your mind?"

"He's lying, Billy. You know it as well as I do."

"He couldn't have known we were going for a warrant."

"He guessed," she said. "And you know what? He guessed right. And now all we're going to find here is some weak evidence that's meaningless."

177

Kate shook loose from Billy Ray and followed the commissioner into the burned-out shell of the home.

"The fire burned white-hot here," he said, pointing. "If you look here through the floorboards, you can see that the piping is melted. That's not copper. It's cast iron—and it melted."

"I'm not a fire expert," Billy Ray said. "What does that mean?"

"It means that the fire was burning at over twenty-four hundred degrees Fahrenheit in this spot."

"So there was something here, some type of material," Kate said.

"Should have been," the commissioner said. "But, so far, we haven't found any residue."

"What else?" Kate asked. "Is this the only anomaly?"

"No," the commissioner said. "There are six spots like this scattered about this room. We call them hyper-burns. No pattern, no rhyme or reason for placement. Look for yourself—here and over there."

"Yeah, I see," Billy Ray said. "Can you give us a second?"

As the commissioner nodded and walked out, Kate began walking around the room. There were strange shapes to these hyper-burns. One, up against the stone hearth, almost looked like the outline of a person.

She bent down and picked up some burned material and then tossed it back on the ground.

"What do you think?" Billy Ray asked.

Kate shook her head in disgust. "I think we're a day late and a dollar short, and now more people are going to die. I think, wherever Vivian Dasher is right now, she's laughing her ass off. She played us and she knows it, and I'm pretty sure we'll never see that bitch again."

Billy Ray agreed.

Kate looked around, feeling defeated. "Come on," she said. "Let's go report the latest disaster."

Chapter 28

New Orleans, Louisiana

NIGHT BENEATH the Midnight Sun was different. The darkness was chased from the streets and forced beneath the overhangs and into the narrow back alleys. Out in the open, things seemed brighter and safer. But the danger wasn't gone. It was only hiding, biding its time in the deep, dark places of this world.

As he strolled the back streets of the French Quarter, Drake Castillion knew this to be true, for he was part of the darkness itself. He traveled slowly for now, wandering past flickering gaslights and wrought iron balconies covered in hanging plants, easing his way toward an address he had not called on in forty years.

Drake felt at home in New Orleans, but to live here, as so many of his kind had tried to do, was a fool's choice. The Church always watched this city, afraid of its lingering connection with the dark arts. At least, for the moment, Drake wasn't worried about the Church. He was looking for someone who owed him a favor.

He turned down a side alley and made his way to a set of stairs that led up to a door. A shingle rested on the far wall. It was old and weathered by time, like the man Drake had come to see. The sign read, JACKSON'S SOLES.

Stepping back into the shadows, Drake waited. A short while later, the door swung open. An older black man in his mid-sixties came out of the shop. He carried a cane and was accompanied by a teenage kid.

"Oh, sure, Miles was great," the older man said, "and so was Clifford Brown, but none of them could play like Dizzy."

"You saw them in person?" the teenager asked.

"All the time."

"That's pretty cool."

They reached the bottom of the stairs and began walking away from where Drake stood. A few paces later, the older man stopped dead in his tracks. He put a hand on the teenager's arm and began to look around, eventually facing back down the alleyway.

"What is it?" the teenager said.

The older man didn't reply. He stepped into the darkness and took a deep breath, as if tasting the air. His face soured. "You best run on home now," he said to his helper.

"But I always walk you home. Ma says you can't find your—"

"I said go home, Charles." The voice was surprisingly powerful for such a frail-looking man. In a softer voice, he added, "Don't worry, I'll be along shortly."

The teenager looked startled, but he did what he was told. He moved away, heading for the end of the alley, glancing back a time or two before disappearing around the corner.

Drake spoke from the shadows. "Terrance Jackson," he said. "It's good to see you again. But tell me, how is it you know I'm here? The sighted walk right past me."

"I can feel your presence," Terrance replied. "The air is always a little bit colder when one of your kind is around. And I can hear the thoughts in your unquiet minds, they reach me like whispers on the wind."

Drake was impressed. "Ah yes," he said. "The presence of a vampire and the senses of a blind man do not mix."

Terrance shifted his weight, turning and honing in on Drake's voice, facing him dead on. Another trick the sighted could not master. "We had an agreement," Terrance said curtly. "You were never to come here again."

"Forty years ago, you called me," Drake said. "You reached into the dark and asked for my help, because you wanted something. I gave it to you. You always knew I would demand repayment someday."

"You took Vivian with you," Terrance said. "That was your payment."

"That was an installment," Drake replied.

Terrance stood a few yards from Drake, clenching his jaw, grinding his teeth. "I'm old and worn-out now, Drake. Not much help I can give you these days, unless you're wanting some shoes repaired."

Drake smiled. "Time may have eroded your physical strength, but not your spiritual abilities. You're like a musician in his prime—like your idol Mr. Gillespie, hitting notes others could only dream of. And make no mistake, you're the only one who can do what I ask, so I will force you to if I must."

Terrance was silent.

"Don't look so glum," Drake said. "I offer a gift as well. Do as I say, and Vivian will be returned to you."

The old cobbler's face softened a fraction. "Is she here?"

Drake knew what Terrance pined for; he would give out the taste in small increments. "Just walk with me, old friend."

He took Terrance by the arm, supporting him much like Charles had been doing, and the two begin to walk the French Quarter.

"I need you to reenact the ritual of the calling," Drake explained. "Only, this time, you will perform it indefinitely."

"Indefinitely?" Terrance shook his head. "I don't think you know what you're asking for."

"I assure you I do," Drake said. "An entity of great power has recently crossed over from the other side. You may have even felt the tremors. It walks among us somewhere. I need you to bring it here. I need you to lure it to the woods, as you once lured me. The calling is the only way."

Terrance stopped in his tracks. "What you ask is not something to be taken lightly. The taste of life does not discriminate, especially if you plan to keep it going for days on end. You'll bring everything that's trapped in the void, everything that hasn't passed over."

"That's not my concern."

"But it's mine," Terrance said. "The most powerful of those caught between worlds will come first; they'll feel the scent of the ritual before the rest of them do. You expect me to bring that down upon this city? Upon my family? Out there in the woods? Alone?"

"Most of the Fallen will not be able to get here so quickly," Drake assured him. "The ones that do will feel my presence. Trust me, they won't come near you as long as I'm out there."

"They'll drift into the city instead," Terrance said. "New Orleans will become a slaughterhouse."

Drake's anger flared. He grabbed Terrance by the back of the neck like one might grab a cat. "You know, if you weren't blind, we wouldn't have to play these little games," he said. "You'll do what I ask, and you'll do it for as long it takes. You'll do it because, if you don't, I'll be forced to pay a visit to some of your grandchildren. You'll do it because, as high priest of the Santeria, you've always wanted to test your power, and I can think of no greater test than this. But most of all, you'll do it because, once the abomination appears, I'll allow it to touch your beloved Vivian. It will turn her back into what she once was—the wife of your youth, human and frail."

Drake released Terrance, and a look of anticipation crept over the blind man's face. Drake had taken Vivian from him forty years ago, after Terrance had used the calling to lure him to the swamps and begged him to save her from a deadly fever that the doctors couldn't cure.

"It won't be a simple matter," Terrance said.

"Do whatever you need to," Drake said. "If you need a human to sacrifice, I'll bring you someone."

"That isn't our way," Terrance said. "We don't steal lives or destroy them. That's what your kind does."

"Very well," Drake said, putting Terrance's hand on the post of a street-light. "Gather what you need. I'll meet you out there tomorrow night."

Terrance felt around him. He couldn't be sure where he was. "You're leaving me here?"

"Despite your orders, Charles is not far away," Drake said, having spotted the young man up ahead of them, glancing out from behind some trees. "Nor will I be."

Chapter 29

LEROY ATHERTON stared at the notice on the door of his dingy apartment. He tried to focus on the words, but for some reason, he couldn't make out the letters, as if they were scrambled. It didn't matter; he knew what it was. He'd already been given three others like it.

Eviction notices. He was pretty sure this would be the last one.

He tried his key, noticed it didn't work, and then realized there was a shiny new lock where the old tarnished one used to be. Furious, he stepped up and busted in the door.

It was dark inside. He stumbled around. Some of his stuff was gone, but some of it was still there. He flicked on a light switch, but nothing happened.

"Damn it," he mumbled.

He had a headache. In fact, his temples hurt like someone was pressing on them with their thumbs. He made his way down the hall to the bathroom.

The lights were on in there. Not bright, but dimly lit and bluish-green in tint. He twisted the old four-pronged faucet. At first, nothing happened. He turned it one way and then the other and then the other. Nothing, not even a sound, emanated from the faucet, and then, finally, cold water started running.

He splashed it on his face, but he didn't really feel it. He cupped his hands under the water and scooped a couple of mouthfuls, but he couldn't really taste it. He found he was still thirsty.

Leroy looked up into the mirror and dried his face off with an old brown towel that was in his hand. He opened the medicine cabinet. Lots of bottles. He looked through them, turning them and sliding them and looking for a familiar label. Nothing—no Tylenol, no aspirin, no Advil.

There had to be something for pain, he told himself. He continued shuffling through the cabinet until he noticed something strange. The vertical fluorescent lights on either side of the mirror were dimming and then growing brighter and then dimming again.

It almost looked like they were breathing.

Leroy closed the mirror and then cautiously tapped one of the bulbs with his finger. The light stabilized, and Leroy looked up. Reflected in the mirror, he saw a figure standing behind him.

He swung around. "Tre?"

Leroy could hardly believe what he was seeing. He stared at his son— with no bullet holes, no blood-soaked clothes. He wanted to grab him. Somehow, he knew he couldn't.

"What are you still doing here, Dad?"

"What am I doing here?" Leroy said. "This is our home."

"Is it?"

Leroy was surprised. His son spoke very calmly.

"Why are you here, Tre?"

"To bring you a message."

"What kind of message?"

"You don't belong here anymore," his son told him.

"That's just a damn eviction notice," Leroy replied. "They have to take me to court first."

Tre didn't answer; he just stared at his father. He seemed to be throbbing with energy, just like the lights. It was the same pattern, the same pace.

"Just listen for the sound," Tre said. "When you hear it…You'll know what to do."

The image of his son began to blur and fade.

"Wait!" Leroy grabbed for him, but the boy was gone. He fell to the floor and woke up to the sight of a weathered, tan-faced man shaking him by the shoulders.

Leroy glanced around. The open floor of the homeless shelter was filled with cots. A hundred people were looking in his direction. It was the middle of the night. The man who'd woken him was a Navajo Indian.

"You were shouting," he said. "Are you all right?"

Leroy focused. He was right where he'd fallen asleep, in the shelter he'd come to after finding himself locked out of his apartment. "I'm okay," he said. "I had a dream about my son."

"It was more than a dream," the Navajo man said. "I saw the light descend upon you. It was breathing."

"Breathing?"

"Yes," the man said. "The great sprit wants something from you. That's why he sent a messenger, to help guide you down the right path."

Leroy listened intensely, but a young man from two cots over broke his train of thought.

"Man, ain't no light came running around here. That crazy old Indian is a fool, and your dumb ass is keeping the whole place up."

A few snickers and laughs came from other men on various cots.

The Indian man put a finger to his lips and then whispered. "What did the dream want? What did it ask you to do?"

"I don't know," Leroy said, throwing off his blanket. "But I know one thing for sure, I'm not gonna find out around here."

He pulled on his old shoes, grabbed his coat, and then stood.

"Can I have your blanket?" the old Navajo asked.

"It's all yours," Leroy said, smiling, and then he turned and made his way to the front door.

He had no idea where he was going, or any idea why, but for the first time in as long as he could remember, he was moving with a purpose and he knew he didn't want to stop. He knew inside himself that he had somewhere else to be.

Chapter 30

THE LIGHT of the supernova continued to burn in the sky, but it had been dimming each night since its initial appearance. Its reflection shimmered off the waters of the bayou, the almost-perfect image lying flat on the surface until Terrance disturbed it by cupping the water in his hands and wetting his lips.

It had been a long, hard walk for the old man. Terrance felt around for his partner, a woman in her fifties, Bella Jackson, his second wife.

"This walk is beginning to take its toll on me; I'm not as young as I used to be."

"You're also not as good-looking," Bella said. "None of us are."

"It's a good thing I'm blind, then," Terrance said as he struggled to his feet, with Bella giving him a hand.

"It's not much farther now."

They were heading for an area deep in the bayou, far from civilization. Even the service roads got you only so close.

After the Civil War, small plantations had sprung up in the area, often divided into sections for sharecroppers to work the land. But it was hard to make a living on forty acres. The soil was poor and the crops weak. When it came time to pay, there often wasn't enough. In time, the land was sold off and given to other uses.

A couple of buildings, now dilapidated by time and the elements, sat on the property. One was an old juke hall, from a time when the nights seemed to never end and they were filled with laughter and music.

Today even those buildings sat empty. The only thing that took place here now was the ritual of voodoo rites that were best done where no one would see them.

As Terrance and Bella approached the site, a low drumbeat could be heard. And through the trees, the flickering orange light of fires could be seen burning. As they stepped into the clearing, Terrance could feel the heat, and he could see the arrangement in his mind, a group of six fires spread out in the open. They formed two perfect triangles—one for the living and one for the dead. Each of them was encircled by a line of mystic ash that cut them off from the rest of the world.

The triangle was an ancient symbol referring to the meeting of mind, body, and soul, which many religions used even today. Some even considered the Trinity of Christianity to be derived from a similar line of thought.

"How will it work?" Bella asked.

"There are two realms," Terrance explained, "the living and the dead. Most things exist in one realm or the other, but the Nosferatu and certain other entities are caught in between, trapped in the void. They need nothing, much like the dead, but they want the taste of life, a hint of what was torn from them, their living souls. But now something else has crossed over, something Drake said has the power to turn them back. He called it an 'abomination,' but considering the source, I think it's something brighter."

"Is he afraid of it?"

Terrance thought about that. There was fear in Drake, but it wasn't the angel he feared.

"No," he said. "Drake wants me to bring it here, to call it like I once called him. But to call those in the void, we need a scent, and the only scent powerful enough to draw in the undead is the burning of the dead and the releasing of their souls."

Decaying animals lay on the ground around them—road-kill, in some cases, as well as downed farm animals and dead things from the swamps. He didn't tell Bella, but his followers had dug up graves and thrown old human bodies on the fires as well. As the bonfires rose, their ashes were sent high into the night's sky. The winds would do the rest.

In the triangle of the living, a naked couple danced seductively, high on a concoction of wine and aphrodisiacs. Soon they would begin to make love. Terrance couldn't see them, but he could feel their presence. He could feel the scent of life flowing from the place.

"Drake had better be right about his presence warding off the others, or we'll have a problem," Terrance said. "Can you take me inside?"

Bella led him past the ritual to one of the old dilapidated buildings. Once inside, she guided him to a wooden table near one of the rooted-out windows. She pulled a tumbler and a bottle from her coat pocket and poured him a drink of whiskey.

She then looked to the darkest corner of the room. "I don't suppose you drink," she said.

"Leave us," Drake replied.

She tensed, but Terrance touched her arm. "It will be okay."

She put the bottle down and stepped back and out into the night.

As she left, Drake came forward.

Terrance said nothing. He just took off his hat, placed it on the table, and drained the half-filled tumbler.

"Does she know?" Drake asked.

"Know what?" Terrance said.

"That you're doing this to see Vivian again."

"I told her what you told me," Terrance said, "that Vivian could come back, that her children—our children—were in danger if I didn't do what you said. But I'm not a fool, Drake. I know Vivian wouldn't stay with an old man like me. That don't mean she deserved what you did to her."

"She chose, just like all of us."

"She was a child."

191

"Old enough to be with you."

That she was. Terrance pushed the glass forward. "Mind doing the honors?"

Drake took the bottle of whiskey and refilled the glass. "That's all incidental now," he insisted. "If you want Vivian to live again—in human form—then you'll finish your part. Things will come full circle, and our business will be finally settled."

A long pause seemed to hold both parties in check, their uneasy relationship wearing thin. Drake slid the glass in front of Terrance, who picked it up and held it in Drake's general direction as if getting ready to make a toast.

"I'm an old man now," he said to Drake. "I don't have many natural years left, so I don't care much if you keep coming around me. But my family, I won't have that. So you listen and listen good. You took an oath to leave us alone. As far as I'm concerned, you took another one when you asked me to do this. I'm doin' it. I'm doing my part. But so help me, if you don't keep your word this time, I swear to you—with all the power I possess—that, when I pass on, I'll reach back into this world from the next one and make sure you're sorry."

With that, Terrance tipped the glass back, knocked the whiskey down, and then banged the glass firmly back on the table.

Drake paused, but his thoughts moved quickly.

Perhaps he had pushed this too far. Perhaps he had played with this voodoo priest for too long. The truth was, Terrance was powerful, a master. If anyone could cross back over the void and create trouble for him, Terrance would be the one.

The thought flittered away as quick as it had come. Drake didn't fear Terrance. In a way, he was almost fond of him. He poured Terrance another shot. "You have nothing to worry about, old man. When this is over, you'll never see me again."

Chapter 31

A COLD drizzle fell over Baltimore, not enough to do anything but keep the people inside. For James Hecht, that was a problem. Disfigured from his battle with Christian, he couldn't show his face—or what was left of it—in the places he was used to frequenting. And with no one on the street, he was desperate for a fix.

He stumbled through the night, his clothes muddy, his hair matted to his head. He crossed through back alleys in the tougher parts of town, but still hadn't found anyone. Finally, he came to an underpass. A small fire burned underneath it, stoked in a dented orange-and-white highway barrel. Three homeless men stood around it trying to keep warm, wrapped in whatever they had scavenged.

Hecht limped up to them, his side still aching from the knife wound Christian had left him with. It reminded him of a similar pain he'd felt a hundred and fifty years before.

The homeless men watched him suspiciously.

He held up his hands to show them he had nothing. "Okay if I join you?"

One of them nodded. A second one moved around the side, making space for Hecht.

Hecht stepped out of the drizzle and moved toward the orange-and-white barrel. It smelled of gasoline and plastic—things they'd probably used to get it going. Two-by-fours and a broken chair back seemed to be the main source of wood.

The men held their hands over it, warming them on the heat of the fire. *The irony*, Hecht thought. It had been one of his favorite feelings.

Hecht mimicked them, though he felt nothing.

"You new here?" one of the men asked. "I ain't seen you around."

Hecht nodded. "Down from New York."

As he watched one of them chew on some food from a dumpster, Hecht's mind began to churn. What he would do to feel the heat, to taste the food. Even food from a garbage heap was more than he could imagine. These men were the bottom of the human chain. And yet, their lives were like kings compared to his.

He held his hands closer to the fire. He sensed the flames licking him, but he felt nothing, no warmth.

"What's up with your face?" another one asked, spotting the back alley stitch job on Hecht's nose.

"Nothing," Hecht said.

"That's gotta hurt."

Hecht ignored him, pressing his hands closer until the flames were singeing his palms, melting his skin. Still, he felt nothing. The anger boiled up inside him.

"Hey, man, what are you doing?" the guy with the sandwich said.

"Trying to get warm," Hecht said.

"You gonna burn."

One day, Hecht thought. *One day I will. But not today.*

The man closest to Hecht grabbed his hand and pulled it back. Hecht looked up at him and snapped. He lunged forward, knocking over the barrel in the process.

Burning wood and sparks and kindling flew through the air. The barrel clanged down loudly ten feet away. The other two men scattered as Hecht landed on the first with his hands around the man's throat.

"What do you feel?" Hecht shouted.

The man's eyes bulged. He couldn't move or speak.

Hecht glanced up to see the other homeless men running out into the rain. He was alone. Just as he wanted to be. The man in his clutches gurgled and fought, but his strength was nothing compared to Hecht's.

Hecht yanked him up and dragged him over to where the remnants of the fire burned. When life coursed through the Nosferatu, different passions came out. Some liked sex, others food, but James Hecht only wanted to feel the warmth of a flame running across his palm. It reminded him of his real life, a time before electricity, when fire was heat and light.

He could barely wait to feel it again. He reached into his pocket and pulled out a knife. He flicked it open, but before he could use it, a strange sensation came over him. He felt dizzy for a moment.

He hesitated, tried to clear his mind and looked at the man in his grasp.

The wave of dizziness floated over him again. His ears began to ring. His mind began to waver. He couldn't really place it, it was no more than the slightest tone, like the sound of silence.

He stopped what he was doing and glanced around, looking for the source of the noise in his mind. The underpass was empty. The rain still fell beyond the shelter of the concrete above, but there was nothing to see.

Hecht considered the possibility of madness. *Who had more right to madness than him?* But even as he looked around and tried to ignore it, the ringing in his ears grew stronger.

Hecht looked down at the man he was about to bleed, released him, and stood up. He stepped back, feeling a little dizzy. He stumbled around from one side of the underpass to the other, looking out into the misty rain. It seemed like something was out there, calling to him.

As Hecht stumbled around, the homeless man got to his feet and scrambled away. Hecht didn't hear him running off, he didn't see him and didn't care. He was studying the steel beams above, as if the ringing was coming from them or maybe from the road up on top. There was a power to that sound, a power he needed to find.

He stepped out into the rain and scrambled up the muddy embankment to the road above. He looked left and then right. There was nothing to be seen.

Finally, he began to understand, began to feel the depth of the world. The tone was coming from somewhere else, somewhere far away. It was calling him, offering him some form of sweetness he could hardly remember, it was offering him… life.

With great conviction, Hecht turned his eyes to the south, and without looking back, he walked off into the night and the pouring rain.

Chapter 32

ELSA'S WORDS flowed like water in Christian's mind.

The calling will test you and tempt you and try to break your will as nothing before ever has...If you chase the moment you seek, it will hide. But if you wait, if you lie quiet and still, it will come to you.

He'd been prepared himself, but he'd never expected the calling to feel as it did. After forty-eight hours of fighting against it, the sound rang in his head like a deep bass drum. It whispered to him like a lover. The invisible scent of life was like the fragrance of a feast to a starving man.

Despite his discipline, Christian felt what all Nosferatu felt—the pull of a life they no longer possessed. Denied long enough by one who possessed enough willpower, the hunger for life faded, but the energy reaching him from the forest had reawakened something within him. And even as Christian gripped the reins of resolve with an iron fist, the desire to cross the void and feel alive once again pulled at him.

With candles lit around him, he meditated in a quiet apartment on Frenchman Street. He focused on Elsa, on her words, on her love, and on the task at hand. He would not give in.

But the drums continued to sound, never stopping, and soon the walls began to close in.

There has to be a way, he thought. *There has to be a way.*

An image flashed into his head—a memory of blinding pain, of something more powerful than Drake's voice, of something more powerful than the drums and the calling that now weighed on him. Desperate like he'd never been before, Christian stood abruptly and marched out the door.

Twenty minutes later, he was walking down St. Bernard Avenue. It was 3:00 in the morning. The streets were deserted. Finally, he found what he was looking for—a small church in the old precinct. It appeared dark and deserted.

In there, the pain would die.

He stood on the sidewalk for a moment, trying to gauge the sanity of what he was about to do. And then he stepped onto the path.

As he approached the church, the drums banging inside his skull were joined by the high-pitched sound of the Cruciatus. As he reached the door, the two sensations became evenly matched.

He reached for the handle, turned it, and found the door unlocked. Surprised and suspicious, he opened it slowly. The church was dark inside except for two security lights high in the rafters and a row of candles burning at the far end by the altar. It appeared to be empty, but it was hard to tell. Christian felt his eyes failing once again.

He hesitated, but pain and blindness were preferable to a craving that he could no longer resist. He pushed through the door and stepped inside.

The white noise rose up, and Christian pressed forward until it drowned out the pounding drumbeat from the forest. He stopped and squinted, blinded as if looking at sunlight on the snow. He felt around with his hand, touched the edge of a pew, and sat down.

He put his hands on the row in front of him, steadying himself and fighting against the waves of anguish that washed over him. Strangely, there was relief in this pain, like a muscle long cramped finally easing. Christian soaked it in, his eyes closed and unmoving. He lost all track of time, until a voice broke the silence.

"You're not a member of the faith."

Christian straightened. The voice had spoken quietly from behind him. He turned his head slowly.

Two rows back and across the aisle, he could just make out a figure in black.

"No," Christian said. "I'm not one of you."

"Do you know who I am?" the figure asked.

"Are you a priest?"

"Once," the man said. "Now I lead the order. My name is Simon Lathatch."

Christian tried not to react. But it was almost impossible that this man did not know what he was.

"And what name do you go by?" Simon asked.

"I'm called Christian now," he said.

"Really? Do you mock us?"

"I didn't choose the name," Christian said. "It chose me."

The priest looked at him skeptically.

"A dying soldier asked that I take it," Christian said. "He was an honorable man. He had no children, no brothers or sisters. He wanted his name to live on."

"And you needed a new identity," Simon suggested.

"I did."

"I see."

"If it bothers you," Christian said, "call me by another name. I was known as Tiberius once."

"Who am I to decide what you should be called?" the old man said. "Perhaps the name is correct. You are here, despite the pain this place must cause you."

Christian wondered if that would prove to be a grave mistake.

"In a way, I envy you," Simon added. "I have faith, but have not seen or felt what you must know firsthand—the power of God. I would be interested to know how it feels."

Christian saw no reason to hide the truth. "Blinding noise," he said. "Blinding light, so bright it hurts the eyes."

Simon's eyebrows went up. "And yet, you've chosen twice to expose yourself to such blindness, to risk what I would have believed impossible. What is it that compels you to seek out our holy ground? What do you expect to find here? Or do you think us so weak?"

Christian blinked. It was difficult to move, as the slightest effort was painful. He tried not to show it. He wondered how many hunters might be hidden in the blinding light. They were probably all around him.

"I don't find you to be weak," Christian said. "Nor do I find your order to be particularly righteous. I've seen the pain you cause, the arrogance and hypocrisy. You talk of love, but your history is dominated by cruelty and murder."

He got the sense that Simon was staring at him, not in anger to what he'd said, but more like Christian was a curiosity, something to be studied and pondered. Instead of signaling the attack that Christian assumed was coming at any moment, Simon Lathatch took a deep breath and looked to the altar and the crucifix above it.

"Our hands are not bloodless," he admitted. "In fact, they are drenched in it. I often wonder how many tears Christ must have shed while watching his children stray."

The surprise Christian felt at hearing this admission could not be measured.

"Nevertheless," Simon continued, "we're not as we once were. We have evolved. The Pope is no longer a king with lands and desires. Our concerns are for spiritual welfare. We have returned to our task of saving souls. And while the number is unknown, the truth is your kind have damned millions throughout their time. Given the chance, you'd spread your curse like a virus, to the whole world if you could."

Christian struggled with the accusation, partially because he had no way to refute it and partially because he knew it was Drake's plan. For many centuries, he'd helped Drake to do just that. Christian himself had turned many to the darkness in his attempt to assist Drake. He wondered if they looked at him from the fires of hell now, waiting for him to join them.

"That isn't my way," he said. "I too have evolved."

Simon seemed to accept that. "Then I ask again," he said, "what do you seek? What does a demon look for in the house of God?"

Christian hesitated. The answer seemed absurd, but it was the only thing he could come up with amid the blinding light, and it was also the truth. "Peace," he said finally. "In a way you could never possibly understand."

"Perhaps I understand better than you know," Simon replied. He moved to a spot directly across from him, pausing. He changed the subject, speaking more quickly and more directly. "You are the one who fought Drakos," he said. "Tell me why."

"Why does it matter?"

"It is rare enough for your kind to leave humans unharmed, but we have never seen one of you challenge your master. You bow down to each other like animals, the alpha always getting its way. Yet you fought him, and more surprisingly, you still live."

"Our world is not as simple as you'd like to believe."

"Do you seek to usurp him?"

"No," Christian said, growing angry at the game this man seemed to be playing, and stood abruptly. "Why are you asking me these things?"

Simon stepped back. Christian saw that he was unarmed. And he was old and slightly lame. His right arm seemed withered.

"Where are the hunters?" Christian asked.

"Out looking for you, and for Drakos, and for the dozens of Nosferatu who now run amuck in this city. You must know you're not alone here."

"But you are," Christian said, guessing at a fact he could not be sure of. "And yet, you're not afraid. Why?"

"Because I believe your coming here was not by chance. Because I believe you wandered into this particular church, on this particular night, at this exact hour, for a reason. Perhaps I'm wrong, but I feel you're here not to fight with us, but to face Drake once again."

The surprises continued. Christian wondered how much he should say. It seemed this aging hunter was astute and farseeing. He was also cagey and most likely had yet to reveal all his thoughts.

Christian chose to remain silent. Simon did the same, shifting his weight and leaning against the back of the wooden bench. The old pew creaked and groaned. It was tired and worn down, like the former priest himself.

"I know of the prophecy," Simon added. "But the Midnight Sun, shining above us now, is slowly burning out. The newspapers say we won't see its light more than a day or two longer."

"You know of the prophecy," Christian said. "But do you believe what it promises—forgiveness for my kind?"

"Yes," Simon replied plainly.

"Then why do you fight us?"

"Don't fool yourself," Simon replied. "Most of your kind would not take forgiveness even if it were offered."

Christian didn't dispute that. "But some would," he said. "I would. If this angel has come from God, those who would accept the gift should not be denied its mercy."

"And what would you do to bring it to them?"

Christian hesitated. He remembered what Elsa had said. His death could bring nothing to pass, but his life…Perhaps his existence, even in this twisted form, could have meaning.

The ex-priest came to the point. "Would you destroy Drakos?"

He nodded. Of course he would. That, he'd do for nothing.

"Can you?" Simon asked.

This was a deeper question. If Elsa was right, he didn't have the power within him to do so. Four times, they'd fought. Four times, Christian had barely escaped with his life. "My powers come from him. I cannot overcome him."

"But you don't give in to him," Simon noted.

"My will, at least, is my own."

202

Simon nodded thoughtfully. His gaze dropped. "We have also failed to destroy him."

"So then he cannot be destroyed," Christian said. "There must be another way."

Simon looked up. He seemed to come to some decision. "We have a weapon."

"What kind of weapon?"

"The greatest relic of our order," Simon explained. "Its holy power will weaken Drake merely by its close proximity to him. He will feel like you feel right now, but worse. If we're right, it will affect him far more than any other Nosferatu, including you."

Christian knew the order had relics and old-world items, some of incredible power and strength; the Staff of Constantine was one, the sword of St. George another. But he could see no reason for Drake to fear these any more than Christian would.

"What weapon are you talking about?"

Simon took a deep breath. "A sword. Forged with the nails that pierced the hands of Christ. Like the pain you feel now, or that of the sunlight, it will bring agony to Drake. You entered the vault in Cologne. Surely you know the origin of your curse. Surely you must understand why this artifact would affect him more than any other."

Christian froze, his mind turning in circles of wonder and disbelief. Yes, he could understand it. "Why are you telling me this?"

"The champion of our order should wield it against him," Simon said. "But I'm too old and worn-out. I could not stand before Drakos even with this weapon in my hand."

"So give it to another."

Simon shook his head. "The one who would take it stands at the edge of his own abyss. Power and its very nature obsess him. If the sword were in his hands, I fear to think what might occur. Drakos would destroy him, or take his mind, or turn him and all he knows against us. At the very least, he would fail in a different way than I, but just as disastrously. You, on the other hand—you who've set foot on holy ground and lived, you who've faced Drakos and survived—my heart tells me you could wield it like no other and bring a final end to him and this dark curse."

Christian could barely focus. The request seemed like madness. He and the Church were mortal foes. And yet, they seemed to have a common enemy now.

"Are you sure you know what you're suggesting?"

Simon nodded. "They will banish me for this," he said, "but I have peace with the decision. If you would have it and use it in your clash with Drakos, I will place the Sword of God in your hands."

Christian did not know what to make of it. It was too new an idea, too radical. He thought of Elsa and Ida, both of whom had suggested he must find another way. Could this be it? He thought of the danger to them and to others and to the world at large. If it was possible, even slightly possible, how could he refuse?

He tried to get his bearings and clear his head. He thought of looking for Elsa again, seeking her out and asking her advice. But even if he could find her in time, she wouldn't choose him.

The sound of latches unlocking at the rear of the church reached him.

"The hunters return," Simon explained. "You must leave."

Christian wanted to speak further.

"You must go now," Simon whispered sharply, "or they will destroy you."

He had no choice. He began to move to the front of the church. His head was spinning from what he'd been offered as much as it rang with the pain and noise of the holy light.

As he reached the front door, Simon spoke again.

"If you accept, return two nights from now at midnight. I will leave a single light on, which you will see. The outside lights will be dark. If anything is not as I say, do not come inside."

Christian nodded and stepped out through the door. The calling from the marshlands returned, but something new had entered his soul: hope, given to him by the most unlikely of allies; hope that there was a way to end this madness; hope that he could destroy Drake and save those who would choose to be saved. It filled his mind and dulled the drumbeat that fought to lure him away.

He moved quickly down the street, disappearing into the shadows, never realizing that his conversation with Simon had been overheard.

Chapter 33

THE AIR was crisp and cool at 5:30 in the morning as Kate Pfeiffer walked across the ramp at Washington National Airport. The noise and bustle of the airport were beginning to rise, and the unmistakable smell of jet fuel scented the air.

Kate walked with a purpose, the heels of her shoes clicking hard on the tarmac. She carried a briefcase in one hand, a large cup of coffee in the other.

If she ever thought about it, Kate would have pegged dawn and the first light as her favorite time of day. At this hour, the ledger of progress was still a blank sheet yet to be scribbled on with wasted meetings and hours spent chasing dead-end leads. At this hour, it seemed anything could happen. Today they could catch a break. Today they could bust the case wide open. Today had limitless possibilities.

And while most days ended in failure, leaving only grim determination to keep going, that single thought always returned: *Tomorrow could be different.* To keep ahead of her, the bad guys had to win every day. She only had to win once. Today seemed like it might just be that day.

Billy Ray caught up to her, huffing as he tried to match her pace. "Easy, Kate," he said. "The plane's not leaving without us."

She dialed the pace back a notch. "Just anxious," she said.

"You want to tell me what's going on?"

"Didn't anyone brief you?"

"Kim Tan called me at four o'clock and told me to be here by five. He also said you'd catch me up on the details. I'm guessing we got a break."

"Yes and no," she said, thinking how everything in this case was one step forward, one step back.

"All hell's broken loose in New Orleans. A dozen people have gone missing in the last three days. On a tip from a junkie, NOPD checked out an abandoned house in the Ninth Ward. Since Katrina, FEMA has never let people back into the area, so it's become a ghost town and haven for drugs and crime. Inside, they found six bodies, all matching the MO in our case."

"Six?" Billy Ray said.

She nodded.

The number was shockingly high. They'd never found more than two in a single place.

They reached the jet, climbed the stairs, and flashed their IDs to the pilots. Moments later, with Kate and Billy Ray strapped in, the jet began to move.

"They've ID'd three bodies from their prints," Kate said.

"What about the others?"

"Nothing yet, but New Orleans PD can't do too much because I asked them not to."

Billy got that suspicious look in his eyes. "Why?"

"They think the bodies were dumped on different nights. That means the killer keeps coming back to the same place. So I told them to leave everything exactly as it was—no police tape, no presence. All they've done is slip in a medical examiner for a quick look."

He shook his head. "Kate, you can't do this. You can't leave bodies rotting in some house."

"They're going to come back, Billy, I know it."

"They?"

"It can't be one person. It's got to be a cult, or at least a group of people with the same sick ideas. Maybe even our missing executive from Boston."

Billy Ray glanced out the window. "It doesn't make sense. She's probably making a million dollars a year. Even if she was involved, could she really be stupid enough to dodge a bullet up here and then immediately go on the rampage down there?"

"How many times have you seen a defendant walk, only to do something worse months later? Sometimes dodging a bullet makes people think they're invincible."

He nodded. They'd both seen that happen plenty of times.

"You've got a camera team on the way, I assume?" Billy asked.

"Out of Shreveport. They're sending everything, including infrared equipment."

By now, the jet had reached the end of the taxiway and turned onto the runway. The engines were spooling up, accelerating the aircraft like an expensive sports car.

"You're taking a big chance here," Billy Ray said.

Kate thought about that as the aircraft raced along the runway and pulled free of the ground. It was a big risk, but playing by the rules had gotten them nowhere. And whether she wanted to admit it or not, she was getting desperate.

Chapter 34

LEROY ATHERTON was back on foot, hiking his way to the Greyhound bus station. At least he had his shoes on.

High in the sky and off to the east, the supernova was rising over the horizon like a full moon.

When it first appeared, people were afraid. Now, after days of news reports explaining what a supernova was and that the exploding star was forty thousand light-years away and posed no danger to the earth, people looked forward to its return every night. As Leroy reached the bus station, at least a hundred waiting passengers were outside staring at it, taking pictures and commenting.

Unlike the moon, which orbited the earth and was often seen in the daytime, the supernova maintained its exact position almost directly opposite the sun in the sky's constellations. It appeared every night, thirty minutes after sunset, illuminating the darkness once again. It lingered all night, riding highest at midnight and setting just after dawn.

Because its light came from an expanding field of plasma, it changed slowly every day, and by the time it came out, it often appeared remarkably different than it had the night before. Leroy noticed that orange and red tints had begun to fill its spreading arms.

He found it comforting somehow. A lot had happened to him over the last year. After so many monotone days, it felt as if colors had begun seeping back into his life.

He stepped inside the station. With everybody staring at the night sky, there was no one at the ticket counter except an employee who had to be there.

"Where to?" the guy asked.

"I don't know," Leroy said. "When's the next bus outta here?"

The ticket master punched a couple of keys and looked at his computer. "We got one leavin' in thirty minutes."

"Where's it going?"

"Lost Wages," the man said.

Leroy gave him a blank look.

"Vegas," the man said. "Las Vegas, Nevada."

Leroy thought about that. He'd been to Vegas before. "What else you got?"

"The next bus after that leaves at midnight," the guy said. "It's heading east." He looked at the schedule. "Tucson, Las Crucas, El Paso, Houston," the guy said, reading off the stops. "Ends up in New Orleans."

New Orleans—a place he'd always wanted to go. Cool jazz. Warm, humid nights. And something else. Leroy turned, facing east. *Yeah*, he thought, *that is the way*. It just felt right.

"Put me on it," he said to the ticket man.

He pulled out his wallet and began to count out some cash. That was the way, all right. East to New Orleans. He almost felt as if the city were calling him.

Chapter 35

THE PINE forest north of Lake Pontchartrain bordered some of the largest swamps in the state of Louisiana. Deep within the forest, a small fire burned. It gave very little warmth or light, but that was not its purpose.

Drake stood nearby, and not far behind him in the shadows cast by the moonlight was his second, Lagos. There, they waited for the Brethren to show themselves.

Drake felt them, knew they were out in the forest just beyond his field of vision. They approached slowly. He could sense their fear, and they were right to be afraid. In their own worlds, they were kings, but here, tonight they came as servants, confused by recent events, but propelled on by the power of the calling.

"You have nothing to fear this night," he said. "I know why you've come this far from the homelands I gave you to rule."

From Drake's left, the sound of pine needles being crushed under heavy boots was heard. A huge African man named Kwese appeared. Drake had turned him three hundred years ago in a slave port as he waited to pass through the Gate of No Return. When the ships finally arrived, Kwese destroyed the whites and turned the other slaves into his first soldiers. To this day, rumors of that event circled the West African countries, tales of demons that drank their enemies' blood.

Of all the Brethren, Kwese was the boldest and the most loyal. His clans spread through the failed nations of West and Central Africa, where locals called them "devils of the darkness." Even the continents' endlessly clashing armies avoided certain areas.

He stepped forward, all six foot four, two hundred and fifty pounds of him. He wore a black leather cloak beneath which a curved scimitar of the Barbary Pirates remained hidden. He reached a position on the other side of the small fire from Drake and bowed his head in acknowledgment of his master.

One by one, the others came forth. Xi was next. His original home was in the small seaside fishing town north of what is now modern Hong Kong, but he had long since hidden himself deep within the mainland of China. He had flourished since the time of Genghis Khan, and his clan spread throughout Asia, from the killing fields of Cambodia to the peasant lands of Western China.

Dressed in gray silk, he carried a samurai sword made by the same master who'd forged Drake's.

Anya Ericson was the third to appear. As fair as a ghost with hair of golden blonde, she looked almost like a porcelain figurine. She stood farthest away from Drake, the small fire barely casting its light on her. She was as cold as the land she came from, a place so far north that, in winter, when there was no sun, she never had to sleep or hide.

Her clan was the smallest, and because of this, her presence was only guessed at by the Church. Twin daggers, eighteen inches in length, hung from a belt at her waist.

All Nosferatu were naturals at stealth and concealment, but Anya was like a spirit even among them. She was Drake's specialist. Her skills were covert, both physically and mentally.

For reasons Drake could not understand, her mind was closed to him. She could hear his thoughts, but searching her mind was like sailing in an endless fog. He had never yet found the shore. A certain amount of distrust remained between them. But such power made her valuable. And Drake chose to use it to his advantage.

Xi spoke first. "What is this new trickery? How have you been able to lead us here against our own will?"

Anya's dark eyes flashed from Lagos to Drake to Xi. Her hands remained on the daggers at the ready. "Reasons matter little. We are called to serve, so we come."

Kwese nodded.

"Not all of us are here," Xi said. "Where are Drovan and Hecht?"

"Drovan is dead," Drake said, "murdered by the Church. As the time grows closer, the death squads will grow more active. They know what is to come, even more clearly than we do. The world is sliding from their grasp."

"And Hecht is lost," Anya said. "He was always careless. Too little control. Too much boasting. He indulged in the blood of the mortals despite our law."

"Perhaps," Xi said, looking across the fire at Drake. "But they are not the ones I speak of."

Of all Drake's disciples, Xi was the wisest. He saw the bigger picture.

"Where is Christian?" Xi asked. "It is rumored that you and he clashed in Germany."

As their creator, Drake could sense their thoughts. He knew they would ask about Christian, as the images and words had begun forming in their minds.

"He lives," Drake said, "for now."

"Why?" Xi asked suspiciously.

"Because I choose to let him."

Drake looked from face to face. As his eyes found theirs, each of them cast his or her gaze down onto the earth.

"I understand your desire to confront him," Drake added. "But I can destroy Christian whenever I wish. Something more important is at hand. A being has entered this world—an entity more dangerous to us than Christian could ever be. The same way you were drawn here, unable to resist the call, this *being* will also draw you out eventually. It will tempt you with the life you long ago rejected."

"What are you saying?" Xi asked.

"The Church calls it a messenger," Drake said, "a wingless angel. But, to us, it is an abomination, sent to unravel all that we've done. Each of you has built empires in the dark under my guidance. Can you imagine them being eaten away bit by bit as your minions are turned from you?"

None of them looked happy about that.

"We can kill it," Kwese said.

Drake shook his head. "If you see it, if it looks you in the eyes, you will fall."

"Then how do we fight it?" Kwese asked.

"Through cunning and guile," Drake explained. "To our advantage, this seraphim does not yet know its purpose or strength. Though, even now, its power grows. This calling will bring it to us. I have a plan. A victim it will seek to heal. When its heart and mind are focused on this broken soul, we will strike. And when I have destroyed it, Christian will rejoin us and retake his rightful place."

"And me," Lagos asked. "Do you expect me to relinquish my place at your side to Christian so easily?"

Drake studied Lagos. "No," he said. "I expect you to sharpen your sword and be ready, for he most certainly will be."

"What if he refuses?" Lagos asked.

"Then the four of you will kill him together."

They seemed uneasy at the answer. Even Lagos, for all his boasting, hesitated at the thought. None of them truly wanted to meet Christian in battle.

"So what is you bidding now?" Anya asked.

"Your brothers will stay with me," Drake replied. "But I have a task for you, my ghost."

As Drake conjured the thoughts in his mind, Anya bowed, never low enough that her eyes came off him.

Placing a hand on each dagger, she nodded. "I will do as you command."

Chapter 36

CHRISTIAN DROVE a borrowed Cadillac Escalade through the streets of New Orleans. The sound of the calling still rung in his head, but he'd beaten it back now, replacing it with the belief that he might finally have a chance to defeat Drake.

To feel any kind of hope was odd. It brought on a sense of tension and even fear. To have hope meant hope could be destroyed. He'd been there before.

Well aware of the Nosferatu flowing into New Orleans, Christian took to the streets. He now felt an even greater duty to prevent the murders his kind was committing. He'd stopped one murder the night before and broken up another gathering of bottom-feeders who might have gone on a rampage.

He destroyed them in a whirl of violence and then dodged a group of the Church's hunters a short time later. By the pile of ashes he found, it appeared as if they'd happened upon another of the Nosferatu and sent it into the abyss.

Like no time or place he could remember, this city had become an undeclared war zone, with dusk and dawn as the borders of the battlefield. The police were out, and in some sections, men sat on their porches with guns, but neither group had any idea what they were dealing with. Official numbers of the missing were high, but they missed most of the victims, those who were homeless and others who'd fallen off the grid.

A vehicle passed him going the opposite way, and Christian sensed a familiar presence at the controls.

Hecht.

Christian made a U-turn and began to follow. They were heading straight for the Ninth Ward.

—⟋⟍⟍—

The abandoned house in the Lower Ninth Ward looked a lot like all the others scattered about: surrounded by chest-high weeds, covered in graffiti, and boarded up over its broken windows.

At the end of the block, a similar house had been transformed into a command post. Kate Pfeiffer, Billy Ray Massimo, and four members of the FBI's Shreveport Tactical Squad were holed up inside it. They shared the space with radios, flat-screen monitors, and other pieces of equipment, none of which included a fan or an air conditioner.

Kate looked at her watch. It was almost 3:00 a.m. She looked over at her partner; he was wiping his head down with a towel.

"Is it me, or does it get hotter at night down here?"

"Welcome to the South," Billy Ray said. "I've seen nights where the walls dripped."

The seasons were on the cusp of changing. Eighties and humid in the South. Fifties up North.

Kate looked back at the screens in front of her; two monitors, each divided into four panels, displayed camera shots from inside and outside the dump house down the block.

The stench inside the house had been horrendous, as much from the rotting wood and furniture as from the bodies. The roof had holes, and the floor was covered in mud from the original flood, and every time it rained, the decay got worse.

"Can't believe they haven't demolished these places," Kate said.

"After Katrina, the Ninth Ward pretty much became a wasteland," Billy Ray said. "They can't rebuild it, because it sits below sea level. No insurance company is ever going to touch a house in this part of town again. From what I heard, that's half the reason some of these places are still standing, because the arguments over who's gonna pay haven't been settled yet."

"Meanwhile, this place becomes a war zone."

NOPD had warned them about gangs and drug houses and even dogs that roamed the streets in packs late at night. It was a dangerous place, but as lawless and secluded as it had become, it was almost paradise for a killer.

Or killers.

"You know, they could have other houses," Billy Ray said.

"Don't remind me," Kate said.

"Or they could have moved on," Billy Ray added.

She turned back to him. "What's the matter with you?"

"I'm just trying to be the voice of reason," he said. "All these cops, all these reports on the news of missing people and investigations—if I were a criminal, I'd be on the next train out."

"Let's hope our killers aren't that smart."

Billy Ray unscrewed the top of a thermos and poured some coffee. "You know, if we don't catch these guys, it's pretty much our jobs."

He was probably right. Whispers had made their way down to her from friends high above in the agency who thought this case was killing her career. Before she could reply, the radio crackled. A voice shot through the speaker.

"We have the target. Incoming vehicle making its way into your area. Male driving, with a female in the passenger seat."

Kate snapped her head around and back to the screens. She tapped a keyboard and brought up the cameras that were watching the street. In the dark, all she could see were blazing lights coming toward them.

"Get ready," she whispered.

Billy Ray tapped the leader of the tactical squad, who had his men up and running already. Quietly, they began to assemble themselves.

Bulletproof vests were pulled on and strapped tight. Gun belts carrying all sorts of attachments—radios, extra clips of ammo, flashlights—were wrapped around their waists.

Kate was already armored up, but she opened her pack and pulled out a small aerosol container. It looked like a can of mace or pepper spray. It was not much larger than those weapons, but it was bulkier and heavier. A small symbol on the front showed three triangles in a circle.

"Where'd you get that?" Billy Ray asked.

"You don't want to know," she said.

"Vehicle pulling to a stop."

Billy Ray stared at her, shook his head, and then went back to what he was doing.

Kate turned back to the screen. The car had parked in front of the dump house and doused its lights. A man and woman climbed out.

"Should we take them?" the team leader asked.

"Not exactly being coerced," Billy Ray said.

Kate agreed. "Let's make sure they're not just a couple of joyriders."

Billy Ray grabbed the radio. "Nobody move until we give the signal."

The other team members replied from different spots.

"Roger that."

"Ten four."

The two figures started walking toward the door of the abandoned house. The woman hesitated, and then the man put a hand on her arm.

"That's not Vivian," Billy Ray noted.

Kate had realized that.

They moved closer to the house, traveling in a strange sort of slow-motion dance.

"Their steps are matched exactly," Kate said.

"What?"

"She moves her foot exactly when he does. She stops exactly when he stops. It's weird. People don't walk like that."

"Is he dragging her?" Billy Ray said.

"It doesn't look like it."

"Maybe she's drugged."

As they crossed the overgrown remnant of a yard, every instinct in Kate's body was calling out for her to hit this guy now, to take him down before he got the woman inside that death trap. But she had to wait. Right now, they didn't even have him on trespassing.

The guy put his hand on the door. Kate lifted the walkie-talkie to her mouth. She was about to give the signal to rush the house when another radio call startled her.

"We have a second target inbound," the spotter said. "A white male on foot."

She flicked her gaze back and forth between the screens. She didn't want to take her eyes off the woman or the suspect, but a quick glance at the street camera showed her nothing. "On foot? Where? I don't see anything."

"He's off camera," the spotter replied, "not on the street. He's headed right for the house, moving cross-country."

The radio went silent.

"It's your call," Billy Ray said. "What do you want to do?"

Kate wasn't sure.

"First target is going inside."

Kate hesitated. She believed these crimes had come from a group or even a cult. She wondered if others would arrive for some kind of sick ritual. They still hadn't seen any sign of Vivian Dasher, their prime and missing suspect.

"Kate?"

"We hold," she said. "We wait and see who else shows up."

"You're putting that woman at risk."

"We have cameras. If anything happens inside, we go, but not until then."

Billy Ray rubbed his temple and shook his head. He gave the order anyway. "No one move," he said. "I repeat, no one move. Do not break cover. We're holding to see who else comes to the party."

SHADOWS OF THE MIDNIGHT SUN

He sat back down, racked the slide on his gun, and then holstered it. "You'd better be right about this. You're playing a game with that girl's life."

"And if we spook these guys and lose them, and ten more people die," she replied, "what good have we done then?"

—ↈ—

Moving through the abandoned yards, Christian focused on the couple entering the dilapidated house. He now saw what he had only felt as the car passed. The man at the door was James Hecht.

There might have been several dozen Nosferatu prowling the streets of New Orleans tonight, but none were as deadly or as powerful as this one. Normally, Hecht was a master of caution. It had taken Christian months to track him down in New York. Tonight, however, in a city on the edge of panic, he was reckless. Then again, the other Nosferatu had become similarly bold. It must have something to do with what Drake was brewing out in the bayou.

Up ahead, Hecht had the woman at the door. She was even thinner than Christian had thought. Probably a junkie of some kind. Hecht's preferred type.

Hecht opened the door, and she hesitated. It would make no difference; Hecht had her mind entangled. He put a hand on her back. He didn't even have to force her. She relaxed and entered willingly.

Christian watched as the door closed. Hecht wouldn't wait long. He couldn't. He was a junkie too, just like the girl.

Chapter 37

AS THE suspects entered the house, Kate switched over to the interior cameras. They were infrared and battery operated, because the house was dark and had no electrical power.

Camera 2 flared a bit, and Kate saw the woman's heat signature as she moved into view.

"Where's the guy?" she asked.

Billy Ray shook his head. "I don't see him. He must be blocked." He keyed the mike on his radio. "Anyone got our first suspect?"

One of the spotters replied. "First target is inside with the girl. Second target is still outside, twenty yards from the house, approaching cautiously."

Kate switched from one camera to the next. Only the woman's shape appeared on the screen. She turned to the tech who'd set up the cameras. "I thought you had every inch of that place covered?"

"I do," the tech replied.

The woman was there. She looked like she was smoking something. A bright spot showed a lighter sparking up and then going dark. At least she was still alive.

"Second suspect is approaching the house."

The woman's image faded for a second, as if something had passed between her and the camera; then it brightened again.

They could hear voices, tinny and slightly muffled, on the audio.

"You got something else besides cigarettes?"

"Unless she's talking to herself, he's in there," Kate said.

"He must be in a blind spot," the tech said.

"From all the cameras?"

"I don't know what else it could be. All systems say they're working."

"Second suspect is at the door."

Billy Ray drummed his fingers. "I think we need to go, Boss. I don't think we can wait."

The tech was working on the problem to no avail. "There's nothing wrong with the feed," he said.

On the screen, the woman's image was obscured again, and then, suddenly, the sound of scuffling broke out. The infrared cameras caught muzzle flashes from a gun as three shots echoed, quick and sharp. The third blast was followed by a crashing thud and then the horrible sound of someone screaming.

"Go!" Kate shouted. "Go! Go! Go!"

Chapter 38

CHRISTIAN HEARD the shots and raced the last twenty feet to the house. He kicked through the door and rushed inside. Hecht was crouched over the woman, gulping down her blood as fast as he could get it into his system.

"Hecht!"

Hecht released the woman from his jaws and looked up at Christian, his face and neck drenched in red. He flung something at Christian and then raced toward a boarded-up window, launching himself and crashing through the plywood and out into the night.

Christian rushed to the girl. She was still alive, barely. He ripped off part of her shirt and wrapped her neck with it, but the bleeding would not stop. As some of the blood poured over his hands, Christian retreated, like he'd been scalded with boiling water.

Beside her, he noticed the source of the gunfire—a cheap 9mm automatic with a stubby barrel.

Christian grabbed the gun, ran to the window, and hopped through. He ran three steps before getting cut off by a man in body armor.

"Freeze!"

Christian raced past him, slamming a stiff arm into his chest and sending him flying into the outside wall of the house.

The man crashed to the ground, spun, and fired.

As the blaze of fire erupted from the agent's rifle, Christian felt the bullets rip through his body, felt his coat fly as they tore holes in the fabric. The well-aimed shots would do the agent no good. The Nosferatu existed in suspension, one foot in this world, one foot in the world beyond. In truth, they phased rapidly back and forth, like an alternating current. The result was something like looking at a spinning fan or propeller. It might have been common knowledge that there were solid blades whirling rapidly in front of the person staring into it, but it looked for all the world like an empty, perhaps blurred, space.

It was the reason the Fallen blurred and vanished in mirrors and other reflections. The reason they appeared ghostly on anything but extremely high-speed film. And the reason they cast no shadow. Anything that moved at high velocity went through them and out the other side as if it were passing through empty space. That included bullets and arrows and light. Only weapons that lodged and held, like swords or knives or simple wooden stakes, could affect them.

With the agent wondering how he'd missed, Christian dashed across the street, chasing Hecht, who was already out of view. More shots rang out after them, but it was too late. Both Hecht and Christian had broken containment. Their pursuers would be left far behind in the blink of an eye.

—✲—

A small army of federal agents charged the abandoned property from all sides. Kate busted in through the front door right behind the main assault team.

Flashlights scoured the walls. There was no sign of movement. The agents fanned out, heading into separate rooms.

Gunfire boomed outside.

"Over here!" an agent shouted from a corner of the building.

Billy Ray rushed to the victim. Kate ran to the broken window.

She glanced outside, the 9mm Glock tight in her hands and ready to fire. She saw no sign of the suspects, but a member of the assault team was injured.

"Man down," she called, clearing the alley and climbing out through the window.

Two more bursts of gunfire rang out, the sound echoing from the front of the house.

Kate rushed to the injured agent. He was alive, but he looked to be in great pain. Still, she saw no sign of the suspects.

"What happened?" she asked, crouching beside him, her eyes darting around.

"My ribs," the guy said, "I think they're broken."

"What happened to the suspect?"

"I hit him with a burst," the agent said. "He didn't even slow down."

The agent tried to get up, fell, and began coughing up blood.

Billy Ray's voice came over the radio. "Victim's bleeding out."

"Emergency units are on the way," another voice answered.

Sirens were already wailing as unmarked cars screeched to a stop around the house. The paramedics wouldn't be far behind.

She keyed the radio again. "Does anybody have eyes on the damn suspects?"

A long silence followed.

"Anyone?"

"Negative. Negative. We lost 'em. They ran north, but we lost 'em."

Kate slammed her fist into the soft ground. "Damn it!"

Keeping her eyes down, she noticed tracks in the mud heading north. Looking north, she paused for a second, And then without a word, she took off running.

Chapter 39

KATE RAN north as fast as she could. She heard the ambulances and the squad cars heading for the house behind her. She heard other emergency units in the distance. If the suspects had any sense at all, they'd be keeping off the roads. She did the same, cutting through the vacant yards and alleyways, crossing overgrown, weed-covered lots.

She felt as if both suspects were ahead, maybe racing toward some prearranged meeting spot or even another vehicle. She had no idea how they'd gotten past the assault team and the spotters, but she wasn't giving up that easily, not this time.

She hopped a low fence and ended up on a greenbelt that might have been designed to catch runoff from the rain. She sprinted on, scanning the area but heading north with reckless abandon.

Half a mile out, her side began to cramp, and her lungs were soon screaming in rebellion. But she ignored the pain and the rational part of her mind that told her she was way out on a limb to be chasing two suspected killers alone, on foot. All that mattered was finding them. She had to.

She had to.

—m—

A full mile ahead, Christian was tracking Hecht like a bloodhound chasing a scent. Somewhere up ahead, he felt James Hecht slowing. Under normal conditions, Hecht could have run almost forever. The Nosferatu had great strength and speed. But Hecht had made a crucial mistake.

By feeding off human blood, he'd taken a step back from the void in which the Nosferatu lived. Hecht was now becoming human again, with all their weaknesses. Just as blood gave the Nosferatu the feelings of life they so craved, it also gave them human mortality as it coursed through their veins.

For this reason, most preferred hidden lairs to open and public killings. They chose places where they could easily disappear while enjoying their fix. But James Hecht was on the street, running for his life, and the human blood in his system was stealing more of his power with every second that passed.

Two miles from the drop house, Christian caught sight of Hecht for the first time since he'd gone through the window. Hecht was stumbling, trying to run. Falling to his knees beneath a lone streetlight, he began to wretch.

He was trying to throw up the blood, a desperate last attempt to bring himself back from the edge, but it was too late. The life force he'd stolen from the young woman had reached its zenith within him. He was fully human now, with everything that came along with it.

Christian moved in.

Hecht snapped his head around. He scurried backward, up against the lamppost. He tried to get up but couldn't. His chest heaved and fell as his mortal body begged for oxygen.

"No point in running now," Christian said. "You can't get away like this."

Hecht looked up at Christian through sullen eyes. "I didn't think…I would see you…so soon."

The pale color of Hecht's skin had flushed with pink. His dead, black eyes softened to a warm, brown color. A tear even formed and ran down his face.

Christian had never been where Hecht was right now, but he'd been told that the rush of feelings was hard to control. It was said many wept over the bodies of those they had killed, partially out of joy and partially because, suddenly gifted with feelings once again, they were stricken with guilt and remorse over what they'd done.

"Don't look at me like that," Hecht said. "I'm no more a monster than you."

Christian ignored Hecht's barb. He looked at his watch; it had been about four minutes. The high could last an hour or so, but Hecht hadn't drawn much of the girl's blood. And he'd thrown up some of it. It wouldn't be long before his strength started to return.

"You could have chosen a different path," Christian said.

Hecht laughed, his whole body shaking. "That's a good one," he said. "Like I ever had a choice."

He propped himself up a little better and pulled a lighter out of his pocket. "When Drake found me, I was lying in a pile of the dead at Gettysburg. A bayonet had split my liver in two. The blood was so black, the pain was so intense, I wished I were dead. I couldn't bear it. But Drake didn't kill me. He turned me, like he did you. He promised me life without pain."

"That's not the choice I'm talking about," Christian said.

"You don't know what it's like to feel this," Hecht spat. "You don't know what it's like once you've tasted life again."

"You'd be surprised what I know."

Hecht ignored him now, reveling in his human feelings. He flicked the lighter to life and brought the flame up, running it across the palm of his hand. At times, his face showed a sense of pleasure from the warmth; at others, a brief spurt of pain ignited as it got too hot.

"It's so empty when it leaves," he explained, "like this place, with all the people gone."

James was burning himself with the lighter now, leaving it in one spot until the palm of his hand blackened and smoked and the smell of his own flesh melting began to scent the air. Only now did Christian realize that Hecht's palms and forearms were covered in burn scars, somewhat like Elsa's.

"I've killed thousands just for this feeling," Hecht said, turning angry again. "But I didn't want this, any of it. Before Drake found me, I was good man. All those lives I took—I'll pay for them in eternity, but I lay their blood on his hands."

At that moment, Christian felt empathy for Hecht. He was a murderer who might well deserve death a thousand times over for all he'd done. But he was also cursed.

"There's another way," Christian said.

"What are you talking about?"

"A chance at forgiveness is coming," Christian said. "This curse can be lifted. I don't know what awaits any of us beyond this world, but you don't have to die like this. Come with me. I'll keep you from—"

"No!" Hecht said, angrily pulling the lighter away from his hand. The pain seemed to have grown too strong. "Nothing will stop me from killing. I know. I've tried. Not even Drake could keep me."

"You can be healed," Christian said. "Forgiven."

Hecht started to laugh. "I wish I could believe that."

He switched hands with the lighter and began to burn his other palm. "You know, I've tried to kill myself—tried at least a hundred times. But I can't…I can't do it."

Hecht looked up, his eyes slowly turning darker. His soul dying once again. "So why don't you do it for me?"

Christian stepped back. He couldn't wait much longer. His hand tightened around the automatic he'd grabbed from beside the victim. "Are you ready?"

Hecht looked around, as if he wanted one last glimpse of the earth, even in this decaying, forgotten place. After endless amounts of time, he had only a precious few moments left. "I am," he said. "Do it now. So I can feel it. At least I can die like a human."

Christian raised the pistol and pointed the snub-nosed barrel at Hecht's chest.

—⁂—

Kate Pfeiffer crouched behind an electrical junction box, breathing hard and trying not to give herself away. Forty yards ahead, a lone streetlight illuminated the two figures beneath it. She couldn't figure out why they'd stopped, but one of them was down.

She called for backup, gave Billy Ray her location, and inched forward. She watched as the tall blond man stood, and she heard what he said next.

"Are you ready?"

The guy leaning against the lamppost seemed to reply, but Kate couldn't make out the words.

She saw him nod, and figured the blonde one was going to help him to his feet. A wave of shock ran through her as the blond raised a pistol and pointed it at the other guy's heart.

As if in slow motion, the gun barrel flashed. The slide recoiled, and a shell casing flew out into the air, catching the glare from the streetlight as the booming sound shattered the silence. The blond man raised the gun and fired again, this time at the suspect's head.

The sitting man's head snapped back from the second shell, hitting the light pole. A spray of blood exploded out the back of his head like mist. He slumped over, falling to the side.

It happened so fast Kate had no time to think. It was the last thing she'd expected. She stepped from the shadows.

"FBI!" she shouted. "Put down the gun!"

The blond man turned and looked directly at her, but she had her eyes on his gun. If he flinched in the slightest, she would blast him.

"Put it down!"

In a slow, casual move, as if he didn't need it anymore, he tossed the pistol to the street.

"Get on the ground," she said.

She was only twenty feet away from him now. She could see that the dead man was the first suspect, the one who'd taken the girl into the house. *What the hell is going on here?*

"I said get on the ground!"

The man didn't move. "You have no idea what you're dealing with here," he said. "The best thing you could do is just walk away."

A weird feeling inside her told her to do just that, but the fires of her determination overrode it. "You get on the ground now, or I'll force you down by putting a bullet in your leg."

As she got within ten feet, she sensed the man trying to stare her down. He was gazing into her eyes. For reasons she couldn't explain, she averted her own gaze, looking at his chest and his arms and his hands.

Suddenly, with great speed, he moved. His right hand snapped toward her. It found her gun, grabbing the barrel. She pulled the trigger out of instinct and fired two shots right into his chest before he snatched it away.

She saw the fibers of his coat burst and fray where the bullets had hit. She saw the flap open with the recoil. But in the next instant, she was up against the lamppost. He held her throat with one hand and her weapon in the other.

"Look at me," he demanded.

She wouldn't do it. Something told her not to.

Look at me.

This time the words were in her head, just like the moment in the conference room in Boston. It made her feel sick and dizzy, yet she still refused.

"I'm not what you think I am," the blond man said.

"You're a murderer," she said.

"He's the killer," the man said, pointing to the dead body.

"I heard you talking. You knew him."

"I don't expect you to understand," he said. "But trust me when I tell you, there are darker things in this world than you know. Let this go. You've got your man. There he is."

She was starting to get her wits back. She realized he was holding her neck tight, but not crushing it. She couldn't understand why he was still standing; he should have been writhing on ground or lying dead, flat out. His coat was thin. He couldn't have been wearing a vest underneath. Even if he had been, the shots would have knocked him down.

Her mind went back to the incident in New York and all the gunfire that added up to nothing but dead men who might as well have been shooting at a ghost.

She heard the sound of cars approaching fast. She hoped it was Billy Ray.

The blond man heard it too. He glanced down the alley as the headlights swung onto the street. In that instant, she grabbed the small spray can from her belt and aimed it at his face.

He dropped her and spun away. She triggered the can as she fell, blasting a stream out into the air. It coated the back of his jacket and the back of his hair, but just like before, he was gone in a flash, vanishing into the dark by the time she hit the ground.

Headlights swung onto the street, and two cars raced up to her. One slid to a stop; the other sped up in an attempt to follow the suspect.

Billy Ray jumped out and ran to her. "Are you all right?"

She nodded.

He looked at the dead man. "What the hell happened? Did you shoot this guy?"

She struggled to get the words out. "The blond suspect," she said, "he killed this one."

"What?"

"He killed this guy before I could stop him."

Billy Ray helped her get up. "Where's your gun?"

"He got it away from me."

"How?"

"I don't know how," she said defensively. "It happened so fast…I just…"Her mind cleared and she realized the advantage they'd gained. "I got him, Billy. I doused that son of a bitch with the tracking paint. All we need is access to the satellite, and we can follow him wherever he goes."

Chapter 40

CHRISTIAN HAD put the FBI and NOPD far behind him. They would find the Escalade and trace it to a couple who'd parked it at the airport before boarding a plane to Cancun. The airport security video would be remarkably blurry when it came to his face, though the FBI agent would probably give a better description. It didn't matter. He'd be hidden in minutes, and he'd remain that way until it was time to meet with Simon at the old church.

Still, he was wary.

Back in the French Quarter, walking briskly along a side street, he felt a presence stalking him. He glanced behind him and across the street.

The feeling vanished.

He moved more cautiously now, sensing something odd was afoot.

Half a block down, he felt it again, as if someone were opening a window for him to see through and then closing it before he could focus on anything inside, but this was a window into someone's soul. He stopped in his tracks and waited. A woman stepped from the shadows in front of him. She was beautiful and pale and blonde. She was a vampire, like him.

Christian knew of Anya. He'd heard word of her as the most recent of Drake's chosen Brethren. But he'd never seen her, having been gone long before Drake turned her. Only directly in her presence did he sense what she was.

"I know who you are," Christian said. "But I have no quarrel with you yet."

"And none you shall have," she replied, moving toward him, unafraid.

Christian tried to read her mind, but he found nothing but mist. "What is it you want?"

"I want many things, but they remain for another day's discussions. Tonight I come only to deliver a message."

She stopped in her tracks five feet away. He tried again to pry into her mind. But she held fast.

She held up a small wooden box, presenting it as if it were a gift. "From Drake."

When he didn't reach for it, she put the box carefully on the ground.

Christian recognized the ancient Chinese puzzle box. Only those who knew its secrets could open it without destroying it. This box had been handmade for Drake. Christian remembered him receiving it a thousand years before, when they were learning the ancient art of sword making and practicing it with members of the Song Dynasty.

He advanced toward the box, feeling Anya's gaze upon him. He looked up, catching a glimpse of her eyes. He felt as if she were in pain and in need of help. The instant the thought flowed through his mind, Anya took off running. He knew better than to follow her.

He picked up the box and ran his hand across the smooth finish. It had held up well. He unlocked it and opened it. A dagger lay inside.

This Roman dagger was an elegant weapon—long, thin, and sturdy, with serrated edges made to tear and rip as one pulled it out of his enemy. The handle of this type was usually made from steel, but this one was made of ivory. Christian knew this dagger and knew it well. It had cut his throat seventeen centuries ago.

When he joined up with Drake, it had been given to him as a token of peace—and then taken from him when the two had clashed over Elsa.

A note lay beneath it, written in Drake's hand.

> *There is much that must be discussed. I suggest a momentary truce with the possibility of reunification. By now, you know what is upon us. We shall meet in the daylight at*

high noon so there will be no conflict, from either side. There is an old abandoned oil platform sixty miles off the coast, south-southeast of New Orleans. I'm sure you can get there. Tomorrow at noon. I offer the dagger I could have punctured your heart with all those years ago as proof of my veracity.

Drakos of the Legion.

CHAPTER 41

SIMON LATHATCH and Henrick Vanderwall waited at the Lakefront corporate air terminal, the original commercial airport in New Orleans. Time had mostly passed it by, as the airlines and the freight companies had migrated to Louis Armstrong International when it was built.

Still, the small airport had charm, Simon thought. It was a quieter, more secluded place, one where the arrival of a jet with the papal seal on its flank would more than likely go unnoticed.

On the far side of the runway, the waters of Lake Pontchartrain shimmered with the afternoon sun. This day, like others before it, had been filled with rest for Henrick's crews of hunters, but with the coming of night, they'd go forth and scour the city once again.

"The men are growing impatient," Henrick told Simon.

"Does that surprise you?"

"Your orders are restraining them," Henrick said. "They are trained to do one thing—hunt the Nosferatu. They have sworn their life's blood to the task, and yet, here at this crucial moment, you've taken the sword from their hands. We should be looking for Drakos, not shadowing these bottom-feeders."

At Simon's direction, the men were to identify any Nosferatu they found and then track them. None were to be destroyed unless caught in the act of attacking a human. And none were to be captured and forced to endure the Cruciatus in an attempt to learn the whereabouts of Drakos.

241

"Are you suggesting the men know better than I?"

Henrick did not answer immediately. If Simon guessed rightly, he would not challenge the order outright, only try to subvert it.

"Of course not," Henrick said. "But they chafe at the harness."

Simon clenched his jaw. He was tired of going through this. "Drakos undoubtedly knows we're here," he said. "He hides and bides his time. You will find no path to him through these scavengers. But their lives are exactly the ones this angel is sent to transform. Do you understand?"

Henrick's eyes suggested he didn't understand or care.

"I know it's difficult," Simon added. "But the only way to find the angel is to witness the transformation it brings. It will not appear with wings of gold and the glory of heaven in its eyes. The prophecy tells us it begins as a childlike soul, unsure of its power or purpose as of yet. Only as it begins its task will it begin to understand. For that reason, the effect of its touch is the proof we seek. A member of the Nosferatu transformed, walking in daylight, crying endless tears. That is the only way to confirm the angel's presence. By its fruits, we shall know it."

Henrick was silenced for a moment. But his displeasure was still evident. His jaw was clenched tight, and his eyes were set forward. He gazed out onto the tarmac where the Vatican's aircraft, a white-painted Dassault 2000, was turning off the runway and taxiing toward them.

Simon pressed the issue to its logical conclusion. "Why don't you just speak plainly, Henrick?"

Henrick bristled and finally allowed his anger to break through. "Messini was wrong to extend your term," he said. "If I were in your position, this would not be occurring. It's almost as if…"

Henrick checked his anger and held his tongue. Simon could only guess what else he was about to be accused of.

"But you're not in charge," Simon pointed out. "And if these are the last days of the curse, you will never be in charge of this office, for it will no longer be needed. I wonder if that's what angers you."

The jet was taxiing closer, and by now, the engine noise was too sharp and piercing for any more speech to be heard. At any rate, Henrick didn't reply; he only stared coldly at Simon.

The jet stopped. A member of the ground crew threw chocks in front of the wheels. The engines shut down, and the wailing noise they produced faded rapidly.

When the door to the jet opened, two guards in black suits came out and positioned themselves on either side of the ramp. Bishop Messini appeared next, taking the stairs cautiously. He reached the bottom and paused.

Henrick turned and walked toward a waiting Land Rover as Simon went forward to meet the bishop. The two embraced.

"Any signs?" Messini asked.

"Nosferatu everywhere, but nothing of the angel."

"It is said they will be thick like flies at the end," Messini replied. "So perhaps you are right. Perhaps the final days of the curse are upon us."

"There is darkness here, but soon there will be light," Simon told him. "I'm sure of it."

"I wish I were sure," Messini said, "but I will trust your judgment. I grant your wish. The Sword of God shall be yours to wield."

Another pair of guards came out of the aircraft. They carried a narrow protective case, which was four feet long and made of polished stainless steel.

Henrick pulled the Land Rover up, and the guards placed the sword reverently inside.

"Protect it, Simon. This is one of our greatest treasures."

"No," Simon replied. "Peace and the Word are our greatest treasures. This is only a valuable tool."

Messini nodded, but there was no joy in his face.

"We approach a moment of God's glory," Simon reminded him. "But you seem so dark."

"Men in your position have fought with Drakos for seventeen centuries. Four have found him, and they did so with large numbers of hunters alongside them. Mathias even wounded him a thousand years ago, but all of them were killed, and Balthazar was turned and had to be hunted and destroyed himself."

"You fear for me."

"I've dreamed of your death," Messini said. "You are not the man you used to be any more than I am. Perhaps Henrick's zeal and strength would be better suited to this challenge. Perhaps, filled with rage, he can stand up to Drakos. He has a fire in him that burns hot, while ours cools."

Simon glanced toward the Land Rover. Despite his clashes with Henrick, he had considered this. But strength of body and anger would not prevail against the King of the Fallen any better than a gaggle of hunters had been able to five hundred years ago. He could not inform Messini of his decision—the Bishop would never understand or allow it—but Simon believed he'd found a better champion.

"Henrick covets the sword as he covets power," Simon explained. "I fear for him in the presence of Drakos."

"But how can you hope to defeat Drakos alone?"

"None of us can do anything alone, Bishop. I will do what I can and trust in the Father. I believe he has shown me the way."

Messini embraced Simon and kissed him on both cheeks. "I will return to the Vatican and await your news. May the peace of God be with you."

"And also with you."

Messini turned and began climbing the stairs back into the aircraft. Simon watched him go, hoping he would live to see his friend once again.

Chapter 42

KATE PFEIFFER stared down at the Y-pattern incision on the dead man's chest. The cut had been stitched with black sutures, creating a clear contrast against the man's white skin.

Kate had seen so many bodies in her day that this one shouldn't have affected her, especially considering that he had been in the process of murdering a young woman shortly before he met his demise. But everything seemed different this morning. As if her world had changed. As if, somehow, the boundaries of reality were no longer as firm as they'd once been.

The bullet hole from the first gunshot had been drilled dead center into his chest and the second right between his eyes. It left a small hole in the front of his skull, and the coroner had sewn on what they'd found of the back half of his skull. His face had scars, with his nose half-missing.

She reached down and opened the man's eyelids. Last night, they'd stared at the barrel of a gun as the man did nothing to prevent his own execution. Why? Why would anyone, even a killer like this man had obviously been, not fight for his or her life?

"What the hell are you doing?" a voice snapped from behind her.

She turned to see a man in a lab coat—John Black, the coroner. He was short, about five foot two; he wore glasses as thick as bottle caps, and his hair was gray and thinning. From what she knew, he was also a Southern Baptist preacher and had been the county coroner for twenty-seven years.

Kate turned, pulling out her badge. "My name is Kate Pfeiffer, and I'm with the FBI."

"I know who you are," he said, walking over to the table. "That don't mean you can go touching the guests."

Kate felt as if she was being scolded by a teacher in grade school, but she was more angry at herself. She knew better. "I'm sorry."

The coroner studied her face and then turned to the body in front of her. "You look spooked," he said. "Can't say that I blame you. This is some of the most bizarre stuff I've ever seen. And we get it all down here."

"Did you find anything wrong with this guy?"

He cocked his head to the side. "They don't come to me in perfect health, Agent Pfeiffer."

"I'm not talking about the obvious," she said. "I think this guy was our killer, but I watched him sit on the ground and let another guy shoot him in the face. What I'm wondering is whether he was drugged. Was he paralyzed somehow? Was his back broken?"

"No, no, and no. None of the above," John Black said. "The only thing in his stomach was blood—the woman's blood. So if she dies, you're right, this guy was the murderer."

"Blood?"

"Yes, blood," the coroner said.

"He drank her blood?"

"So it would seem."

Kate felt sick. The whole thing was becoming more demented every moment. It made her think of the other bloodless victims. It made her think of the blond man's words.

"There are darker things in this world than you know," she muttered, repeating them.

"Sadly, you're right," the coroner replied.

"Not my words," she said. "The blond guy. The one who shot him."

"Oh yeah," he replied. "Your mystery vigilante."

"Maybe," she said. "Except, they knew each other. I know they did. This doesn't make any sense."

The coroner laughed. "You want to hear about some things that don't make sense? Come over here, young lady."

She moved around the other side of the body.

He pointed to a scar on the man's side. "Big knife wound," he said. "Right between the ribs. As far as I can tell, it lacerated his lungs, liver, and left kidney. Can't think of a reason why he wasn't already dead from such a wound, especially as it seems no one ever cleaned or stitched it."

While Kate took that in, the coroner pulled back the sheet, exposing the man's leg and pointing to another small incision he'd made. "When I moved his calf, I felt something inside the muscle tissue, about six inches below this point. I had an X-ray taken, and then I cut out what we found."

He held up a glass vial. A little round ball rolled around inside.

"What is it? A marble?"

"A musket ball. Solid lead. Fifty caliber."

"Who gets shot with a musket ball?"

"I don't know," he replied, "but I searched every inch of his leg, and there's no sign of an entry wound—no scar, no damaged tissue, no calcium deposit on the bones."

"What do you mean?"

"A ball like this should shatter bone and rip muscle out in huge chunks as it goes in. Don't see any of that in this guy."

"So how'd it get in there?"

He shrugged. "Then there's this," he said, holding out a vial of liquid. It looked like rusty water, the kind that came out of a pipe that hadn't been turned on in years.

"What is it?"

"His blood."

"What?"

"This is the guy's blood. It's coagulated. It's as thick as molasses. The cells are all deformed in a way I've never seen."

Kate looked at it as she turned the vial upside down, and the blood ran slowly to the bottom like syrup. "What would cause this?"

"I have no idea," he said. "But if this was the consistency of the blood in his body before he got shot, I can't see how his heart was pumping it."

"Meaning what?"

John Black looked over his glasses. "Your suspect should have been dead instead of running a four-minute mile in the Ninth Ward."

Kate found herself getting more confused. "So it happened afterward," she guessed. "Right?"

"It had to," he said unconvincingly, "but I still don't know how or why."

"Could drugs have played a part? Could he have been exposed to some toxin?"

The coroner looked over his chart. "No drug I've ever heard of could cause something like that."

She sighed. "Anything else?"

"You want there to be more? This guy is already a giant medical mystery."

Kate almost laughed, a feeling she'd forgotten existed. "No, I don't want there to be more," she said. "I want there to be less—less of everything. Then maybe something would make sense."

The door swung open, and Billy Ray walked in. He looked bad, rubbing the back of his neck like he was fighting a knot or a pinched nerve. He'd been in the ICU all day, guarding the victim and waiting for her to come around.

"I'll leave you two alone," the coroner said and then pointed to the body. "No touching."

As the coroner stepped out, Kate looked into Billy Ray's eyes. "What did the girl say?"

He shook his head. "She didn't say anything, Kate. She went into cardiac arrest a couple of times. The last episode started an hour ago. She died on the table without ever waking up."

Kate felt as if she'd just been punched in the gut. "Damn," she said.

"There's going to be hell to pay for this," Billy Ray said. "We could have stopped them."

248

"You were right," she said. "We should have gone in."

"Yeah," Billy Ray said. "If we had, she'd be alive right now." He looked down at the table. "And so would he. And we'd be getting something out of him."

She looked away, remorse overflowing from within. "I'm so sorry," she said. "But you know there's something bigger going on here. Thirty missing persons cases in the last five days. A dozen victims in Boston. I thought it was worth the chance. All we have to do is find the guy I painted last night, and we'll break this case. He knew this guy. He holds all the answers."

"You just don't get it, do you?" Billy Ray said. "We've got zero. We broke all the rules, and we got people killed. There is no next time; there is no finding this blond guy. You're damn lucky not to be lying on the slab down here yourself."

A long silence hung in the air. He was right.

"Come on," he said. "We have to go. We have a conference call scheduled with Director Tan's office in an hour."

She'd never seen Billy Ray so angry. She felt the need to apologize more, but her mind was still working the evidence. Even things that didn't add up could tell you something. And nothing was adding up to her right now.

"Why'd he do it?" she whispered.

"Why'd who do what?"

"Why'd the blond guy let me live? Why am I not down here on a slab?"

"I don't know, Kate," he said. "I can't tell you what these psychos think—"

"He wasn't a psycho."

"He executed this guy in cold blood."

"After what we saw this bastard do, do you really have any qualms with that?"

Billy Ray exhaled sharply. He looked at the dead body once again. "No," he said finally.

Kate felt something changing, some bit of clarity growing within her.

"He had my gun," she said. "He obviously wasn't afraid to kill. And he must have had an escape plan already set up, or we'd have nabbed him. He was calm, he knew what he was doing, and he obviously didn't want to get caught. So why let the only person who's seen you up close live to tell the world? Why let someone who's trained to remember details and sworn to arrest you if she sees you again get out alive? It makes no sense. He has to know an accurate description of him will be out within an hour. So why not kill me and prevent all that?"

"Maybe he doesn't care," Billy Ray said. "Maybe he's already on a plane to South America."

"Or maybe he thinks we're on the same side."

Billy Ray just stared at her. "Are you out of your freaking mind?"

"Look, I'm not saying *he's on our side*," she explained, "just that *he might think so*. Arsonists sometimes think they're on the same side as the firefighters. Domestic terrorists think they're out to save the country. This guy might be thinking along the same twisted lines, and that might play to our advantage."

"More likely, he's part of it," Billy Ray said. "And he's trying to kill off anyone or anything that connects him to this stuff."

She didn't think so, but it was a possibility. "Even better," she said. "That means if we find him, we can find the rest of this cult."

Billy Ray continued to stare. "Tracking paint," he said.

She nodded.

"They'll probably arrest you for using it without authorization," he said. "Even if they don't, they'll never let us use the satellite. It's military."

Kate shook her head, growing more confident once again. "If they want to end this, they'll do whatever we ask."

Chapter 43

LEROY ATHERTON had never seen the wetlands or the deep bayou before. But something had drawn him here, and even as the shadows grew long and afternoon turned to night, he'd continued to hike deeper into the great swamp.

Now that darkness had fallen over him, he began to think he'd made a mistake. He'd begun on a trail but had long ago wandered off it. Now he was lost.

Strange birdcalls pierced the night, startling him. Bullfrogs and crickets and a thousand other kinds of insects kept up a background noise that was so odd and all encompassing it made him feel dizzy. Bright eyes reflecting the moonlight seemed to stare at him from all sides.

He pulled the hood of his gray sweatshirt up over his head after the tenth mosquito buzzed in his ear. A few seconds later, he jumped back as something scurried out from under a bush and raced into the water.

"Water rat," he muttered as the thing disappeared.

It struck him as funny. He'd lived his whole life in the badlands of Compton. He'd been in fights, seen people shot and killed. He'd been harassed dozens of times by overzealous cops or threatened by punks in the neighborhood. He'd seen bigger rats in kitchens and alleys, and yet, he felt utterly ill at ease. He guessed it was the difference between the danger you know and the danger you don't.

"What am I doing here?" he asked himself.

He was about to turn around when a light in the distance caught his eye. He lifted his head in an attempt to see better. The point of light was moving, coming closer. It flickered like a candle.

Unsure of what to do, Leroy crouched down behind a great cypress, trying to see what was coming his way.

The source of the flame came into focus. It was a torch, like the kind lynch mobs ran around with in those old movies. Fear suddenly gripped Leroy. He wanted to run but felt as if he were paralyzed.

A figure holding the torch slowly came into view—a woman dressed in white. She seemed to glide across the water's surface, and the mist gave her a ghostly effect. She stopped about twenty yards away, stepping onto a dry mud bank.

She didn't look like she belonged in a swamp. *How many people are lost in this place?* Leroy thought.

"You're not lost," she said out loud, as if reading his mind. "Nor am I. Both of us are right where we're supposed to be."

Her voice sounded like a song, like a melody. And Leroy found he was free of his terror almost instantly. He came out from behind the tree. "Who are you?"

"My name is Elsa," she said. "I'm here to be your guide."

Leroy almost laughed. "My guide," he said. "Well, I am in the middle of a swamp, in the middle of the night, without a flashlight or a map. I guess I need something. A guide would be good, or maybe to have my head examined."

She smiled. "I'm your second guide, Leroy. I'll take you part of the way. If you don't give in to fear, a third will take you the rest."

As she spoke, the moonlight reflected off her face. She was beautiful. She had the brightest eyes he had ever seen.

"Second and third?" he asked. "Who was the first?"

"Your son," she said plainly. "Tre."

"My son?" Leroy didn't know what to make of this. The dream of his son had been so real, but he was pretty sure it was just a dream.

"He sent you forth," the woman in white added. "You have been chosen for a great task—chosen because of the mercy you've shown. You are honored with freeing the souls of those who've been enslaved."

Leroy thought back to that night he was going to avenge his son. At the moment he was about to pull the trigger, he remembered feeling sympathy for the kid—this lost soul—a product of his environment. It had all started then, at that very moment.

He considered the feeling that was drawing him deeper into the swamp. It felt as if others in great pain were waiting on him. "They're out there," he said. "That's why I've been drawn here."

She nodded, but the look was sad. He thought he could guess as to why.

"There's danger where I have to go, isn't there?"

"I'm afraid there is," she said. "Danger and death lie ahead in your path."

He looked past her. He felt it. He knew she was right.

"What do I do?" Leroy said.

"Walk with me a little while, and I'll tell you that which you need to know."

Chapter 44

KATE STARED at the drab cinder block wall of the hallway. It matched her mood perfectly. Her request to use the satellite to search for the suspect she'd painted had ignited a firestorm. She'd already been raked over the coals by the local FBI brass. Now the big dogs—Kim Tan, the FBI's director of operations, and Doug Salome, the head of Homeland Security—would get their turn. As a conference call was being set up, she was made to wait in the hall like a kid outside the principal's office.

This is probably the end, she thought, *firing time or at least reassignment to some miserable desk job.* Something painful enough to make her quit.

She was almost fine with it now. She could see more time with Calvin on the horizon. She could see the fights with her mother fading to a subtle, passive-aggressive *Isn't this better?* victory smile on her mother's face.

But even if it was better for her, there were others it wouldn't be better for.

She took full responsibility for everything that had happened in the Ninth Ward. Despite that, Billy Ray was out on the same limb and about to get chopped off with her. He hadn't said much in the past few hours, staring at his phone most of the time, texting and e-mailing and reading the responses with a scowl on his face. It felt like their friendship was gone, another casualty of the case.

And then there was the other issue. Who would take the case next? Probably someone competent. But months of effort, knowledge, and boots-on-the-ground experience didn't just transfer with the files. She and Billy

Ray had been learning from every mistake, getting closer and closer. She felt they had the killers on the defensive for the first time. She felt they were so close to ending this.

The new agents would be back at square one, and the killers would get some breathing room. And who would pay the price for that? More victims. More daughters and sons and brothers and sisters. More wives and husbands, like hers.

A year ago, she hadn't gone home when she should have. How the hell could she go home now?

She glanced at a small picture she kept in her purse. It was Calvin. He was three, and his dad was holding him. How far away that moment felt. She tried to conjure up the joy and contentment she'd felt back then, but it was nowhere to be found. It felt alien—in fact, as if it were someone else's life. Maybe that would change if she could just finish the damn job.

The elevator door opened, and Billy Ray came out carrying two cups of coffee.

She hid the picture away. "Thought I was going to the guillotine alone."

"Got caught on the phone upstairs," he said, handing her a Styrofoam cup. "Here. Consider it a peace offering."

"Thanks," she said, taking it. "But you don't owe me anything. The way things are going, I've probably gotten us fired and ruined that political career your father wants you to have."

He smiled. "Well, then perhaps some good has come of this, after all."

Billy Ray seemed to be himself again. Thank God for that.

He took a sip of the coffee and made a terrible face. "That's…just… awful. I don't even know where they get off even calling it coffee."

Kate studied her partner's face. "What is it you're not telling me?"

Before he could answer, the door to the videoconference room opened, and Charlie Gallagher, the regional director, snapped his fingers at them to come inside. "It's showtime."

They stood, and Billy Ray held the door. "In case you're wondering, I've got your back."

Thankful to hear that, Kate sat down in front of a fifty-inch flat screen. A second identical screen sat to the left. On one screen was Kim Tan, the director of the FBI, and on the other was Doug Salome, the secretary of Homeland Security.

Kim Tan spoke first. "We all know each other here, so we'll dispense with the pleasantries. There are two main questions we have to answer. One concerns your continued employment with the FBI, but to answer that, we have to get to the bottom of a few things. To begin with, what the hell were you doing with the radioactive marker paint?"

"It was checked out to me under standard protocol," she said.

"Three months ago," Kim Tan said. "For another case!"

"When I packed equipment for this assignment, I realized I still had it," Kate said. "It seemed prudent to use it if we got the chance."

Salome broke in. "This equipment was issued only to be used in connection with a terrorist plot here in the continental United States. It's beyond expensive, and it's also classified. It's for tracking terrorists and guys smuggling plutonium and WMDs."

"With all due respect," Kate began, "if you don't consider eighteen horrific murders and thirty missing persons to be domestic terror, then I'm not sure what qualifies."

The secretary of Homeland Security looked shocked at her response. He fell silent. She hoped that was a point in her favor.

Kim Tan didn't react much either way. "We'll let history decide if you made the right call," he said. "In the meantime, the question becomes what we do now."

The room fell quiet.

Salome didn't say a word. There was a slight buzz from the phone on his desk.

Kim Tan stared directly at the agents. "We're waiting."

"You're asking us?" Kate said. "I thought we were getting fired."

"I ought to fire you," the director told her. "But if I do, I have to fire the senator's son. And if I fire him, I have to explain myself to his budget committee. And quite frankly, I don't want to do that. More to the point, getting rid of you means I screwed up by giving you the case in the first place."

She thought she saw a hint of a smile crease Kim Tan's face.

"Besides, if it ever came out that we did anything less than everything in our power to stop this madness, I could kiss my own ass good-bye. So, in a way, your lunacy has given me cover. And since the suspect is already painted, we're going to look for him." He paused. "Doug, you want to take it from here?"

The secretary of Homeland Security cleared his throat. "The NSA is going to give us use of a military satellite designed to track this marker for the next twenty-four hours. They insist that this time limit is absolute. It's not the first time they've helped us out this way. When the Beltway Sniper was running loose in DC, they did a similar thing, loaning us a bird that watched for muzzle flashes. It didn't solve the case, but at least it gave us precedent to ask."

Kate could hardly believe what she was hearing. She looked at Billy Ray. He'd definitely gone to bat for her, probably twisting arms right up until he'd arrived with the two cups of the world's worst coffee.

She caught his eye. He smiled.

Kim Tan spoke again. "The satellite will be in position by nineteen hundred hours, but the team needs some basic information to complete the setup, so get your butts over to Communications and give 'em what they need."

Kim Tan smiled at her.

Salome added a word of warning. "Don't forget, this activity is not to be spoken about outside this building."

Kate nodded. Billy Ray did the same. A moment later, they were out the door, headed down the hall to another part of the building where the remote surveillance feeds would be monitored.

"This was all your doing," she said.

"I don't know what you're talking about."

"Uh-huh," she said. "And you don't want to be a politician."

Billy Ray nodded. "Never," he said. "And just so we're clear, that's as far as my pull goes. If we mess up again, we're both flipping burgers."

She looked Billy Ray straight in the eyes. "Don't worry," she said, "I won't let you down again. Tonight we end this case, one way or another."

Chapter 45

AS THE hour of noon approached, Christian hid in the darkest shadows of the decaying hulk of an oil platform. Abandoned after Katrina, it sat and rusted, becoming a home for birds, corrosion, and mold.

He'd made his way there in a rented powerboat, coming under cover of darkness and hiding in the catacombs of the huge structure as day broke. When and how Drake would show himself, Christian didn't know. He'd searched the rig from top to bottom. Neither Drake nor any of his drones were there. At least it wasn't a trap.

Finally, he heard the sound of a helicopter approaching. He guessed it would be carrying Drake or some messenger.

Christian moved forward to the edge of the shadows. Even here, reflected sunlight began to weaken him and bring on a gnawing pain.

He watched the aircraft approach, moving across the brilliant blue sky. He found a stairwell and climbed until he stood half a deck below the helipad. The sound grew louder, and the old structure shuddered as the helicopter came in for landing.

Christian watched as it touched down and the blades began to slow. Soon enough, a door on the helicopter's side opened. The pilot got out and then helped what appeared to be a frail old man climb down.

As the withered man set foot on the platform, Christian realized it was Drake. He was covered from head to toe in black garb. A cloak draped over his shoulders. He even wore a head scarf, as if he were a Bedouin in the desert. He stepped forward, walking with a cane.

Christian had never seen Drake in the daylight. He seemed crippled by it. The fearsome creature of the night was just a tired old man by day.

He tried to read Drake's mind, but there was nothing there, nothing to hear.

Christian stepped forward, climbing the last few stairs. He gripped the railing and prepared to dive back into the shadows if anything happened. He felt the weight of the sunlight pressing upon him, felt his strength ebbing rapidly.

"Tell him to leave us!" he shouted, nodding toward the pilot.

It was odd, Christian thought. The roles were reversed: the titans of the Nosferatu race cowering in fear of an average human man. The pilot could have easily killed them both in their current states. No doubt he was under Drake's control, but for Christian, that was all the more reason to send him away.

Drake waved a hand toward the helicopter, and the pilot got back inside and fired up the bird. As it lifted off and moved away, Christian stepped forward, keeping to the shade. In front of him, Drake's hand shook as it gripped the cane that held him up. Seeing him this way, Christian felt sorry for him.

"Our enemies would not show us the compassion you feel for me now," Drake said.

Christian ignored the comment. "Why have you asked me here?"

Drake unbuttoned his facial cloth; his skin looked weathered and aged. Christian's own face was faring little better.

It had been said enough time in the sun would reveal the Nosferatu's true age. Christian doubted that, but he didn't want to stick around to find out.

"I've called you here to give you one last chance to rejoin us," Drake said. "For where else can you go?"

Christian believed he had somewhere else to go, but until the right moment, he wanted to keep that from Drake. He did what he could to block his thoughts. The best way he'd found was to focus on something else. He focused on their first meeting, the night when Drake had turned him. Drake read it quickly.

"Still living in the past?"

"You deceived me," Christian said. "Right from the start."

"You were already separating from the world," Drake said. "Running from the legion. Heading for the wild lands and the Goths. You murdered the prefect and the general, and you slew his guard to reach him. I watched as the guilt swelled within you. You only realized the foolishness of what you'd done afterward. And fearing you could not hold the power you'd grasped for, you ran."

Only now did Christian understand why Drake had turned him and why, as Tiberius, he'd been so filled with fear that he'd allowed himself to be turned. He'd even begged for it.

But while Drake was right about much, he was wrong about the truth of that moment.

"You misjudged me," Christian said. "I killed the prefect and the commander of our legion, that much is true, but the only guilt I felt was for the innocent guards I had to strike down to get at them. That's my sin. If any form of hell awaits me, it's for that reason and that reason alone."

"You grasped for power," Drake countered, "but realized you could not hold it."

"No," Christian said firmly. "I never wanted it, but Trajan was worse than a fool. He wasted the men on battles they could not win. Sent them to war with no objective beyond his own glory. While he basked in it, the men swam in blood—their own. I killed him to save them, not to rule them or write my name in history."

Drake's face showed a look of surprise that Christian had never seen before. He knew from searching Christian's heart that the words Christian had spoken were true. He'd never sensed this before, perhaps because it was buried under the waves of guilt Christian felt for slaughtering the general's guard.

"You wanted power," Drake insisted. "I felt it!"

"Yes," Christian admitted. "Power to stop the waste and mindless slaughter. After two years of carnage, I realized it would never end. Trajan could not be swayed, could not be convinced of any other form of action beyond what he desired."

"You were a traitor!"

"To Trajan, yes. To the power of the politicians, yes. But to my men, to the honor of Rome, no!"

He had never said these truths before. Just speaking them seemed to give him strength. And strangely, they seemed to strike fear into Drake. For the first time ever, Christian sensed confusion in his old master's eyes. Surprise and miscalculation had put him off-balance.

Drake put a hand to the railing, grasping it for balance.

"You are the master of deception," Christian said. "It seems you have deceived even yourself."

"No," Drake said. "It is you who fails to see the truth."

For the first time in seventeen centuries, Christian felt the balance of power turning. He stood on the brink of wielding a weapon that would destroy his old master, a weapon that would weaken him and wear him down worse than the sunlight was doing now. The path was finally clear, the end game of this journey finally in sight. Christian's confidence swelled with the thought.

"You forget our history," Drake warned, sensing Christian's confidence and suddenly returning to his menacing form. "You live only because of my mercy. I thought that lesson I taught you on the White Cliffs of Dover would have made a deeper impression. If you couldn't kill me filled with rage over your poor Elsa, you will never have the strength to do it."

"I've found a weapon more powerful than rage," Christian insisted.

Drake's anger was bringing him strength. He stood taller. "There is no power that will bend my knees," he insisted, "not the Church, not this so-called angel, and certainly not you!"

Drake had missed it. He thought Christian was referring to the angel, not the sword of God that would send Drake straight to hell.

"Your end is coming, Drakos," he said. "It's not going to be the Church, nor the angel that finishes you. It's going to be me. Seventeen hundred years ago, I killed Trajan to end the slaughter of the legionnaires, and when the Midnight Sun fades, I'm going to kill you to end the carnage you've brought to the world."

As the words came from Christian's mouth, the wind picked up across the water. It whipped around them and tugged at the cloak, Drake wore. It brought the sound of the helicopter returning to Christian's ears.

The two goliaths stared each other down.

"You will fail," Drake said calmly.

"We shall see."

With Drake still in the light, Christian backed into the shadows until he reached the stairs. He moved down two flights and then a third before disappearing into the unlighted catacombs of the huge rig.

He waited, but the only sound from up above was that of the helicopter landing. Neither Drake nor anyone else followed, and by the time Christian reached the bottom level of the platform, the black helicopter was lifting off high above and banking away to the north.

Any chance at reconciliation was forever gone now. There would be no more truces, no more talks. A small part of him wished things were different. The angel brought what Drake had begged for so long ago. But his old friend had been churning the bitterness in his heart for two thousand years. He would never turn back; he was too far gone, just like Hecht.

And just like Hecht, Christian would have no choice but to destroy him.

Chapter 46

SIMON LATHATCH knelt before a small altar in the tower room of the church on St. Bernard Avenue. His eyes were closed, his hands folded around a rosary, his chest rising and falling slowly. His lips moved in a silent prayer, one he repeated over and over again.

I hope to act righteously, Father. I hope my will has conformed to yours. If my path is true, please show me a sign, for my heart trembles at what I have proposed to do.

In front of him, held in clasps of the purest gold, was the sword into which the nails of the Crucifixion had been melted. The Ignis Purgata believed this sword carried the blood of Christ within it. They believed it held the power to end the curse of the Nosferatu.

All those who'd held Simon's position had been entrusted with it. None had ever dared to use it in battle. And none of them would have even considered what he was about to do with it.

My heart trembles at what I have proposed.

Simon wondered if he had taken leave of his senses.

He opened his eyes. The sword glistened in all its brilliance, the metal polished to a mirror finish. It was beautiful. It was perfect.

Legend held that the nails from Golgotha had been recovered by one of the Roman soldiers as Joseph of Arimathea retrieved the body of Christ from the cross.

They remained in this soldier's possession for seventy years, until he died at the age of ninety-one. They were passed down to his son and then to his grandson, each of whom kept them secret as the Romans tried to destroy the Christian movement. Ten generations later, after the establishment of the Church, a young man who'd become a priest offered them as a gift to the papal envoy.

The Church council met, prayed and sought a sign of their own. Shortly thereafter, the petition of Drakos reached the council. In response the leaders of the Church deemed the nails a divine gift, preordained to help them destroy the scourge of the Nosferatu.

They were hidden away for centuries afterward. Then, during the Dark Ages, with the Nosferatu running rampant in the plague filled world, a hunter named Ishera had a vision that the nails of the cross had become a sword of iron and steel. In his dream, this sword shone through the night like a beacon, and the hunters followed it, sweeping the Nosferatu from the earth.

The greatest sword makers of Europe were called. They forged many prototypes before one craftsman was selected and given charge to create from the nails and the strongest metals known, the sword that would end the curse of the Fallen.

Simon had pondered this often. He wondered what the Prince of Peace would think of their actions, of turning the nails that tortured him—as he allowed himself to be a sacrifice for all the world—into a weapon of destruction.

It was a conflict the Church had always struggled with, from the Crusades, to the actions of the Ignis Purgata. What place did warriors have among those charged with praying for their enemies? If the Church was the body of Christ, the instrument of peace, then why were they so often at war?

Simon caught sight of his own reflection in the gleaming blade. He saw himself wrestling with the decision, trying to come to his own conclusion. He closed his eyes again, trying to remove himself from the equation.

Not my will, but yours, Father. Not my desire, but yours. If my way is righteous, please show me a sign... Please show me a sign.... Please show me a sign...

The sound of the door opening ended his prayer.

Simon turned to see Henrick letting himself in. He made no request to enter, and offered no apologies.

Frustrated at the disturbance, Simon crossed himself before the altar and got up, his old knees hurting as he stood. Henrick said nothing. He just started past Simon, looking toward the sword.

"Why have you interrupted me?" Simon asked.

"One of the hunters wishes to speak with you," Henrick said. "He reports a sign—a Nosferatu walking in daylight. He believes the demon has been turned back into human form."

Simon's heart swelled with hope. "Are you sure?"

Henrick seemed contrite. He nodded slowly, as if admitting that he might be wrong and that Simon might possibly be correct after all these years. "You should speak with him and decide for yourself."

Henrick opened the door and stepped out. Simon followed, closing the door behind him and moving to the stairway. Henrick marched in lockstep at his side.

"If this is true," Simon began, "then we must do all we can to protect the angel."

Henrick nodded as they took to the stairs. "In which case, I ask you to think about the moment at hand. Even with the sword of God, your strength will be no match for Drakos. Your body is frail; your arm is withered, Simon."

"Withered because I ripped you from the grasp of a demon that was trying to consume you."

The incident was twenty years ago. Sometimes it seemed to be all that bonded the two men anymore.

Henrick nodded his appreciation. "All I ask is the chance to return the favor."

Simon was unnerved by Henrick's manner of speaking. The man was usually brash and arrogant. He demanded; he did not request, even as a subordinate.

"You're full of tact all of a sudden."

"I only desire what should rightfully be mine," Henrick said. "The honor and danger of carrying the sword into battle. In return, I offer you the chance to reconsider the madness of your decision."

"What *madness* are you talking about?"

"You know what I'm talking about," Henrick said.

The tact was gone, the edges of Henrick's cool fraying as they reached the bottom of the stairs. "Either lie to me boldly or speak the truth," Henrick demanded . "But hide your actions no longer. Tell me —here in the house of God—what are your plans for the sword?"

By now, they'd stepped out onto the floor of the church. Standing there, Simon noticed one of the hunters who was supposed to be out tracking the Nosferatu.

Two other hunters emerged from the back. While across the church, by the front door, three more appeared . They stepped from the shadows and moved down the aisle toward him.

There was no point in answering Henrick's question. Clearly, he already knew of Simon's plan.

As the men moved approached, Simon's heart filled with sadness. Some of these men he'd trained, all of them he'd known for years as they progressed through the order. The look on their faces suggested confusion, anger, and betrayal.

Henrick had done his job well, but then Simon had made it easy for him.

"Nothing to say?" Henrick asked. "Then let your silence convict you." He turned to one of the men. "Upstairs, in the tower room. Secure the sword so I might take it from this place."

Simon could not protest. He could not fight or even attempt to explain. As the hunter ran off to get the Sword of God, Henrick and the men glared at him as if Simon had become a demon himself.

The other hunters moved closer—five strong men, apparently more loyal to Henrick than to their oath or to Simon. Soon he was surrounded in the small space by the altar. The room became silent and the air awfully still.

"This is mutiny," Simon pointed out. "Do you even fathom what you're doing?"

"Do you?" Henrick replied sharply. "Perhaps this demon has cracked your mind. Perhaps you're under his control."

"I'm not!" Simon insisted. "My will is my own."

"That only makes it worse."

The lone hunter came back down the stairs with the sword in his hand. He delivered it to Henrick, who held it aloft. "The Sword of God will not be turned over to the enemy."

The rest of the group nodded approvingly. Even if Simon tried to explain, he could not expect the mutineers to change their minds now. He held silent, and Henrick pointed the sword at him.

"Now," Henrick said, beginning his reign, "we're going to need some information concerning this new friend of yours."

With that said, two of the hunters forced Simon to his knees. He said nothing, prompting Henrick to step forward and strike him in the face with a gauntlet covered fist.

Simon looked up, his nose broken, his lip bleeding. He gazed into Henrick's eyes. Fear filled his soul. Not for himself, but for the world at large, for those who would suffer, and for the single Nosferatu who had dared visit the house of the Lord.

A second blow jarred him, snapping his head to the side and splattering his blood across the floorboards. Dazed but conscious, Simon eyed the crimson stain of his life's blood. Slowly, a sense of peace came over him. By the time he turned back to his tormentors, a faint smile had found its way to his damaged face.

Henrick noticed quickly and grabbed him by the hair, tilting Simon's head back. "You have nothing to grin about, old man."

"I… have… understanding," Simon managed.

Henrick released Simon's hair with jerk. "Understanding of what?"

"I asked God for a sign," Simon whispered. "A sign that my path was righteous. He sent me a betrayer, at the head of a mob, to take me away in chains. What greater sign could He possibly give me?"

Henrick glared at him, quickly calculating the significance of the statement. As he realized what Simon was suggesting, Henrick's eyes contorted with rage and he reared back and smashed Simon's face once again, this time with all the force he could muster.

Chapter 47

NIGHT HAD fallen over New Orleans. Unlike other nights in the past week, this one was as black as ink. The moon would not rise until nearly 4:00 a.m., and the Midnight Sun, which had faded in magnitude with each passing day, was gone. Without a telescope to view it, the supernova was little more than a grayish wisp in the sky.

The once-in-a-thousand-years event was now just a memory. The end of Christian's long wait had come, and he was glad of it. Glad he'd fought the calling and sought refuge in the old church. Glad he'd met a man who could see past the long history of war and into Christian's heart. Glad he would soon be in possession of a power that would overcome Drake and end this madness.

He stopped a half block from the front of the church. A single light was on in the upper room, just as Simon had promised. All other lights were out.

Christian stepped forward and began walking. The familiar pain began to wash over him, but he welcomed it now. It felt like penance or even proof of the humanity that still lived somewhere deep inside him. He wondered if that's what Hecht had been after when he held the flame to his hand. To feel anything was a gift; to feel nothing was the cruelest part of the curse. Dead but alive. Entombed in one's own body.

He ran up the old stone steps to the church's entrance, his body stoked by the fires of purpose and destiny. He pulled on the handle and opened the heavy wooden door. His head was buzzing, his senses failing. He stood gazing inside.

The church was dimly lit. It appeared empty, just as it had before. Almost.

Down the long aisle, at the altar, in front of the crucifix, Simon Lathatch knelt. His dark robe draped the floor, his clasped hands resting on the communion rail in front of him. His head bowed, he seemed to be trembling.

Christian glanced around the church and moved inside. He walked forward, conscious of his own footsteps at first and then losing even them to the clamoring in his head. It was like tunnel vision affecting all senses at the same time.

"Simon," he whispered, continuing forward.

The closer he got to the altar, the brighter the pain was and the weaker he felt. He legs trembled and shook, threatening to give out on him. He fought forward, reaching his newfound ally and placing a hand on his shoulder.

"Simon."

Simon turned his head. He looked like a fighter who'd just gone fifteen rounds and lost. His face was bloody and bruised, his nose broken, one eye swelling shut. His hands were tied to one another and tied to the rail of the altar. His mouth was taped over, and his feet and knees were bound to keep him in a kneeling position. Tears flowed down his weathered face.

A spike of adrenaline surged through Christian. He reached for the tape and pulled it free.

"Run!" Simon managed, his voice cracking. "Run!"

The sound of the main doors banging open turned Christian around. Two men stood there now—hunters in all their deadly glory.

From the side and back doors came four others. And then from the nave, where the choir might sing, came a sixth man. In his hand, he carried a gleaming sword. Christian felt a new wave of pain.

"Is this what you're looking for, demon?"

"I'm sorry," Simon whispered to Christian. He seemed to gather his strength for one last plea. "Henrick, please. You're making a mistake."

Henrick ignored Simon, addressing Christian instead. "You may have corrupted his mind, but your actions will not bring you victory. You have come here to find only your destruction."

Christian stood up slowly, his whole body shaking. His greatest fears were realized. With his head ringing and his strength drained, he had no chance. He was dead and he knew it.

"Not so dangerous in here, are you?" Henrick said. "Perhaps I should thank our disgraced former leader for luring you to this spot."

Christian fought to clear his mind. Despite a desire to protect Simon, he stepped back. Distance from the altar would help, if only slightly. "I want what you want," he said. "Drakos is our enemy."

Henrick stepped forward, unafraid. "The wicked will say what they can to avoid the fires of hell. But lies are still lies."

Christian continued to back up, but other hunters were coming at him from behind and the side, closing in on him from all fronts, closing the net.

Christian stumbled, but caught himself by grabbing the backrest of one of the pews. His eyes darted around, going from Henrick to the men on either side. A quick glance behind told him the hunters at his back were only three rows away.

He pulled his sword from its sheath beneath his long coat.

One of the hunters stepped forward with a palladium whip and cracked it, snatching the sword from Christian's hands. It was child's play. A second whip snapped forth, wrapping his arm and pulling it taught.

Christian turned, startled, unable to think or react, or even see clearly.

"Drakos will destroy you," Christian said in a desperate effort to influence this Henrick. "His greatest desire is revenge on the Church."

"I will kill him myself," Henrick said, "as I'm going to destroy you. All you have to do is tell me where to find him."

Christian didn't speak.

Henrick raised his hand, and the hunters watched for his signal. "You have one chance to make it easy on yourself."

Christian said nothing and steeled himself for the inevitable.

The hand fell. And the hunters charged.

Three from the rear of the church moved forward quickly. The two in the aisle charged as well, one swinging a whip that lashed around Christian's leg, the other swinging a barbed staff.

To avoid the blow of the staff, Christian ducked and bent his body to the side. It saved his head, as the barbed staff obliterated the back of a pew, but the whip was yanked backward and his leg pulled out from under him.

Christian fell, crashing into one of the pews and knocking it over.

The hunter who'd snared him tried to drag him out into the aisle, but Christian managed to pull loose. He kicked free of the lash and rolled over. He tried to scramble away, only to have another of the hunters leap over the pew and land a blow with a heavy club to his ribs.

Christian heard and felt his ribs cracking. He slammed the palm of his hand into the man's chest, sending him flying. Before he could get up, another whip lashed around his arm. And then a blow from another weapon to the back of Christian's leg dropped him down. A third hunter lunged for him with a palladium chain in his hands.

Christian spun and heaved himself backward and managed to throw off the men but could do little more.

Desperate to reach the exit, he tried climbing over the back of a pew. It tipped over and fell, and he dropped into the space between it and the next bench.

He heard laughter from the altar of the church.

"Look at your champion," Henrick bellowed to Simon. "A child could take him."

Simon was sweating and crying. "Please, Henrick," he begged. "Have mercy. You don't understand."

In some corner of his battered mind, Christian recognized the significance of Simon's act. He could not have imagined a member of the Church pleading on his behalf for any reason, but this broken man was begging his usurper to show pity.

Christian's will to live rose up. He had to escape, had to live, if just to prove Simon was right about him, if just because the dogma of two thousand years was cracking and the truth was meeting the light of day.

He climbed the next wooden pew and then the next. The hunters followed, two on either side of the row, as if waiting for him to decide which way to turn, to choose which group would be his destroyers. He fell off the last pew and sprawled out, facedown, on the old stone floor.

A thud hit him in the back, and then another on his leg, and then a third near his head. They would beat him into submission and then chain him in palladium and force him to divulge all he knew. Their final act would be the Rite of Ignatorium, where they would destroy him like a rabid dog.

As blow after blow rained down upon him, Christian found he could no longer fight, he could no longer reason. He tried to stand and was knocked back down. He began to lose consciousness under the blows. He covered up and felt something jab him in the ribs, something inside his coat.

An image flashed into his mind—the Glock pistol he'd taken from the FBI woman in the Ninth Ward. It was in his coat pocket. He'd forgotten he had it.

He slid his hand into the pocket and wrapped his fingers around the carbon grip. Another blow struck his back, another beside his head. He took a breath and rolled over, drew out the gun, and began firing blindly in all directions.

The booming sound of the weapon shook the church. Shocked faces were replaced with agony as Christian began blasting holes in the men who were clubbing him. Three quick shots dropped the closest group. In seconds, the others were running, scurrying like rats in every direction.

Christian fired away at them, gunning down two more.

Henrick reacted with great speed. He sprinted for an open door at the back of the church.

Christian stood and aimed through the glare of light that blinded him. He fired twice, but Henrick disappeared with the sword in his hand.

Turning from quadrant to quadrant, Christian looked for enemies through the haze. He saw none. He lumbered forward to where Simon's battered figure remained tied to the altar. Christian tore the ropes free, releasing Simon's hands and legs.

The old parish priest fell back as if he were a rag doll.

Christian caught him and draped him gently to the ground.

"They've broken my back," Simon whispered. "I can't move."

Sorrow, an emotion the Nosferatu did not normally possess, flowed through Christian. But this man had tried to bridge the gap. And his presence in this holy place seemed to bring back some of Christian's humanity.

"I can keep you from dying," Christian said. "The wounds will heal."

"No," Simon told him. "I will not take it. I'm not afraid of dying, just of failing at the gate."

Christian nodded. He understood now. Those with fear and doubt more easily accepted the offer of the Nosferatu. But this man, like Elsa, was not afraid.

"You must leave quickly," Simon told him, coughing up blood as he spoke. "The hunters will return with reinforcements. You must not be detained. You must destroy Drake, or none of this will matter."

"But how?" Christian asked. "I don't have the sword. Send the hunters, the ones who are loyal. I'll tell them how to find him."

"None of them will trust me now," Simon explained. "I cast my lot with you. Besides, they will look for you now, not for Drake. You are their greatest enemy. The invader of churches. The would-be thief of their most precious relic. They will hunt you like no other as long as you live. You must go and go quickly. You must do so before it's too late."

"I have no weapon," Christian said. "What can I fight him with?"

Simon's chest heaved and fell. Each breath was agony. "The Staff of Constantine," he whispered. He was barely breathing now. "In the tower... with the journals. They're all...I have left...to offer you."

Christian stood but hesitated.

Simon looked into his eyes. "You must know..."

"Must know what?"

Simon could not speak. He was coughing and spitting blood. Christian tried to view his mind, but he couldn't, not in the church, not through the pain.

"I must know what?" he asked desperately.

"Who…you…are," Simon managed. His eyelids slid down until they were no more than slits. His head lolled to the side. His mouth opened as if to speak, but Christian could barely make out the whispers. "And that… you're…not…alone."

Simon's mouth opened again, but no sound came forth. His eyes closed, and his shallow breathing ceased.

Some kind of alarm went off, and Christian knew he had to hurry. He marched raggedly up to the tower and found the staff. When he touched it, a new spike of pain shot through his arm. He held it anyway.

A few feet away, he spotted Simon's journals—four old books, leather bound and held together with elastic twine around them.

He grabbed the journals and then made his way down the stairs. Quickly, he moved toward the front of the church. His strength grew as he neared the exit. And by the time he pushed out into the cool night air, he could feel his heart pounding and his mind racing.

He knew what lay ahead. He'd baited Drake and boasted to him, teasing out his anger. He'd done so believing he would be carrying a weapon of incomparable power. Now he had to fight with less, much less, and his foe was riled to the top of his rage, primed and waiting with everything he had.

Doubt flooded Christian once again, as if a dam had burst. In his heart, he knew he could not defeat Drake, not with the weapon he now carried. But even so, he could not turn back.

Simon Lathatch had died trying to help him, and even if it meant his own death, Christian would try to complete his end of the bargain.

He sprinted down St. Bernard Avenue to another stolen car he'd grabbed. He needed to reach the swamp and break up Drake's calling before the angel found it. There was little time left to lose.

Chapter 48

AT THE FBI's New Orleans field office, Kate, Billy Ray, and Section Chief Gallagher had been watching computer screens all night searching for any sign of the radioactive dye marker.

The operation wasn't easy. The signal from the invisible radioactive dye was too weak for the satellite to pick up on a wide-angle scan. It was designed to be used in tracking a marked package, not searching for a needle among six hundred thousand others. So they had to pan and scan.

They'd scanned the streets of New Orleans for hours, back and forth, several blocks at a time. Never knowing if they were missing the target in one section of town while studying another. It was tedious, mind-numbing work, and after five hours of it, Kate began to think the suspect had left town.

Then the computer reported a hit.

By the time they zoomed in on the area, the target had vanished. Playback showed the subject entering a church. They kept the satellite's cameras focused on the street, hoping it wasn't a mirage or a glitch.

"We have movement!" Billy Ray shouted several minutes later. "On the side of the building."

Kate saw a man running out through a side door. "Is that him?"

"Negative," a technician said. "No paint. It shows up in neon green. Not a lot, but enough to tell him from the others."

Two more men ran out the back door, and a third stumbled after them.

"What the hell is going on?" Billy Ray asked.

"Let's get NOPD down there," Kate said. "Let's not wait."

The section chief was tied in to NOPD on a direct line. He covered the phone. "They're already rolling. They've had three nine-one-one calls. Shots fired. People running in all directions."

"We'd better get down there," Kate said.

"Look," Billy Ray said, pointing.

On screen, a figure shaded in effervescent green came running out through the front door of the church. He disappeared each time he raced beneath a tree and then reappeared on the other side.

"That's our suspect," Kate said.

They watched as he jumped into a car and sped off without turning on the lights.

"Track him!" Kate said.

On screen, the satellite feed widened and pulled back a bit. The SAT team knew what they were doing. They were able to track the car as it raced off to the south and then turned hard to the northwest.

"Where's he going?" Billy Ray wondered.

"Nothing that way except Lake Maurepas," the chief said.

Kate wasn't waiting any longer. "Get the chopper up," she said, grabbing her new pistol from a desk drawer and slipping it into her shoulder holster. "Let's bag him before he disappears."

—✺—

Out on the old plantation, the drums continued pounding. Smoke and ash and sparks drifted through the air. Still sitting inside the old juke hall, Drake's patience had begun to wear thin. The scent of life was testing even his control.

Suddenly, Terrance raised his head.

"What is it?" Drake asked.

"Don't you feel it?"

The old blind man looked at Drake, his white eyes floating as if adrift on the sea.

"Feel what?"

"Something different out there," Terrance said. "Something passing through the markers."

A sense of concern filled Drake. He thought he'd feel the presence of the angel as it approached, the way magnets sense their opposite. "I feel nothing," he said. "Are you sure?"

Terrance spoke slowly. "The images of two I see."

"Two?" Anticipation surged through Drake, but the Santeria priest liked to talk in riddles. Something that filled Drake with fury. "Speak plainly, or people you love will suffer."

"The images are the same, but reversed, like a reflection. It comes across the water, but where I saw two, there is only one now."

Drake's arm shot forward. His fingers curled around Terrance's neck.

"Get off him!" Bella shouted, stepping forward wielding a machete.

Drake spun, never letting go of Terrance. His free hand caught her wrist and yanked the machete away. It flew across the room and clattered to the floor. He pulled her close and then backhanded her across the face, sending her into the wall.

She crumpled to the floor, concussed and woozy. Drake yanked Terrance out of his chair and slammed him down onto the rotting floorboards. He tightened his grip, squeezing harder and harder.

Terrance dug at Drake's hands.

"I warned you once," Drake said. "Tell me what you sense."

Before Terrance could speak, the drums stopped beating. Silence swept through the door and into the old room like a cold wind. Only the crackle of bonfires remained.

"Go...see...for...yourself," the voodoo priest managed.

Drake let go and stood up. Terrance rolled onto his side, choking and gasping for air.

Drake left him there and walked to the door. Now, finally, he felt a presence. Something that triggered feelings very unlike those he got when other Nosferatu were near. With a sense of destiny filling his dead soul, Drake stepped through the door and out into the night.

Chapter 49

KATE AND Billy Ray were in a car, racing at top speed along an empty street on the outskirts of New Orleans. Reports from the satellite team had the suspect hitting a marina and taking a boat onto Lake Maurepas.

They charged into the same marina and skidded to a stop.

Kate got on the radio. "We're at the marina."

"The suspect's on the water, heading northwest on the lake. After that, it's just swamp. Not sure what he's doing. Once he gets across, there's nothing but swampland and a winding river that cuts through it. He has fifteen minutes on you."

"What about the chopper?" Kate asked.

"We had to round up a sharpshooter. The chopper will be wheels up as soon as he's on board."

"And the rest of the troops?"

"On their way," the chief said. "It's your call if you want to wait. We can track the guy from here."

"Unless he goes for a swim," Kate said.

Billy Ray nodded. "I'm with you. This is our best chance."

"Have the backup teams cut off any exits," she said into the radio. "We're grabbing a boat."

The rental shack showed little signs of life. Considering the hour, Kate figured they'd have to kick in the door. She pounded on it once.

To her surprise, it opened. Standing before them was a scruffy-looking guy with spiked hair and a three nose rings.

Kate flashed her badge. "We need a boat."

"A fast boat," Billy Ray added.

"You guys chasing the lunatic with the spear?"

"A spear?" Kate said.

"Yeah. He came running through here with a spear, and I thought, 'Damn, this guy is some kind of wacko or something.'"

The guy was stoned like a Rastafarian on holiday. But Kate didn't doubt what he'd said.

"Can it get any stranger?" Billy Ray wondered.

"Not sure we really want to know," she said.

The rental guy grabbed a set of keys and threw them at Billy Ray.

"Which boat?" Kate asked.

"The blue one on the end—it's the fastest one I've got."

—⁂—

Christian reached the far side of Lake Maurepas and the edge of the swamp. Finding the narrow channel that cut through it took only a minute, and soon he was racing up the slender river as fast as he possibly could.

Finding Drake would be the easy part. But then what?

As he grew closer, the calling became so loud that his whole body felt as if it were shaking. He clutched the Staff of Constantine as a counterweight to the effect—pain to distract him from the pleasure. It left him numb, operating solely on determination and willpower. The strength of his mind, that was all he had left.

He began to smell smoke. In the far distance, he saw firelight through the trees. He turned the boat toward the shore, cut off its noisy engine, and coasted into the muddy bank.

He could hear drums now and feel the pull of the ceremony like the undertow from a great wave drawing him in.

And then, suddenly, the calling ceased, and Christian's mind cleared.

He had no idea what was happening, but he didn't like it. He sensed time was running out. He jumped off the boat and began to run toward the flickering light.

Chapter 50

THE DRUMMERS stood exhausted in the humid night air, their hands blistered and raw, their brows dripping with sweat. They seemed surprised at their surroundings. With their minds released from Drake's grasp, they stared blankly, like sleepwalkers woken from a dream.

Drake ignored them. He scanned the trees around the clearing. Everything seemed to be moving in the flickering light. A force of life stronger and more potent than the mere human chattel around him had drawn near. The angel was out there, just beyond his view.

He walked into the circle of the living, his boots scuffing the circle of ashes that divided it from the outside world. Within it, a naked woman stood with her man—Terrance's disciples. Young, virile, and passionate, their dance had ended with the drums.

"Leave," Drake said.

They scampered off, and Drake turned slowly. He held out his hands, palms up and empty. "We wait for you," he boomed. "If you've come for us, there's no reason to hide."

He glanced toward a dilapidated building across from the juke hall. "Bring Vivian to me."

One of his slaves appeared in the doorway, leading Vivian down the cracked wooden stairs. Chained, shackled, and scarred, she looked bedraggled and skeletal, more like a neglected animal than the woman Terrance had once loved or the queen Drake had cultivated her to be.

As if to see her, Terrance came to the door of the juke hall, leaning on Bella's arm.

"Begin the chant," Drake said to one of the drummers.

The drummer struck his instrument a single time. A low boom echoed across the night, dying just as the drummer hit the skin once again. He kept that rhythm, slow and heavy.

Boom...boom...boom....

Each stroke was harder and deeper, each echo longer, until it seemed they were on top of one another.

Drake looked to Vivian. "Come to me."

The slave released her chains, and Vivian obeyed her master. She stepped into the circle and moved toward Drake.

At that very moment, a figure appeared at the edge of the tree line. The figure was cloaked like a monk—its face hidden beneath the shade of the hooded sweatshirt, its arms folded and crossed in front, its hands hidden inside the cuffs.

Drake could feel the power of the approaching figure, the power of life, of love, of redemption—things he wanted no part of. They were attributes of the weak and needy. But Vivian seemed to feel them also. She seemed to want them. She raised her head, looking toward this being.

Drake sensed that she'd do anything to be human again, to feel, to love, and to be rid of him as her master. The angel seemed drawn to her, as if it could feel her pain.

Perfect.

He took a step back. As he did, the hooded figure took a halting step forward. It moved cautiously, like a newborn foal on unsteady legs.

Drake took another step back, and the figure moved forward again, matching his rhythm, keeping its hidden face toward Vivian.

Soon, Drake thought. *Very soon.*

—⁘—

Kate held on to the dashboard of the boat as the wind and spray whipped past. They'd made it across the lake and were now following the narrow river through the swamp. Kate kept track of their location on a GPS receiver. In her other hand, she held a radio.

"How much farther?" Billy Ray asked.

She repeated the question into the radio.

The regional director's voice cut through the static. "We're downloading the suspect's last position to your GPS right now. Just so you know, we've lost him in the foliage. You're on your own, unless he pops up again."

"Terrific," Kate said sarcastically. "What happened to 'He won't get away this time'?"

"Trees are a problem," she was told.

She waited for the GPS to refresh. When it did, a red line appeared over the screen.

"Five miles," she said.

"I don't get it," Billy Ray said. "What's he running this way for?"

"Maybe he's looking for a place to hide and lay low," Kate guessed. She held the radio close to her mouth to block the wind. "Anything up here?"

"Not much," the director said. "A couple of old plantations that were flooded out fifty years ago. A few abandoned shacks here and there. According to the SAT team, there are a few heat sources up ahead. They register as large bonfires."

"Death cults and bonfires," Billy Ray said. "Great."

Kate checked the sky behind them. "Where's the chopper?"

"Spooling up now," the chief said. "It'll be on-site in fifteen minutes. Suggest you wait until then before moving in. We also have a makeshift tactical team heading your way. State troopers are going to block the roads out, and the tactical team will move in from the southwest. They're twenty minutes behind you."

"Well, that's something, at least," Billy Ray said.

Fifteen minutes for the chopper, Kate thought. *Twenty before the arrival of any backup.*

She turned to Billy Ray. "If something is going down up there, fifteen minutes is gonna be a lifetime," she said. "I don't want to wait like I did before."

Billy Ray nodded and kept the boat's throttle pegged.

Kate put the radio to her mouth. "Get everyone here as fast as you can," she said. "We're gonna crash the party as soon as we get there."

—ɯ—

Christian was picking his way through the trees. The gash in his leg from the fight with the hunters was taking its toll on him, but anger and desire pushed him forward. He sensed Drake up ahead, but heard nothing in his mind, as if Drake was so focused on the task at hand that he didn't feel Christian coming.

Now, he thought, *this is my chance.*

He pressed forward, but suddenly found himself surrounded. Two figures appeared in front of him and one to either side. A fifth came around from behind. Drones. Lying in wait.

They roared like animals and then rushed in.

Christian thrust the spear forward, impaling the first of the demons. A second drone swung an ax for his neck. Christian ducked and the ax head plunged into the thick wood of an oak tree. Christian sidestepped the beast and plunged the spear into the creature's back. It dropped to the ground and burst into flames, along with the first one.

He yanked the spear out of the dying beast and swung, just in time to deflect a blow from a third member of the group.

A fourth attacker almost got him, but Christian dropped down and swept its legs out from underneath it. Before the beast could hit the ground, Christian gave him a roundhouse kick, sending him flying toward another of his kind.

With a moment to breathe, Christian stepped back and whirled the staff into a ready position.

There was a long pause as the simple minds of these animals studied the situation. Two of their brothers were dead and burning, another lay gasping for air on the forest floor, and their foe carried a weapon that even these most brainless of creatures recognized.

Christian noticed their hesitation. He moved forward, brandishing the weapon of the Ignis Purgata. His arms trembled and burned as the razor-sharp edges of the spear begged the drones to challenge him.

They stepped back in unison.

"Leave," he growled.

Their minds broke down. They turned, running into the shadowy recesses of the bayou. The way now clear, Christian raced forward.

Chapter 51

IN THE clearing, Drake continued to back off slowly. As he left the circle of ash, the hooded figure moved around it. It focused on Vivian as the fires flickered and the drum continued its heavy beat.

Vivian looked up, her hands in chains, her beaten and broken body waiting and longing to be freed. Drake could feel the desire inside her, the desire for peace. He could not have planned this better.

The angel drew near to Vivian and stopped.

It was almost too easy now. Under Drake's long black coat, he griped his sword, ready to slice this angel's throat.

The hooded figure stopped. Vivian inched toward it, like an animal in unfamiliar surroundings. Drake's grip on the samurai sword tightened.

The figure held still, all but hovering over Vivian.

What is it waiting for?

Much like the stare of the Nosferatu, the angel was foretold to have mesmerizing powers. Drake could not trust himself to face it alone. He could not look it in the eye and have it gaze into his soul. If it did, he might falter. He might crave what Vivian was now longing for, or he might be smote down by power he did not understand.

To steal its strength, he needed the angel to be engaged with another. He needed it to be distracted and defenseless.

Patience, he told himself. *Patience.*

Finally, the angel stretched out a hand.

Vivian looked up as if awaiting communion.

Drake inched forward.

Vivian's shoulders slumped, her posture softened as if she were relaxing, finally beginning to let go of the pain she'd felt for so many years. Her eyes closed, and she began to tilt her head back as if feeling the release. He could sense her drifting.

Now, Drake thought.

He rushed in across the circle of ash, raising the sword.

The angel spun around. The hood covering its face dropped.

Instead of kindness, Drake saw pain. Instead of peace, he saw anger, vengeance, and a woman's face, twisted with scars. It shocked him enough to throw him off-balance.

The woman raised a stone dagger and thrust it toward him. Only his great speed allowed Drake to knock the dagger free.

She spat at him, and his rage flared. He thrust his free hand to her neck and lifted her off the ground, forcing her to look into his eyes.

"Elsa," he said, finally recognizing her, "the years have not been kind to you."

She laughed, a sickly sound coming from her constricted throat. "How wrong you are," she said. "I've lived long enough to foresee your destruction."

"We both know that is but a mere possibility," Drake said. "But if you were truly gifted, you would have foreseen your own death at my hands."

"I have," she said, "and I welcome it."

Drake ignored her wordplay. He was looking into her eyes, seeing past her hatred to the things she loved. *Yes, Christian, of course, but what else?*

She began to squirm. "No…"

"Release it," he commanded.

"No!"

He pressed his full weight onto her, using the powers of his mind to force the image from where she'd hidden it.

She'd seen the angel. She'd met with him and warned him off. Told him to hide. But now her mind had betrayed him. Drake saw the angel's face, felt the aura of its power. With that alone, he could seek out this being. It was weaker than he'd thought. It was afraid and confused.

"You have given me more than I could have dreamed," he said, raising his sword.

"Let her go!" a voice bellowed.

Drake spun around, holding Elsa's frail body in front of him.

Christian stood at the edge of the clearing, with the fires of determination in his eyes like Drake had never seen before. He appeared to be injured, but in his hands was a weapon that had taken so many of Drake's children.

"So you side with the enemy, after all," he said.

Christian moved closer, circling to the left.

"Let her go," Christian said again. "This is our destiny, our fight. Not hers. Let her go, and we'll finish this together!"

Drake smiled. "I have a better idea," he said. "Deal with your brothers first."

As Drake spoke, new shapes came forth from the shadows. First was Kwese, next was Lagos, and then Xi. Last of all came Anya. They took up separate positions, one of them at each point of the compass, with Christian caught in the middle.

Chapter 52

CHRISTIAN STOOD in the clearing, caught between the bonfires of life and death, caught in the middle, as he'd been for so many centuries.

Christian glanced at the new arrivals, sizing them up. Though he'd once been part of the Brethren, these were not his brothers. And while they would kill him on Drake's command, they knew nothing of honor and loyalty. They would not die for each other, as the men of the legions had once done.

Drake wanted them to rush Christian together, converging on him at once, but he'd miscalculated his own power structure. The hope among these Brethren was that the others would die first in the effort, and then they would clean up at the end, finishing Christian and soaking up the glory.

It made them weak. It made them divisible. So fully did Christian now understand the difference that he didn't hesitate for an instant.

He lunged first at Kwese, twirling the spear in his hands and bringing it down toward the big man's head. Kwese blocked it and tried to rip it from Christian's grasp, but Christian spun in the opposite direction and brought the back end of the staff into Kwese's chest. It hammered his center mass, cracking his sternum and sending the huge man falling helplessly backward.

Anya rushed in next, the two daggers twirling in her hands. Christian ducked, spun, and swept her legs out from under her. She jumped to her feet, but a kick from Christian's boot sent her tumbling backward.

"Kill him!" Drake shouted.

Lagos and Xi were circling the perimeter. They charged from opposite sides.

Christian pivoted and twirled the staff in both hands. Both blows were deflected.

Xi dove to the ground, rolled, and came up hacking at Christian's leg. Christian stabbed the head of the staff into the ground, blocking Xi's swing and using the staff like a pole vault. He leapt over Xi and came down behind him.

Xi turned just as the diamond-shaped tip of the staff plunged into his chest.

He wrapped his hands around the staff and released a hideous cry as he slumped to his knees. His arms fell to the sides, and flames engulfed him.

With that, the humans around the clearing broke out of their trances. They began to run and scatter. Bella grabbed Terrance and dragged him off.

Christian yanked the staff out of Xi's burning shape and turned from point to point. Wounded and spitting the orange blood of the damned, Kwese had come back for more. Lagos stood at the ready, uninjured, biding his time, and Anya had crawled to one of her daggers. She crouched like a cheetah, ready to attack.

As they hesitated, Christian slid a foot under Xi's sword and flicked it upward. The perfectly balanced sword flew to waist height. Christian grabbed it out of the air. He held the sword low in a defensive posture and the spear high like a missile ready to fire.

"None of you have to die for Drake," he shouted. "Leave him to me, and when I'm done, I will lead you all to salvation."

They held their ground.

"You will not turn them from me," Drake said.

As these words came forth, Christian sensed Drake's will upon them. No longer would he let them choose. They moved to new positions, approaching him in a triangular formation, with Lagos in the middle, Kwese on his right, and Anya on the left.

Drake moved in behind them, dragging Elsa with him.

Their approach halted as Drake's will left his three minions and fell upon Christian. Christian felt it hit like a wave of pain and fear crashing over him. He felt the sense of inferiority that Drake had instilled in him so long ago surging forth once again.

Who are you to confront me?

Christian tried to shake it off. He felt his heart pounding in the effort. *You will bow before me, or you will fall and burn.*

The image of his own painful death flashed into Christian's mind. The fires of hell gripping him. The torment of flame. Elsa's pain. The pain he'd trapped her with. He would pay for his sins in kind.

His skin burned, his mind darting from place to place to find a way free. He gripped the staff, trying to draw strength from its power. He fought back, only to have another will fall upon him as Kwese joined his strength to Drake's. Moments later, Lagos did the same and then finally Anya.

The weight of their minds forced him backward, forced him to look downward. The ground beckoned.

Kneel.

The pain in his mind grew as he resisted. Like daggers piecing his eyes, like a thousand screeching decibels wailing in his ears. It became agony. If he just bowed before them, it would vanish. If he just gave in and rejoined them, they'd free him from this mental torture.

He backed to the edge of the clearing and bumped into the trunk of a large cypress tree. He pressed himself against it to keep his knees from bending. The trio of Drake's disciples pressed closer. The weight of the attack grew.

Drake looked on from behind them. "Kneel!"

So clearly had Drake taken control that Christian could see his old friend's mind through the conduit. He saw that Drake had stolen the image of the angel from Elsa, saw how near Drake was to his great triumph.

He could not give in now, or all would be lost. But even if he didn't bend, they would continue the attack until he broke or until Drake ordered one of them to kill him in his defenseless state.

Kneel!

His legs threatened to buckle. He looked at Drake, breathing hard.

I command you to kneel before your master.

Slowly and deliberately, Christian shook his head.

Then die instead.

If Christian would not break, he would be destroyed. Lagos began to move forward. He raised his sword slowly, the executioner to the end.

Christian focused on him and tried to hold him back, but as he did, the pain from the others grew stronger. His body began to shake.. He tried to raise his sword in defense but found his arm would not move as if it were trapped beneath a thousand pounds of iron. His world began to shrink. He was dead and he knew it, until he sensed help from an unexpected place.

Elsa had begun squirming in Drake's grasp, trying to distract him.

Christian managed to look her way. "No," he grunted, shaking his head slightly. "Don't."

She smiled. *Don't be afraid, my love. I'll be waiting for you on the other side.*

"No!" he shouted.

She flipped something into the fire. It flared bright white, like phosphorous in the dark, blinding everyone. In the moment of distraction, she ripped a hand free and raked her nails across Drake's face.

Drake pulled back and, in his rage, plunged the sword into Elsa's heart. She stumbled backward, falling and clutching at her chest. As she dropped, her face changed from the twisted scars she had worn for so long into the beauty she'd once been. By the time she hit the ground, she was a young woman again, in all her beauty.

"No!" Christian shouted.

Fury erupted in his heart. He surged forward, throwing off the combined will of the Brethren. Kwese and Anya fell backward, as if hit by a shock wave. Lagos stumbled but kept his feet, only to have Christian knock his sword to the side and then run him through with the Staff of Constantine.

As Lagos fell and caught fire, Kwese and Anya charged him together, but Christian's madness was beyond their power to contain. He deflected one attack with the staff and then took Kwese's arm off at the elbow with a thunderous chop from Xi's sword.

He spun in time to see Anya's dagger plunging downward toward his heart. The blade grazed his arm as he swung the back end of the staff. It caught Anya in the temple. A bone-shattering crack rang out. She stumbled away, crawling into the brush.

Without hesitation, he spun back in the other direction, slashing with Xi's sword, beheading Kwese in a single cut.

Drake looked on, stunned by the decimation. Christian turned and fired the staff toward him like a missile.

Drake reacted in what would have seemed an instantaneous move to some, but was slow by his standards. He swung his sword and just caught the point of the spear as it hurtled toward him.

The forged steel of the samurai sword shattered. A dozen shards flew from it. They cut into Drake's face and neck and chest. One hit his eye, slashing across it. Another gashed open his cheek.

Christian charged, ready to finish him, but Drake spun to the ground, kicking his foot into the bonfire and sending a hail of sparks and ash into Christian's face.

Christian felt a flash of heat and an instant of blindness. He shook his head, swept the ash from his eyes, and forced them to open. Drake was nowhere to be seen.

Christian ran to Elsa and crouched beside her. Her clothes were soaked in blood—red, human blood. It was almost a relief. Her eyes were still open, her face passive and beautiful.

She was gone, lost to him, but finally free.

Only now did he understand the faith that lived inside her. Only now did he feel an emotion he'd long thought was impossible for him, a sense of peace and of understanding.

She'd given her life to save him and to save the angel, to show him the true strength he possessed. He would not fail her now.

He grabbed the Staff of Constantine from the ground and then the stone dagger she'd carried. It was an odd weapon, a foot-long stalactite that looked as if it had been taken from a cave and then carved and polished by hand for an eternity. By Elsa's hand, he guessed. Had she known all this time that she would need it?

It was perfectly balanced. He decided he would finish Drake with this weapon, repaying him for all he had done to her.

He stood, but before he could move, a gunshot rang out in the night. In its wake, a voice shouted from the other side of the clearing.

"FBI! Everybody on the ground!"

Chapter 53

KATE STOOD with her finger on the trigger, staring into the circular clearing at a sight beyond her imagination.

In the center, near a group of bonfires, a young woman in chains cowered like a beaten animal. A few yards away, the blond man from the Ninth Ward crouched over another female who lay unmoving in blood-soaked clothes. Filling out the madness, three other fires burned in the ghastly shapes of human bodies.

The blond man looked at her. She felt her mind going blank. She held her focus and tried to pull the trigger, but her hands would not obey.

Just then, the helicopter thundered overhead, lighting up the clearing with a million-candlepower spotlight.

The blond man glanced up, and Kate's mind returned to her control. She opened fire, sending a half dozen shots toward him before he disappeared into the tree line.

Billy Ray's shotgun added a pair of blasts.

Once again, she was certain they'd hit him. Once again, it seemed to have no effect.

"Follow the suspect," Kate yelled into a radio.

The chopper peeled off, and Kate began to move, intent on running after the man.

Billy Ray grabbed her arm. "Let the chopper do it," he said. "You have no idea who else is out there. And backup is still ten minutes away."

She pulled her arm free. She would chase this bastard to the very end if she had to.

"Remember what happened last time," Billy Ray added.

Kate stared into the darkened forest and then studied the madness that lay all around them. Her partner was right. They had no idea what they were dealing with.

She moved to the victims. One of them seemed to have been stabbed through the heart. A few feet away, the woman in the chains was alive, but she looked disoriented and was striving to reach the dead one, crawling on her hands and knees, her eyes locked on the pool of blood.

"Team One to tactical," Kate said into the radio. "We have several dead here and one victim alive. Suspect is running northeast, carrying a spear. The chopper is following him. See if you can set a net for him."

"We're on it," a voice called back.

"We got the roads blocked," a second voice said.

"Watch the trees," she said. "We're going to get the survivor out of here. Keep us posted."

Kate reached toward the woman in chains. At her touch, the woman reared back like a startled animal.

"It's okay," Kate said. "I'm with the FBI. I'm getting you out of here."

The woman didn't react to Kate's voice. She just stared at the blood-soaked clothes of the other victim.

"Don't look at her," Kate said.

The woman resisted, reaching toward the other victim with her shackled hands and dipping her fingers in the blood like one might dip his or her fingers in oil on the garage floor to see what it is.

—✺—

Christian raced into the dark, trying with all his might to see through the dense brush. He crashed through tree branches and tangled undergrowth. The helicopter thundered overhead, looking for him.

He didn't care.

It didn't matter to him if the whole act of killing Drake was caught on video and replayed endlessly on CNN and every other network in the world. He would not let Drake live through this night. And if the FBI agents got in his way and tried to stop him, he would kill them too.

—⋙—

In the thin cover of the forest, Drake continued to run. He stumbled out from the dense section of trees onto a muddy riverbank. Half-blind from his wounds, gripped with fear for the first time in two thousand years, he stumbled and fell to his knees, landing in the muck. He crawled forward, trying to reach the slow-moving water.

—⋙—

Kate and Billy Ray backtracked through the forest toward their boat.

"How far?" Kate asked.

"Quarter mile."

With the chaos of the ritual well behind them and the swampland open and empty, Kate slowed her pace.

"Okay, let's see if we can get these chains off her."

She holstered her pistol and went to work on the chains as Billy Ray stood guard with the shotgun. She got the shackles off the woman's feet and then began to work on the handcuffs. As she fiddled with them, the woman seemed to grow agitated. She kept pulling away, wanting to go back to the clearing. She kept her eyes and face in that direction, as if there were something about those fires drawing her in.

"It's okay," Kate said. "We're getting you out of here."

The woman turned back toward her. Suddenly, she looked familiar.

"Vivian?" Kate said.

As Kate spoke, the handcuffs fell off and dropped to the ground, and Vivian sprung free and lunged at Kate with madness in her eyes.

Chapter 54

THE PILOT of the FBI JetRanger circled east for a mile and then turned back toward the clearing. He was on visual. The sharpshooter in the back was looking for a heat signature through an infrared scope.

"See anything?" the pilot asked.

"I got nothing," the sniper said. "Take us back around."

The pilot put the helicopter into a turn and then spotted movement on the riverbank. "You see that?"

"See what?"

"I thought I saw someone running and stumbling down there." He turned the chopper around again and slowed to a hover, aiming the spotlight. "There!"

The marksman lifted his eyes from the scope. "I'll be damned," he said. "Circle left."

The pilot brought the craft around, re-centering the spotlight as he went. The figure on the ground was crawling through the mud toward the river. A trail of his progress led back to the forest.

The pilot saw no weapons. "Victim or suspect?"

The marksman hesitated. "He looks injured. I don't see anyone else around, but everyone right now is considered a suspect. Radio it in."

As the pilot reached for his radio, the figure on the muddy ground looked up at them and held a hand out to block the light. The pilot angled the spotlight away, scanning the surrounding area for targets and giving the figure on the ground a break from the direct effect of the beam.

When the pilot glanced back at the injured man, he saw something odd—a reflection from the man's eyes, like cats eyes in the night gleaming back at him. A thought occurred to him with incredible power, a thought he felt he must obey.

Land.

———

Kate had no time to process what was happening. Vivian launched herself like a wolf. Kate was knocked backward. She heard her gun discharge but had no idea in which direction it had fired. She felt hot breath on her face and something yanking and slashing at her neck as she desperately tried to protect herself.

A shotgun blast rang out again. Kate felt some of the pellets hit her arm. The woman spun off her as Billy Ray fired again and again.

Kate put a hand to her neck; it was slashed, partially torn. Warm blood flowed down and across her collarbone.

This can't be happening.

She felt dizzy. She heard another blast and then the sounds of a struggle.

"Billy?"

She tried to get up and staunch the bleeding at the same time. She fell forward, too light-headed to stand. She fell into the soil, face-first.

Looking forward, she saw the woman dragging Billy Ray off like a rag doll.

———

Christian raced through the forest. He sensed a faint impression of Drake in the distance. He saw the helicopter's spotlight shining down through the trees and descending. He knew all too well what was happening.

—⚒—

The JetRanger was dropping rapidly toward the mud flat below.

"What the hell are you doing?" the marksman shouted.

"Got to…land," the pilot mumbled.

The marksman looked at the figure on the ground. He saw a wounded man crawling, but that didn't prove anything. "This isn't protocol," he said, turning back to the pilot. "We don't know if he's the victim or the—"

His last words were drowned out by gunshots from the pilot's sidearm. The pilot blasted the marksman from point-blank range. The marksman's vest took the first shot, but the second shell hit him in the neck and a third in the face. He fell backward, dead. And when the pilot rolled the helicopter sideways, his limp body poured out through the door, dropping into the shallow water of the swamp.

The pilot slid his sidearm back into his holster and maneuvered the helicopter until he could descend and set down beside the wounded man crawling in the sludge.

The mud-caked figure reached the door and pulled himself into the helicopter.

Take me into the city, the voice inside the pilot's head commanded. *I have someone I must find.*

The pilot knew he had to go. He knew where. The why didn't matter.

He throttled up once again, feeling a strange sense of accomplishment as the helicopter pulled free of the muddy ground and began to lumber off.

—⚒—

Christian ran from the forest, spotting the helicopter as it pulled away. He saw Drake sitting in the open doorway as it climbed.

311

Racing as fast he could, Christian ran to the river's edge and hurled Elsa's stone weapon with all his might. It fired through the air like an arrow of stone, the superb balance of the weapon keeping it on line.

Either Drake had not seen it or was too injured to react. It caught him in the side, puncturing his ribs. Christian felt Drake cry out in shock and anguish. The helicopter shook and began to slip sideways, dropping as the pilot's mind was released form Drake's control.

For a second or two, it looked as if it would crash, but then it accelerated forward, stabilized, and began to rise again. No flames erupted form the cabin, no sign of the Ignatorium.

Christian sensed Drake in agony, but he wasn't mortally wounded—at least not yet. There was a cold sensation to the pain. In Christian's mind, it burned in a blue color, with the brightness of embers in the fire as they were freshened by a breath of wind.

Though he'd missed the kill shot, Christian sensed desperation in Drake. He sensed panic, as if some poison from the weapon was now spreading through his old master's body.

The helicopter changed course, turning away from the city of New Orleans where the angel would be found and heading due north. Drake was no longer racing to his final triumph; he was in pain and running, in search of help. In that, Christian found some sense of victory. At least, for now, the angel would be safe, and hope would continue to live.

He watched as the helicopter grew more distant, until its lights went out and it was swallowed up by the dark of night.

Chapter 55

KATE CRAWLED toward where she'd last seen Billy Ray. She held the wound on her neck as tight as she possibly could. She felt like she would throw up, but she had to keep going.

She came across her gun, picked it up, and then used a tree to help her stand. She lumbered forward, lurching from one tree to another. She heard grunting sounds and other strange noises from the brush just beyond her.

She pushed forward, past some ground cover. Twenty yards away, she saw two shadows on the muddy deck of the bayou. The woman was perched on top of Billy Ray like a vulture. All Kate could hear was the lapping sound animals make when they drink water.

She steadied herself, lit up the flashlight on the lower rail of her pistol, and painted Vivian in the stark-white light of the high-intensity LEDs. The woman's face and hands were drenched in Billy Ray's blood. Without hesitation, Kate unleashed a hail of gunfire.

Vivian's head snapped back as the first shot hit. She tumbled onto the ground, but got up again, only to be knocked backward by three more shots. She hit the ground and began to shudder, but rolled over once again.

Kate continued to fire, her mind flashing to New York and to the Ninth Ward. She emptied the entire clip into the woman, firing until the slide locked itself open and smoke poured from the breach.

Somehow, Vivian still lived, though she shook and screamed uncontrollably.

Kate dropped to her knees, struggling to pull a new clip from her belt. It slipped from her grasp and landed on the ground. Kate reached for it and slumped over sideways, so weak she couldn't even break her fall.

She lay there, unable to move.

At this point, after all she'd seen, she wouldn't have been surprised if Vivian got up and crawled away or stood and attacked her or Billy Ray once again. But it didn't happen. Vivian's convulsions slowed to a shudder, and eventually, her body went still.

Kate lay on her side, trying to keep the wound on her neck from bleeding out.

Time seemed to stretch out. She began to grow unfathomably cold. Her mind wandered to her son. She now understood all the pain her mother had wanted her to avoid. He would grow up alone—no mother, no father—knowing only that both his parents had been murdered.

"I'm sorry," she whispered. Her eyes fell on Billy Ray. His neck was ripped to shreds. "I'm so sorry," she repeated.

It was all for nothing.

Footsteps approached, running quick and soft through the forest. As her eyes began to fail, she caught sight of the blond man. The suspect. The killer who'd warned her to stay away from things she didn't understand.

At first, she thought it was just a hallucination. But he stopped and crouched beside her.

"You," she said unevenly. "You caused all this."

"No," the man said. "I tried to stop it. I tried to warn you."

"Please," she begged. "Get me out of here."

He touched her face. His hands were as cold as ice. Colder than she felt.

"Your wound is too deep," he said, pressing on it and trying to hold the torn artery shut. "You'll bleed out before I can get you help."

"I…have a…son," she said, beginning to cry. She was sobbing and shaking and freezing on that cold, wet ground. "Please…Please…Do something. "

She didn't even know what she was saying anymore. The words were jumbled in her head. The only one that stood out was her son's name. She was calling out to him. "Calvin."

The blond man held her face in his hands. She looked into his black eyes, but they were not as they'd seemed in the Ninth Ward. There was kindness in his eyes, kindness and pity.

It was the last thing she saw. Then her vision failed and a sensation of pain spiked brightly in her mind.

Her final thought was simple. *This is the end.*

Chapter 56

KATE WOKE up to darkness and the feeling of movement. She was rocking back and forth. It almost felt pleasant, except for the hard metal floor beneath her.

She tried to move, but it was painful. Her entire body felt as if it had been crushed and mangled and then stretched to the breaking point. Her head felt as if it were being squeezed in a vice, and her throat and mouth were so dry she thought she was choking.

She rolled over and realized she was up against a wall of some kind. The wall was made of metal. It had some type of raised pattern on it, like a line of rivets. In the distance, she heard the sound of a train whistle.

A train.

She was on a train.

A match flared across from her, bringing light to the space. It was an empty boxcar. Across from her was the blond man from the Ninth Ward.

She looked into his eyes, and it all came back flooding back: the voodoo ritual, the fires, Vivian, and then Billy Ray. *Oh God*, she thought. *Billy Ray!*

She forced herself to sit up and looked the blond man in the eyes. "Where are you taking me?"

"I'm not taking you anywhere," he said.

He held the match to a small stick of wood. It was like kindling. It burned softly. Kate found it was plenty of light to see by.

"Why are we on a train, then?"

"I had to get you out of there," he said. "You needed time to heal. I needed space. It was the only way. With a little luck, they've found my coat by now."

He spoke calmly, matter-of-factly. He seemed almost emotionless.

"Your coat?" she asked.

"The one you painted with the radioactive marker."

She was stunned. "How did you know?"

You told me.

She heard the words clearly, as if he'd spoken strong and loud, but his lips had never moved.

Yes, you can hear me. And I can hear you—at least when we're close.

Kate began to freak out. This was too much. She tried to stand and fell. Her legs were numb. He reached out as if to assist.

"Don't touch me!"

"I'm trying to help you," he said, speaking aloud.

"Then let me go," she said. "I have a son. He's only five. His father died a year ago."

"I know all that," the blond man said. "That's why I...why I helped you."

"Helped me?"

"You asked me to save you. This was the only way."

He touched his neck and pointed to hers. Suddenly, she remembered the horrendous gash the psychotic woman had left in her neck. She put her hand to it. It was closed. Not exactly healed, it felt more like it was scarred over.

"It will heal," he said. "But it's the last wound that will ever heal on you."

She felt as sick as she could ever remember. What the hell was he talking about? It was like a nightmare come to life.

"Look, I just have to go home," she said. "I appreciate whatever you did to stop the bleeding, but I have get out of here. I have to get back to my family."

The train seemed to be rounding a curve. It didn't seem to be going all that fast. The sound of bells clanging told her they were passing through an intersection. She noticed a tiny crack of light coming underneath the door.

As before, the man seemed to sense her thoughts. He seemed concerned with what she was planning to do.

She grabbed the handle and instantly felt his mind commanding her not to open the door.

"Listen to me," he said. "You're about to go through a transformation you cannot possibly understand. It's going to take months. It's going to be painful and disorienting. At times, you won't believe it's even happening. At times, you'll want to die because, against all reason, you believe that it is. Even when it's done, it might leave you in misery. If you try to go through this alone, you probably won't survive."

She gripped the handle tighter. "What the hell are you talking about?"

"For your son's sake," he said, "for the sake of everyone you care about, stay with me—at least until you understand what you've become."

"What I've become?"

"I'll explain everything," he said.

He stood and offered his hand. She wanted to reach for it. His will had a grasp on her that she found hard to resist, but more than that, she wanted to see her son. After all this madness, it was the only thing she yearned for.

She pulled the handle hard and fast and yanked the door open to the blazing light of day. The blond man shrank back against the wall, forced into the shadows. They were moving slowly, maybe fifteen or twenty miles per hour. There was a grass slope outside the railbed. She didn't care if she broke both her legs. She was jumping, and for reasons she couldn't explain, she knew he wouldn't follow.

She flung herself free, landed on the slope, and tumbled down. One ankle rolled hard, but as she slid to a stop, she felt as if she was okay. She looked back. He hadn't jumped; he hadn't followed.

She got up, limping and walking as fast as she could in the opposite direction from where that train was going. She was free. She was safe.

The last car passed by, and the train continued to clatter off down the line. As she looked around, a thought rang out in her head.

You'll need me. I'm your only chance.

She looked at the train as it continued down the tracks. It was his voice in her mind, she knew it. She didn't understand or even want to know how it was possible. She just wanted him to leave, to go.

"Don't follow me," she shouted. "Just leave me alone. I promise they won't look for you. I'll tell them you're dead."

Then the voice appeared in her mind again, weaker and more distant, but she still heard the message clear enough. It frightened her.

I am dead, Kate. And so are you.

Chapter 57

BISHOP MESSINI left Sunday Mass, where the Pope had just finished the service. He walked the halls with an argument raging inside him. He was troubled. He stopped to look upon the great square of St. Peter's.

His phone rang. It was Henrick Vanderwall.

Strange, he thought, that Henrick should call him and not Simon. It could mean only two things. Either Simon was unable to call or Simon didn't know of this call.

Messini answered. "Yes, Henrick."

"I'm sorry for disturbing you, Bishop. But I have news."

"Of course. What is it?"

"I'm afraid Simon Lathatch is dead."

Messini felt his heart breaking. He said nothing.

"Bishop Messini?"

"Yes, I understand," Messini replied bluntly.

"Unfortunately," Henrick said, "I'm not sure that you do. He was killed by a demon—a demon whose spell he'd fallen under. He was going to give the Sword of God to this abomination."

"The Sword of God?" Messini said. "No, Simon wouldn't do that. Even if he did, no demon could wield it. I'm certain of that."

Henrick's voice returned undeterred. "I can only tell you what I saw with my own eyes. We are dealing with a treacherous creature, the one who entered the cathedral in Cologne. He must have powers the others do not possess. He claims the name of our faith as his own. He took the Staff of Constantine."

Messini's hand began to shake. He could barely hold the phone. He had to sit down.

The Staff of Constantine in the hands of the enemy? This was not possible. No demon could touch a consecrated relic of the Church, let alone the weapon that had rid the world of so many. "There must be another explanation."

"I assure you there isn't," Henrick said. "We were lucky enough to fight this demon off and retain the sword. Five of the bravest are slaughtered in the church. I myself have been wounded. This blond demon is our greatest enemy now. He is more dangerous than even Drakos, for at least that one remains in his dark strongholds."

Henrick had a point. It unnerved Messini. "How did Simon die?"

"The creature murdered him."

Messini took a deep breath. "Like John of Alexandria," he said to himself.

There was no question that the reckoning and dark time had arisen, but until this moment, Bishop Messini hadn't imagined how dark it could possibly be. Still, one question remained. A question Bishop Messini feared to ask. A question upon which all things might now hinge.

"And what of the angel?"

Henrick did not respond immediately. "We've found no sign of any such thing," he said finally.

Messini grieved. Simon had died for nothing. Mislead by a demon. Perhaps all of them had been misled, right from the beginning.

"What is your bidding?" Henrick asked.

"Bring the Sword of God home to the Vatican," Messini said. "I will anoint you a second time and enter your name as the ninety-first to lead the order. But you must come immediately. We're now in a footrace with darkness. And I fear we are falling behind."

"Yes, Bishop," Henrick said reverently. "I'll come at once."

Chapter 58

LIKE SO much in his world that was new, Leroy Atherton had never been in the cab of a semi truck before. The view was tremendous, clear and unobstructed. Perched high up, Leroy felt he could see for miles. A glorious day seemed to be laid out in front of him—blue skies, warm sun, just enough humidity to make your skin feel good. Up ahead, the buildings of New Orleans gleamed like the Emerald City.

"There it is," the truck driver said. Mr. Johnny O. Beasley, owner and operator of the semi, had been kind to Leroy since the moment they met.

"That's a beautiful sight," Leroy replied.

"You sure you want me to drop you off there?" the driver asked. "This ain't all that far from where I found you."

Johnny O. Beasley had picked up Leroy outside the swamps, near Lake Maurepas. Leroy had been hiking all night, was soaking wet from the waist down, and was doubting anyone would give him a ride when he heard those air brakes come on.

The trucker had asked him if he was lost.

"No," Leroy had replied, smiling, "not anymore."

Now, Leroy was smiling again. "I've got somewhere to go," he said.

"Okay, then. I'll just hop off the highway near the French Quarter. And, well, I guess you're on your own from there, partner."

"You've been more than helpful."

A couple of minutes later, the semi was parked, and Leroy was opening the door and stepping out onto the running board. He looked back at his host. "Thanks for the ride."

"Anytime, young fellow. Listen, the next time you're in the Great State of Texas, you look me up—if I'm still around, that is."

Leroy reached out his hand and they shook.

"You will be," he said. "I think that cancer thing is gonna work out for you. Next time they take you in for a test, you might want to bet the doctor a twenty spot that they won't find nothin'."

Johnny O. Beasley smiled a hopeful, gap-toothed grin. "From your lips to God's ears, my brother. From your lips to God's ears. Ha-ha-ha."

Leroy smiled, hopped down off the running board, and shut the door.

A few seconds later, the great machine went into gear with a shudder. It soon moved off once again.

Leroy watched it go and then turned and strolled into the French Quarter. He'd never been to New Orleans. He found there was just so much to see.

He passed by antique stores, bars, coffee shops, and hotel entrances. But he didn't stop; he didn't even look in. He just studied the names and kept on strolling.

Eventually, he turned down a small alleyway. No storefronts here, just a shingle by a blue door. It read, JACKSON'S SOLES.

Leroy paused and studied it. That was the name the old lady in the swamp had told him to look for. He took a deep breath, climbed the three short steps, and opened the door to the cobbler's shop.

A bell tinkled. He smelled shoe polish and leather. He saw an old man behind a desk replacing the soles on a pair of heavy work shoes. Across from him, a teenage kid was stitching up a cowboy boot.

The old man looked up. His eyes were white. He seemed to be blind. His smile lit up the room. "I'm Terrance," he said. "Come on in. I've been expecting you."

Leroy wasn't sure what to make of all this, but he had faith now to say what he felt and what he knew. "The old woman sent me. I felt like I was supposed to be out there in the swamp. But she met me and told there was danger and death out there. She took my coat and went in my place. She told me about the gift of healing I have. She said you'd explain how I need to use it and what I should do next."

The old man put the boots down on the floor, lining them up perfectly despite not being able to see. He looked sad for a moment.

"She was a soul of exceeding brightness," he said. "You're fortunate to have met her, as am I."

"I feel like there's a lot of work ahead," Leroy said.

"Yes," the old man said. "More work than you can possibly imagine. Healing, for a part of the world that hasn't known it in two thousand years."

Leroy wasn't sure what that could mean. "I don't understand."

"There are those who've fallen from grace," the old man said. "You've been given the power to raise them up once again."

Leroy sensed this was something more than healing the sick. "You're going to help me, right?"

"Yes," the blind man said. "My task is to show you the way."

Epilogue

THE RAIN fell in sheets across New York City. It soaked the avenues, parks, and buildings. It flooded the streets and dripped from gargoyles perched high above in their endless watch for evil.

Christian Hannover stood in that rain on the South Lawn of Columbia University's main campus. Under the storm's thick clouds, he could bear the daylight hours. The muted pain that reached him was now an almost-welcome reminder, a connection to his human past.

Unmoving and alone, he stared across the wet grass to the Butler Library, an imposing structure that held nine million books, including a collection of rare volumes and manuscripts. He wondered what its curators might think of the journals Simon Lathatch had given him.

After leaving New Orleans, Christian had looked through them in hopes of finding some answers. He discovered, to his surprise, that the writing was not Simon's alone. There were notes and drawings in many different hands. Most of it was written in Latin, some in ancient Greek. He could only guess it was an heirloom of the Ignis Purgata, passed from leader to leader.

He wasn't sure why Simon had wanted him to have it. At first, he thought it might be to keep it from his rival Henrick. But Simon Lathatch was not a petty man. He was strong, tough, pragmatic. He was cold, forged steel on the outside with a will of iron, but he was also a thinker. Simon had chosen to look beyond what he'd been told his entire life and see the possibilities of the future. Proof of this came in his actions and in the last words of the journal, hastily scribbled in Simon's hand and meant, inescapably, for Christian.

You are the only hope. But you are not alone, my midnight son.

There were secrets in this journal, secrets Christian could use to carry the battle forward. But he needed to get at them and understand them to find them helpful. And that had brought him out to Columbia in the pouring rain.

Across the lawn, the library's main door opened. A security guard held it as a woman in a wheelchair came out. Once she'd made it through the door, she opened a large umbrella and slotted it into a holder of some kind. With a flick of the wrist, she started down the access ramp and onto the pathway that divided the South Lawn.

Halfway across the lawn, she noticed him. Her pace slowed for a moment, but she continued on, stopping a few feet from where he stood.

For a moment, neither one of them said a thing. They just stared at one another, accompanied by the patter of the rain on Ida's umbrella.

"How long you been out here, sonny?"

"All night."

"And when I don't work all night?"

"I watch your apartment," he said, "to make sure you're safe."

"Because the others might know about me now? Is that it?"

He nodded.

She sighed. "You know, I'd almost convinced myself this was a delusion—you and your kind, all the things you told me—but then I went through my research again and I heard about what happened in New Orleans. The bodies the FBI found and the massacre in the bayou."

"Sorry for getting you involved."

"I was already involved, ever since I was a child." She smiled sadly and then added, "I was worried about you."

He didn't know why it mattered, but it meant something to him that another soul on this earth was concerned for his well-being. "Thank you," he said. "I'm okay."

"Did you find your friend Elsa?"

He nodded and then looked away. "She's gone now."

"I'm sorry to hear that."

Christian shook his head. "At least she's free."

He told her what had happened, told her of the battle and the FBI and Drake's wounding.

"So what happens next?" she asked.

"I'm not sure," he said. "That's partly why I came here."

He pulled out the journal and handed it to her. Beneath the shelter of her umbrella, she opened it and began to leaf through the pages.

"This is in Latin," she said. "Figured you'd be more familiar with that than me."

"I am," he told her. "The Latin's not the problem. It's written in some kind of code."

She leafed through a few pages. "You want me to figure out the code? What am I—a secret agent or something?"

"No," he said. "Just a resourceful, tenacious woman."

"Not sure I'm up to code breaking."

"Two thousand years of Church secrets in there," he said.

She smiled and looked back at the journal again. "I'll take a shot at it."

"I thought you might," he said.

She looked up at him. "You seem different somehow."

"I'm not afraid anymore," he said. "For seventeen hundred years, I've been fighting against fear. But you can't get anywhere fighting *against* something. You have to fight *for* something. Something that matters. Something like love or faith or justice. It gives you a power that evil doesn't have."

"And what are you fighting for now?"

"For those who can't fight for themselves."

"Sounds like a pretty good cause," she said. "Buy me a cup of coffee, and I might join up. You guys do drink that stuff, right?"

"We stay up all night," he said, moving to the back of her chair. "What do you think?"

She chuckled, and as he began to push the chair, she fiddled with the umbrella holder, raising it higher so he could duck under it.

"You don't need to," he said.

She finished and locked it into place. "I'm guessing you don't catch cold, sonny. But you look kind of silly standing out in the rain like that. There's enough room for both of us under here."

He nodded and ducked underneath.

"I'll carry the shield," she said. "You drive."

"Sounds like a plan," he said, pushing her chair slowly. "But we have to get one thing straight."

"What's that?"

"You need to stop calling me 'sonny,'" he said. "I'm seventeen hundred years older than you."

She laughed again, and Christian found himself smiling at the sound. There was a long road ahead, but for the first time in centuries, he wasn't traveling alone.

14066578R00191

Made in the USA
San Bernardino, CA
15 August 2014